Ross Neil

Carleton Grange

Vol. II

Ross Neil

Carleton Grange
Vol. II

ISBN/EAN: 9783337082239

Printed in Europe, USA, Canada, Australia, Japan

Cover: Foto ©Andreas Hilbeck / pixelio.de

More available books at **www.hansebooks.com**

CARLETON GRANGE.

A Novel.

BY THE AUTHOR OF "ABBOT'S CLEVE."

IN THREE VOLUMES.

VOL. II.

LONDON:
TINSLEY BROTHERS, 18, CATHERINE STREET,
STRAND.
1866.

LONDON: PRINTED BY WILLIAM CLOWES AND SONS, STAMFORD STREET,
AND CHARING CROSS.

LONDON: PRINTED BY WILLIAM CLOWES AND SONS, STAMFORD STREET,
AND CHARING CROSS.

CONTENTS OF VOL. II.

CHAPTER IX.

CHAPTER X.

CHAPTER XI.

CHAPTER XII.

CHAPTER XIII.

CHAPTER XIV.

CHAPTER XV.

CHAPTER XVI.

CHAPTER XVII.

CHAPTER XVIII.

CARLETON GRANGE.

CHAPTER I.

A BLACK SHADOW ON THE THRESHOLD.

IT was a pleasant retreat, Maud's favourite summer-house, nestling among the trees and shrubs of a little knoll overlooking the river, and covered with jasmine and honeysuckle that hung in long fringes over the tiny lattice-window and low doorway. And never had it seemed to Maud more bright and attractive than when she sought it on the evening of the day which, as she hoped, would be the last of Francis Godfrey's stay in Hernebridge. The setting sun, peeping from behind the clustering boughs of the Ormonds-bury trees, shed a warm stream of yellow light through the doorway on to the tiled floor that was quite gladdening to look at, though yet not too dazzling to interfere with the view of that white corner-stone of Ormond Hall which was visible from most parts of the Carleton domains, and which so agreeably relieved the monotony of the waving mass of verdure behind. Then Maud herself was, perhaps, more than usually inclined to appreciate the tranquil cheerfulness of the hour and the spot, for her spirits had been disturbed and depressed in consequence of the morning's conversation with her father, and stood in need of a restorative. To avoid the risk of meeting Francis Godfrey she had remained at home all the day, and in her solitary chamber had been the prey of many anxious apprehensions and misgivings which nothing could tend so effectually to dissipate as fresh air and sunshine. For not only had she been deeply grieved at the evident disappointment inflicted on her father by the frustration of his plans for her future; she had also been tormented with doubts whether it might not be apt to influence unfavourably his reception of Philip Ormond, on the nature of which she felt that all her hopes of happiness depended. But the fragrant freshness of the evening air and the placid aspect of the evening sky contributed wonderfully to calm her spirits; and, as she cast her hat and shawl on the seat beside her, the better to enjoy the cool breezes as they came wafted across the stream, her heart was lighter than it had been

since her aunt had disturbed her by speaking of
Francis Godfrey as of an avowed suitor. No,
it could not be that her father would oppose
her choice merely because she had not been
able to bring herself to submit to his. Was not
the principal aim of his life to make her happy,
as was abundantly testified by his promise to
take measures for ridding her from that day
forth of Mr. Godfrey's society? As she thus
argued with herself, especially when she remembered that she would probably never see the
obnoxious visitor again, a feeling of peaceful
trust crept about her heart; and the mild rays
of the evening sunshine, streaming full upon her
from the direction of Ormond Hall, seemed to
convey a cheerful augury in the soft radiance
which they diffused through the material atmosphere around, and which thence re-acted on
her tranquillised and gladdened spirit. She
accepted the omen, and, drawing forth a volume
of poems from her pocket, composed herself to
read, quietly happy in the present and trustful
in the future.

Suddenly a cloud obscured the sunlit page on
which her eyes rested; the yellow gleam on the
floor was all at once blotted out; and Maud was
conscious of a black shadow interposed between
herself and the bright rays of promise-beaming

light that shone from beyond the white corner-stone of Ormond Hall. She looked up startled ; a dark figure stood in the doorway ; and then her heart gave a great bound of nameless apprehension, for she recognised in the eyes which gazed down on her from under a pair of scowling brows those of the man she had hoped never to see again. The scowl disappeared as her eyes met his, but was replaced by a familiar insinuating smile from which she shrank with tenfold terror and repugnance.

Instinctively she sprang to her feet and endeavoured to pass into the open air. But in this she found herself opposed by the intruder, who, advancing a step or two within the threshold, extended his arm across the entrance—with a deprecating air of respect and deference, it is true, yet so that she could not pass him.

"Pray don't let me disturb you, Miss Fleming. You can't be in a hurry, I am sure, for I was just thinking how quiet and composed you looked. I am glad to see no traces of the indisposition which has deprived me of the pleasure of meeting you to-day."

Maud remembered her father's anxiety to treat his guest with all possible courtesy and forbearance, and so far overcame her agitation as to make an inclination of the head, and stammer forth a few words to the effect that she had forgotten it was getting so late.

"Not so late but that you can spare me a few minutes, Miss Fleming. Even inexorable Fate, you see, has befriended me this evening by prompting me to take my after-dinner walk in this direction; and surely you cannot be so hardhearted as to insist on depriving me of the pleasure she has thus procured for me, especially as it is one which I so highly appreciate."

Maud did not speak. There was something in the man's voice and manner which filled her with a sense of fear and shrinking, and deprived her of the power of framing the coldly civil and ceremonious answer she would have wished to return.

"I see how it is, Miss Fleming; even yet you do not understand me. You do not guess how I have longed for this opportunity, or how rapturously I hail it now that it is found—the opportunity of exchanging a few words with you alone."

In her very desperation Maud gathered courage now to speak. Anything rather than let that man make an avowal of love!

"Alone! there can be no possible reason for your wishing such a thing—no possible purpose which it can serve. Pray let me pass."

"You persist, then, in being blind to the last

—cruelly, wilfully blind, as I cannot but think. You pretend not to know that I love you, that I cannot be happy without you, that I seek you now to learn my fate."

"Mr. Godfrey, you are only causing me needless pain. I cannot say anything which it could give you pleasure to hear—indeed, indeed I cannot. I entreat you not to detain me longer."

"Do you think I am a man to let my happiness escape me so easily? Forgive me, but you must stay till you have heard me plead my cause. A passion such as mine has at least the right to be listened to."

"I do not wish to listen. Mr. Godfrey, it is useless to say more—useless, I assure you."

"Useless is it? At all events, I will make proof of that myself. Come, Miss Fleming, why be so unreasonable? I am ready to devote my life to the task of making you happy, your father approves my suit" . . . . .

"Not now—not now. Oh! if you had but spoken to my father before torturing me thus" . .

"Yes, yes, I know you have been practising on him at my expense, but I need not remind you that a man convinced against his will is of the same opinion still; and you convinced him against his will and better judgment, believe me. You may take my word for it, Miss Fleming, nothing would give your father greater pleasure than to hear that my perseverance had moved you to relent, and that you had consented to an arrangement which would make me the most fortunate and enviable man in the universe, and which at the same time, I flatter myself, would not be without its advantages on the other side also. May I tell him it is so, Miss Fleming—or Maud, I should rather call you—may I tell him it is so?"

She could bear this no longer, and, suddenly confronting him with flushed indignant face, exclaimed passionately:

"Mr. Godfrey, you insult me, and insult me because you find me alone and unprotected. I never liked you, but I did not know before that you were a coward."

His lips turned white, and quivered as though with anger; evidently the shaft had told. But he controlled himself, and answered with a smile— a menacing and dangerous smile, however, more sinister than many a frown.

"Take care, Miss Fleming, my charming Maud, take care. I have a good temper under ordinary circumstances, but if you persist in being so very plain-spoken you may force me to be so likewise, and I warn you that the result would not be an agreeable one. I fear it might considerably startle you were I to state my impression of you with the same delightful frankness which you have shown in characterising me. I will if you wish it, of course, but I should recommend you to think twice before insisting. You see it may happen that I know a little more of you than you do of yourself, in which case I might probably give you something of a shock. Do you defy me, my dear Miss Fleming, do you defy me?"

Maud was silent for a moment, not with fear, but with surprise and indignation, mingled with a certain uneasy perplexity. What could that man mean by his enigmatical menaces? And involuntarily she thought of her father's unwonted manifestation of hospitality, of his forbearing endurance of familiarities which seemed most calculated to rouse his resentment, of his avowed anxiety to avoid giving his guest cause of offence. But she felt that this was no time for indulging in these irrelevant recollections, and, shaking them off with a vigorous effort, boldly confronted Francis Godfrey's inquiring gaze with a proud steady look of contempt.

Yes, she defied him; the defiance of an honest and innocent nature—a nature strong in the consciousness of its own purity—was written in her truthful eyes and on her clear open brow, in characters which he could not mistake for an instant. But unabashed he still kept his insolent darkly threatening gaze fastened on her face, and still stood his ground doggedly before her.

"Mr. Godfrey, I wish to pass. Stand out of my way, or I call for help at once. I may not be so unfriended as you think; there were gardeners at work yonder a few minutes ago, and if you do not yield at my desire, you may find yourself forcibly removed by my servants."

"So, so—you do defy me then?"

"I do." But even as she spoke, her brave words were belied by the beating of her heart; and though she scorned to let the man see the fear with which he inspired her, she felt sick and faint with terror.

"Very good; call your servants then, as you style them, by all means; but first let me tell you what I shall say to them when they come. You are curious to know, are you not? Well then, I shall inform them that they are not under the smallest obligation to come at your beck and call, inasmuch as you are not, as they mistakenly imagine, their lawful mistress, or the owner of the very eligible property out of which their wages are paid—inasmuch, in short, as you are not Maud Fleming at all. Who you really are—that is, to what name you are properly entitled—I should unfortunately not be able at this precise moment to tell them. As you are doubtless aware, illegitimate children take the patronymic of the mother, not of the father; and what your mother's name was I cannot just at present recollect, though I have it noted down somewhere. Well, why do you not call the servants?"

Simply because she had not strength to lift her voice. Without appreciating the full significance of the words she had just heard, for the very reason that that significance was too fantastically horrible to be comprehended at once, she had a vague idea that they conveyed the announcement of some fearful calamity and disgrace, that they were in some way or other the most terribly portentous she had ever heard uttered. Stunned as by a mighty crash of which we only feel that it means danger, without knowing from what quarter it sounds or in what cause it originates, she could not speak, she could hardly think, but could only seek to rush from a presence more than ever abhorrent to her. But Francis Godfrey grasped her wrist and held it tightly.

"No, no, I will have no half-measures. You have had the text, and now you shall have the commentary. Stay where you are, and you shall learn how I come to be so well acquainted with your antecedents; you shall examine me and cross-examine me if you please — the more the better, for it will convince you that there is no hitch or flaw in the evidence."

CHAPTER II.

STILL Maud did not speak. There was a confused whirl in her brain which as yet scarcely allowed her to take in the sense of the words she heard, much less to frame an answer.

" Well, then, Miss Fleming — for form's sake I shall continue for the present to call you so — you shall have my story from the beginning, as it was related to me not many weeks ago by my late honoured father. You have not heard much about my father, perhaps; there were circumstances connected with him which must have rendered him a disagreeable topic of conversation to a certain gentleman of our acquaintance. So I ought to explain that once upon a time he and that gentleman were very good friends—an excellent reason, it seems to me, why their children should be so likewise. They picked each other up in some studio or other, and my father, who was by some years the elder, had pity on the evident

greenness and rawness of his young friend, took
him by the hand, initiated him into the ways of
the world, and in short made a man of him.   Gilbert Fleming knew what life was in those times, I
can assure you, though he chooses to play the ascetic
now.   Well, at last he got married, and from that
day forth left off sowing his wild oats — in public,
I mean — like the prudent and well-behaved Bene-
dict that he was.   To do him justice, he had the
grace not to throw old friends altogether overboard,
and still kept up a kind of acquaintance with the
Mentor who had done so much for him.   But in
other respects he had undergone a total change ;
I have heard my father say he never saw a man so
unlike his former self as Gilbert Fleming on his
arrival from India."

Here Maud made a great effort, and, rousing
herself as though from the influence of a spell,
exclaimed :

"I believe nothing that you say, nothing that
you can say.   Let me go ; your words are lost on
me."

"I understand, Miss Fleming, I have tired you
by the length of my exordium.   But it is over
now, and the story is just coming — such an
interesting one that you must positively stay to
hear it.   Once upon a time, then, as the fairy tales
say — the time was some two or three weeks after

Mr. and little Miss Fleming's return from India—
my father, working in his studio, was interrupted
by the announcement that a young woman, apparently in great distress and agitation of mind,
had called to ask the favour of a minute's interview. A request of such a nature from a lady
my father was the last man in the world to
refuse, and the visitor was at once shown in. And
then he was rewarded for his civility by the sight
of one of the most magnificent creatures he had
ever seen in his life — rich brunette complexion,
large liquid black eyes, glossy raven hair — the
whole face and figure might have served as model
for an Eastern queen. Fancy his surprise when
it turned out that the business of this beautiful
apparition was to ask if he knew the address of Mr.
Gilbert Fleming, who had left London a few days
before for the coast, to try sea-bathing for his
delicate child. Of course my father was too clever
to say either yes or no to such a question from
such a quarter without first getting a little information on his own account; and at last, with a
great deal of difficulty, he managed to elicit that
this mysterious beauty had known Mr. Fleming in
India, that she and her mother were now in lodgings in London, where the old lady had been
suddenly seized with brain fever, that medical and
other expenses had swallowed up a small sum

with which their kind, but not over rich, friend
and protector Mr. Fleming had presented them
before leaving town, and that it was consequently
a matter of life-and-death necessity to her to find
out where he was, that she might appeal to him
for further assistance. She had heard him speak
of a Mr. Godfrey as one of his friends, and had
found a card with my father's name and address
in the pocket of a coat which Gilbert had left
behind at her lodgings; and to Mr. Godfrey she
applied accordingly, in the hope that he might be
able to tell her something of her patron's present
whereabout. It so happened that my father was
in possession of the desired information; but, instead of giving it to her at once, he was politic
enough to promise to make inquiries and let her
know the result — a brilliant piece of strategy, by
which he succeeded in getting the fair stranger to
entrust him with her address. For, before the
first interview was over, he had fully determined
on laying siege to this Indian beauty — hers was
just the kind of dark magnificent loveliness he
most admired; and indeed, from what he told me
of her black gazelle eyes and her smooth richly
glowing olive cheeks, I can't find it in my heart
to moralise too sternly on his conduct, especially
considering that such a treasure was left with nobody to guard it but an old woman laid up with
brain fever."

Curious that, in the midst of the wildest perturbation of mind and heart she had ever known, Maud should find herself thinking of the roadside cottage at Laviston and its strange occupants. Yet so it was; and even with the detested tones of Francis Godfrey's menacing voice ringing in her ears, the features of the woman whose dead hand she had held in the darkened bed-room of that homely dwelling rose up before her as vividly as Francis Godfrey's own.

"But to return to my story. My father was not the man to let grass grow at his heels in such matters, and in a few hours he paid his first visit to the home of his charmer under pretext of bringing her the information she wanted. On thus penetrating behind the scenes, he was surprised to find that there was yet another member of her family, of whom no mention had been made to him — a pretty little girl, apparently about three years of age, whose existence, I need hardly say, confirmed him in the suspicions he had already formed as to the relations between his innamorata and her disinterested benefactor. To satisfy himself still further on this point, he found an opportunity of making inquiries from the people of the 'lodging-house, whose theory as to the character and position of the beautiful stranger quite agreed with his own. It seemed that she had arrived at the house with the child a short while before — it must have been just about the time of her patron's return from India — her mother following a few days afterwards, and that on two or three occasions since her establishment there she had been seen by a gentleman answering the description of Gilbert Fleming. As to the child, she had represented it as that of a married sister who had lately died ; but the landlady was a sharp-sighted woman, and had formed a pretty shrewd guess that the married sister was a myth. For the rest, it seemed that both the old woman and the young one were as close as wax, and could not be got to give the least scrap of information respecting their past life. This my father found to be strictly true so far as the daughter was concerned ; and as regarded the mother, it did not signify much whether she was communicative by nature or the reverse, for she only recovered from her attack of brain fever to fall into a state of hopeless idiocy, so that he had never an opportunity of exchanging a word with her. The interest of the story begins to thicken now, Miss Fleming, does it not ? "

Yes, surely it did, judging from the look of rapt dismayed attention which was gradually settling itself on the listener's face as it proceeded. Was it chance, or was it a fatal testimony to Francis Godfrey's good faith, that the mother and daughter of his narrative bore so close a resemblance to the two women she had seen in the cottage at Laviston?

"Well, time went on, and my father still persisted in his design of netting the beautiful bird whose former possessor seemed to set so slight store on it. His task, however, proved more difficult than he had anticipated under the circumstances; the fair one was colder and more repellent than he had ever found one of her sex before, and at the end of an acquaintance of two or three months he was to all appearance still as far from the attainment of his object as he had been at the beginning. But he persevered, and after a short time was inspired with new hope by the tidings that his friend and rival Gilbert Fleming, who had meanwhile been making a long stay at Linchester, had left England for the Continent, the better to care for the precious health of his legitimate daughter, the heiress of Carleton Grange. And now, Miss Fleming, I come to the cream of my tale, and have to bespeak your most particular attention."

He made a momentary pause, as though to give additional weight to what was to come, and then went on in slow distinct tones:

"One evening, about ten days after the Flemings had left England, as my father was approaching the lodging of his hard-hearted lady-love, he was surprised by seeing her come out of the house, carrying the child in her arms. The evening was black and stormy, and she did not observe him, but hurried on through the dark streets with the quick decided step of a person bound on some definite errand. You guess what my father did, Miss Fleming, I dare say. He did precisely what I should have done under similar circumstances; that is to say, he followed her. His curiosity was thoroughly aroused as to what she could be doing out of doors on such a night, especially with the little girl for a companion; indeed for some time he fancied that she was bent on doing away with herself and the child too, particularly when he found that she made straight for London Bridge. But he was mistaken, for she crossed the bridge without once looking right or left, and then he discovered that she was bound for the railway station. His curiosity grew stronger than ever at this, and, having ascertained that she took a ticket for Dover, he took a ticket for Dover too, and entered the carriage next to that in which she was seated, still without being noticed by her. In course of time Dover was reached, and, continuing to tread on the footsteps of his unconscious and involuntary guide, he threaded one ill-lighted street after another, in the teeth of a pelting storm, until he found himself in front of a second-rate hotel in an

out-of-the-way part of the town.   Here the woman
entered, still carrying the child in her arms.   .   .
You follow me, Miss Fleming?"

Ay, she followed him, followed with a quick
readiness and vividness of comprehension which
he had no idea of. For, as he spoke, long-
dormant memories seemed to stir within her;
and, like the recollection of a dream in the far
away past, there rose before her a vision of long
dismal streets, with dark pools of wet glistening
in the dim light of an occasional lamp, and a
black starless sky sending down pitiless torrents
of rain, driven against the faces of benighted way-
farers by shrill whistling gusts of wind.

"Through the open door of the hotel my father
noticed that she was shown upstairs by one of the
waiters, and, determined to see the end of the
adventure, he went in and ordered refreshment
in the coffee-room, stationing himself at a table
near the door to watch her return. In about
half-an-hour she re-appeared, this time with no
child in her arms, and passed out of the house,
taking the same way by which she had come.
It occurred to him that he would probably discover more by staying to make inquiries than by
following her home again; so he remained behind,
finding occasion to ask one of the waiters who was
the pretty girl that had just gone out. The answer

took him by surprise. She was a nursemaid in the employment of a gentleman then staying in the house, the waiter said, and had come that evening to bring him his little girl, who was to start with him for the Continent the following morning. More the waiter could not tell, the gentleman, it seemed, having omitted to mention his name. But my father was resolved that in one way or another he would find it out, and remained in the house that night in the hope of making a discovery. And sure enough, next morning a discovery was made, for face to face on the staircase he met his old friend Mr. Gilbert Fleming. Of course he expressed great astonishment at the rencontre, on which Gilbert stammered something about an unexpected summons to England on urgent business. And then he was breaking away in a great hurry, when my father, with his usual presence of mind, stopped him for another moment to inquire how the waters of the German Spa were agreeing with little Miss Maud. No sooner were the words out of his mouth than such a change came over Gilbert Fleming's face as was never seen on a face before. He turned pale and red and pale again, and then, half choking himself in the effort, managed to say that his daughter was much better, and likely to do very well. He was in such a hurry that it was impossible to get anything more out of him just then, but my father was a shrewd man, and a word to the wise goes a long way. I am afraid my narrative has been almost too interesting for you, Miss Fleming; you look quite pale."

Pale as death indeed she was, and trembling so violently that she was obliged to lean against the table for support. No need for Francis Godfrey to detain her by force now.

"I have nearly done now, however, so you must try to bear up a little longer. Well, my father took leave and started homewards; but the more he thought of what he had seen and heard, and especially of the singular way in which his inquiries after Miss Fleming's health had been received, the more suspicious he became, and the more persistently his suspicions pointed in one direction. The first thing he did on reaching London was to seek his Eastern beauty, with the intention of subjecting her to a thorough cross-examination; but to his disappointment he found that she had been beforehand with him, and that she and her mother had moved from their lodgings a few hours previously, without leaving any clue by which they might be traced. His suspicions once aroused, however, he was not to be so easily balked, and decided without further ado on following the Flemings to the Continent. This would have been no such simple matter to a less determined man, for, no doubt to avoid an awkward meeting with English friends, father and daughter kept moving about from one out-of-the-way place to another with the most provoking rapidity. But by dint of perseverance the pursuer got on their track, and at last had the satisfaction of putting up in the same hotel where a Mr. Fleming and his child were staying, the latter declared by her talkative French *bonne* to be a rich English heiress. In that child, Miss Fleming, my father had soon an opportunity of recognising the pretty little girl whom he had first seen living with his beautiful Indian enchantress."

She had known that this was coming, and yet her white lips grew perceptibly whiter when she heard it.

"Immediately after thus making sure of his facts, my father confronted his friend without further delay, and plumply accused him of palming off his illegitimate child as his wife's daughter and the heiress of the Carleton property. There was no rebutting a charge capable of being so circumstantially proved, and, after a few vain struggles to break through the meshes of the net in which he had been so cleverly caught, Fleming gave in and confessed. The real heiress, it seemed, whose life he had taken so much pains to preserve, had never even reached the Spa which was reported to have been of such benefit to her, but had been forced to break off her journey at an obscure German village on the way, where she had died after a few hours' illness. And then your father—thinking it a pity, no doubt, that so fine an estate as this should be allowed to go out of the family—very wisely bethought himself of you, who, though a year younger than the genuine Maud Fleming, resembled her sufficiently to be able to take her place in a few years, provided you could be kept out of sight in the mean time. In the village where his child had died, nobody knew whence he had come, or with what family he was connected, or anything of him save his name; and, as the two had travelled alone together from England, there was no chance of what had happened being reported at home. So he made an appointment to meet the new heiress at Dover, bore her off to the Continent next day, stopped a week at the Spa that was to have cured the other one, taking care to inscribe his name in the visitors' book; and then, providing her with a French *bonne*, who of course knew nothing of her except what he chose to say, whisked her about from place to place in triumph, until he had the misfortune to fall in with

my father. You quite understand, Miss Fleming,
do you not?"

Alas! she understood but too well. How could
she fail to understand when through her brain there
rushed a host of childish memories which, vague
and shadowy though they were, invested Francis
Godfrey's words with a dread significance that no
unsupported assertion from such a quarter could
ever have had for her? Yes, she understood that
if the tale she had heard were true (and, if it were
not true, how explain the distant echoes it had
awakened in the chambers of her memory?), she
was the child of shame, the instrument of fraud,
the living representative of vices and crimes which
she shuddered even to think upon. All her life
long she had been deceiving and deceived; the
father whom she had proudly deemed the soul of
truth and honour was a robber and a liar; the
mother whose memory she had cherished and
revered as the type of all virtue and nobility was
a fallen guilty woman, reduced to ask pardon on
her death-bed from her own child—she knew now
why those dark eyes had been fixed so wildly on
her face. And she herself, Maud Fleming, she
who had been so happy in her imagined atmosphere of purity and innocence, was a creature
polluted in her very birth, to be looked on as an

outcast by all who held their own reputation dear, by all whose good opinion she had ever prized, by Philip Ormond . . . . . If indeed the tale she had heard were true.

"You look overwhelmed, Miss Fleming, and I could almost be sorry for you had you been a little less hard-hearted towards me, but I assure you that all is exactly as I have said. The real Maud Fleming died fifteen years ago, and, if necessary, her death may be proved by the doctor who attended her and the people of the house where she died—some half-dozen witnesses in all, who, as I have lately taken occasion to ascertain, have not forgotten the lame little English girl whose death left her father apparently so inconsolable. So you see I come prepared at all points. But take comfort, for, as my father pointed out a way of escape to yours, so am I able to offer absolute safety to you. To conclude, it was agreed that, in consideration of an annuity payable to my father during his lifetime, Mr. Gilbert Fleming should hear no more of him or his awkward discovery. There must have been a spice of romance about the governor for which I should hardly have given him credit, for till within the last few days of his life he adhered rigidly to the very letter of his promise, remaining constantly abroad according to stipulation, and never breathing a word of what he knew—not even to me his only son. But at length, a week or two before his death, either touched with commiseration for the fate of the desolate orphan he was about to leave behind, or reflecting that the sole monopoly of the secret could be of no further use to him, he took me into his confidence, and told me the whole story just as I have now repeated it to you. Of course I re-solved to turn the paternal legacy to the best account I could, and as soon as possible came to England, revolving the terms I should accept in consideration of my secresy. It was not till I had had an opportunity of seeing you, my dear Miss Fleming, that I fully made up my mind what to ask for; but from the time I had the honour of meeting you on your return from a drive I have been troubled with no further doubts on the subject. Your father, like a sensible man, has been willing to acquiesce in an arrangement by which, believe me, your happiness as well as your interests will be secured; and though you have been rather unreasonable at first, I have no doubt that the little history I have just had the pleasure of relating to you will considerably modify your views. But it is not in my nature to hurry a lady, and I will not press you for an answer this evening, especially as just at present you are naturally a little nervous and flurried. So farewell till to-morrow, and let me advise you in the meanwhile to give your best consideration to what I have said."

He was gone now, and Maud was free to wander forth whither she pleased. But not till his retreating figure had finally disappeared from view under the dark shadow of. the trees, did she find power to use her liberty, stunned as she was by a cruel and crushing blow. Then, as one awaking from an evil dream, she drew a long breath and smiled an incredulous smile. For it was not true, the tale she had listened to just now —could not be true, though framed with such wily art as momentarily to impose upon her. And with an access of new feverish energy she quitted the summer-house, and sped through the gathering darkness towards the Grange, making for the tall window on the ground-floor whence shone a solitary light—the window, as she knew, of her father's study. In her father's arms she would find a refuge where no horrible nightmare could torment her more ; at the sound of her father's voice the lingering echoes of fiend-inspired calumnies would disperse and die away.

The folding leaves of the window were standing open as she drew near, and, before he was aware of her presence, she saw her father sitting alone by his table, not reading or writing, but plunged in deep thought. His face looked so pale and ghastly as seen by the dim lamp-light that for a moment she shrank back in dismay, as though Francis Godfrey's words might after all be true. But in the next, drawn towards him by an invincible attraction, she was in the room, kneeling with streaming eyes and clasped hands at his feet.

"Papa, papa, comfort me, or I must go mad. Do you know what I have heard, papa? but no, no, of course you do not; you cannot even guess. That man, that Francis Godfrey, he has told me —But I am not afraid, for I know it cannot be" . . . .

Ere she could say more she felt a shiver run through her father's frame, and, looking up affrightedly into his face, she saw that his eyes were strained and starting as though with horror, and his mouth convulsively twitching.

"Papa! It cannot be—it cannot be."

No answer; and, with a wild cry of anguish and despair, Maud sank fainting on the floor. For silence had been more eloquent than words, and she felt now that Francis Godfrey had not been deceiving her.

CHAPTER III.

THE VOICE OF THE TEMPTER.

THERE was an interval during which all was a blank—during which pain and horror, and even the consciousness of existence, ceased to be. And then, slowly and gradually, Maud became aware that she was lying on the sofa in her father's study, and that her father himself was stooping over her, holding one of her hands clasped in his, and gently smoothing away the hair from her feverish brow. She had never been thus tended by him before, and to find him so near her made her first sensation on awakening a grateful one. But as her eyes, dazzled for the moment by the glow of the lamp-light, became by degrees able to discern clearly, she was struck by the marble whiteness and rigidity of the face which bent over hers; and then the pleasurable sense of peaceful languor died away, and she knew she had awakened, not to tranquil contentment, but to pain and sorrow sharper than had ever touched her yet. In another moment the full tide of life and agonised self-consciousness had returned, and, with a sudden rush of blood to her heart, she remembered everything that had preceded the blessed, but all too short, period of oblivion by which an otherwise unbearable torment had been temporarily lulled. The faculty of suffering came back to her as strong as ever now, strong enough to make physical weakness and prostration seem as nought; and, dragging herself to her feet, she gazed around with dull tearless eyes, as though desperately seeking some way of escape from the miserable reality to which she had awakened.

"It is true then—it is true. Oh! if I might only die!"

Mr. Fleming did not speak, but she felt the cold hand that held hers shake convulsively.

"Papa, papa, help me!" she cried, turning upon him wildly. "What shall I do? what shall I do?"

She wrung her hands; a sob burst tempestuously from her bosom, followed by another and another, and in a passion of uncontrollable grief she cast herself on the ground before him.

He looked at her for a moment sorrowfully and compassionately, perhaps a little remorsefully; then, as if moved by an impulse of fear, glanced towards the door and window, and hastened to secure them.

"Hush, my dear, hush," he said at last, gently raising her and placing her beside him on the sofa. "Maud, Maud, show yourself brave and strong, as I know you are."

But the kind, almost endearing, tones of his voice, the unwontedly tender touch of his hand, the familiar sound of that name which she knew she could no longer rightfully claim, only so far availed in soothing her anguish as to enable it to find new expression; and, covering her face with her hands, she broke into an agony of weeping.

Again Mr. Fleming looked anxiously towards the door.

"Maud, be calm, I entreat you. If your aunt or any of the servants should hear . . . . For Heaven's sake, compose yourself."

"I cannot, I cannot. Let them hear if they please; they will know soon; all the world will know. Oh! that I might die first!"

"Maud, my dear, listen to me, listen to reason," said Mr. Fleming, and he took her hand and held it almost caressingly between his. "This grief has come upon you so unexpectedly that you are overwhelmed, and I cannot wonder—poor girl, I did not think I had the feeling left in me to be so sorry for you as I am. But you must be reasonable—perhaps things are not so hopeless as you believe. Where is the need that anybody should

know what it gives you so much pain to think of?
why should not the future be as the past?"

She looked at him in wondering perplexity, her
tears checked in mid course by sheer bewilderment.
Alas! how was it possible that the future which
rose before her so black and desolate could ever be
as the bright and happy past—that past whose
golden visions and sunny promises had been
rudely and irretrievably shattered as by a dis-
enchanting wand, that past in which nothing had
been real, though all so exceeding fair!

"Hear me, Maud, and you will understand that
there is no occasion for despair. It is in a sense
true—would to Heaven it were not—that we are
at the mercy of a villain, a false, mean, vindictive
villain, for I confess now that you judged more
correctly than I did the character of Francis
Godfrey" . . . . . .

She shuddered; the mere mention of the
detested name made her blood run cold.

"Fear nothing, Maud, you shall not be asked to
sacrifice yourself to that man. Now that I know
what he is, I should feel more shame in being
accessary to a union between you and him than
in standing with my neck in the pillory. But
trust me, there are other ways of dealing with him.
We are unhappily in one sense at his mercy, as I
have said, but then in another he is at ours. That

is to say, all his hopes of ease and affluence depend exclusively on us and our willingness to make terms with him. You understand me ?"

She understood the sense of his immediate argument, but, stunned and bewildered as she was, she did not perceive its relevancy to what had gone before; she did not comprehend how Francis Godfrey's hopes or fears could have aught to do with making the future what the past had been.

" So that let him once be convinced of our readiness to brave all extremities rather than consent to what he wishes, and then he must either betray us, and in betraying us renounce all expectation of profiting by our fears, or he must sell his secresy on lower terms. You shall see, my dear, he will be too prudent to insist longer on his demand when he finds we are determined to refuse it. Leave me to deal with him, and I will undertake that an annual payment chargeable on the estate will make us as free of him as we have been all these years past of his father."

She began to understand now, and she saw that, if tried, the plan would probably be successful.

" And then, Maud, I will do my best to make you forget what you have suffered by my means. I have not been all that I ought to be to you, I know, but I will do better for the future : I will

give myself up to the task of repairing so far as in
me lies the wrong I have done you.   You used to
say you would like me to spend more time at home
—you have always loved me better than I deserved
—well, I will do whatever you wish.   What would
you say to a tour together in Italy ?   You will
need a change, my poor girl, after what you have
suffered to-night.   Your aunt Nicoll shall stay
with her friends in Ireland while we are away, so
that we two shall set out by ourselves, and I. will
introduce you to an unknown world of art at Rome,
to an earthly paradise at Naples.   What think
you, Maud ? we shall be very happy, shall we
not ? "

For a moment the brightness of the ideal
existence thus conjured up was so dazzling as almost
to persuade Maud into a belief that happiness—
maimed and imperfect, and poisoned by a lasting
sense of disgrace, yet still happiness as compared
with the black despair to which her soul had been
but now given up—might perchance once more be
possible to her. If only they could shake off
Francis Godfrey so effectually as never to hear of
him more, and travel to the classic lands over
which nature and history have conspired to cast a
golden spell of poetry and romance—she and her
father together, all in all to each other, unconcerned for what was being said or done among the

far-off scenes they had left behind them ! Such a life, could she but have dreamed of it a few days or weeks before, would have seemed to her a very heaven upon earth ; and even now, in the midst of her anguish and her shame, the idea of it opened to her a hope of comparative peace and rest, a way of escape from the world's scorn, a prospect of solace in the companionship of the only creature on whose love and sympathy she had a claim, which made her long for it as a storm-wearied mariner for a harbour of refuge. Then, overwhelmed with grief and horror as she was, her heart was yet not incapable of feeling a thrill of pleasure on hearing herself addressed by her father, almost for the first time, in the language of affection and tenderness. Deeply as he had wrongéd her, deeply as she felt the wrong, and far as he had fallen from the pedestal of honour and veneration which he once had occupied in her imagination as a kind of superior being, she clung to him still with a love that had undergone no diminution. For was he not her father? ay, and now not only her father, but the one living thing that had no right to spurn her with reproach and contumely? The tie between them was drawn closer than ever now, and even in the depth of her suffering it was pleasant to find that he too felt that it was so, pleasant to look forward to such an existence as he painted to

her—calm and peaceful, over-clouded by no care
save the consciousness of the dread secret which it
would be their joint task to cover from every eye
but their own.   Only for a moment, however, was
she blinded by the brightness of the vision ; in the
next she understood that its realisation would
involve her conscious complicity in a fraud of which
she had till now been but the involuntary and
innocent instrument.   Not even to purchase the
fatherly tenderness she had so long pined for, and
which now, when she stood most in need of it,
seemed to be within her reach, could she connive
at the perpetuation of a wrong.

"Papa, dear papa, you forget.   The truth must
be spoken in justice to others.   I have usurped an
inheritance that is not mine ;   the world must
know what has been done in order that it may be
surrendered to its lawful owners."

And then her heart gave a quick throb of pain,
for she remembered as she spoke who those lawful
owners were.   According to the terms of old Mr.
Carleton's will, the death of Gilbert Fleming's
legitimate child had left Sir Arthur Ormond master
of Carleton Grange and its belongings ; Sir Arthur
Ormond therefore it was whom her unconscious
imposture had for years defrauded of his rights.
The recollection caused her pale cheeks to flush
with a poignant pang of shame.   That Philip

Ormond and Philip Ormond's father should have cause to complain of being wronged by her means was the last drop wanting to make the cup of her sorrow and humiliation overflow. But yet her voice had never sounded more clear and firm than when, after an instant's agonised pause, she continued:

"It is Sir Arthur Ormond who is rightful master here; it is due to him that everything should be told. Dear papa, you must see yourself that there is no choice."

Mr. Fleming's face darkened, but he evidently desired to deal tenderly with one whom he had so grievously wronged, for he answered in tones rather of grave expostulation than of anger:

"I was prepared for some such difficulty as this; for I know that girls of your age are apt to entertain exaggerated ideas of duty—to imagine that the greater the sacrifice they may take it into their heads that they ought to make, the greater the obligation to go through with it. Otherwise I should have deemed myself safe in the love you have always professed for me, and which I will not believe can have been crushed out of your heart at so short a notice. For the question is not whether you will give up or retain Carleton Grange, but whether you will or will not set me up as a mark of scorn and hatred before the gaze of the world.

The question is, will you humble me to the dust at the feet of my enemies, shatter in one moment the fabric of social estimation and regard which I have been laboriously building up for myself by years of toil and self-denial, cover me with a mass of infamy and opprobrium a thousand times more foul than that which they sought to heap on me when they tried to cheat me of the love of her who, in spite of them all, gave up rank and riches to be my wife."

He had worked himself up into a state of strange excitement, of which he seemed only now to become aware, for he checked himself, and went on more calmly:

" You had forgotten all this, Maud, I am sure; you could not else have deemed yourself under an obligation to betray me. And now that you remember it you will make a merciful use of your power, will you not? I can be grateful, Maud, and such a service would bind me to you till my dying day."

There was a pleading tone in his voice, a pleading look in his eye, which made it inexpressibly painful to Maud to withhold instant assent to his entreaty. She called up all her firmness, all her sense of duty, to her aid, and murmured, with lips that almost refused to do her bidding:

"I cannot keep what is not mine. Let Sir Arthur Ormond come—it is his right."

"But it is not," said Mr. Fleming energetically. "Child, believe me, the real right to rule at Carleton Grange is with you, not him. That is," he explained, "my claim to nominate a successor to the inheritance of my dead child, to the inheritance of my dead wife, who was foully cozened of it by vile slanderers and intriguers, is morally stronger than any that senseless parchments can confer. This is not a case to be ruled by law, but by natural right, and the natural right is with me, or with those whom I choose to represent me. Keep Carleton Grange with a clear conscience, and I will take the burden of the fault, if fault it be, on mine."

Alas! was not his conscience already sufficiently charged with faults which, let him palliate them to himself with what sophistries he pleased, must sometimes make themselves felt with only too oppressive weight? But Maud knew that it was not for her to argue with him thus, and simply shook her head and whispered despairingly:

"I cannot, papa, I cannot."

Apparently his patience began to fail him now, for he frowned more darkly than ever, as he answered:

"You cannot! You cannot remain silent when on your silence my safety and my good fame depend; you cannot keep your lips from forming syllables which will make my name a by-word with those whom I have forced to respect it by years of patient effort! You cannot! Rather say you will not."

"Forgive me, papa," was all she could stammer forth.

"Forgive you if you hand me over to shame and ruin! Never."

She was dismayed by the fierce determination audible in his low suppressed tones, and, electrified into new energy by the fear of alienating the one being to whom she could henceforth look for the friendship and sympathy of which she stood in such sore need, fell on her knees in passionate entreaty.

"Papa, papa, hear me before you speak such cruel words again. Why should you fear what they may say of us, papa?—let them rail as they will, we will not stay to listen. We will go to-morrow —to-night—too soon it cannot be—we will fly together to some far-away land where none will know us or take heed of us; thence we will write to Sir Arthur Ormond and confess the truth. He is a kind old man, they say; he will surely not seek to follow us, or wish to crush us more than we are crushed already. And then we will make a home far from them all, papa, in some quiet pleasant spot where we shall see nothing to remind us of what is past. And I will tend you and wait upon you, and work for you if need be—for we shall be poor then, and I am glad of it—and some day perhaps we may even learn to be happy again. You said yourself we might be happy going abroad together, papa, and I think we may when once our terrible secret is gone from us."

He laughed in withering scorn.

"Happy! happy in the knowledge that at home my enemies are triumphing in my fall, that the name my dead wife shared with me is dragged through the dirt by all the ale-house gossips of the county. Ay, truly we shall be very happy."

But Maud did not or would not understand the bitter irony that rang in his tones, and, catching at his words, went on eagerly:

"Yes, papa, I believe in time we may. For we shall love each other more than ever now, and with love all things are possible. You know I love you with my whole heart and soul, papa, and you will love me dearly too now, will you not?"

A fierce vindictive light shot from Mr. Fleming's eyes.

"If you betray me? Never think it, girl. I shall hold you as the deadliest of my foes."

And indeed, as he looked down at her, such an

expression of dark lowering wrath crossed his face as spoke of hatred rather than of love. She shuddered as she saw, and, twining her arms round his knees, sobbed out:

"Papa, I have lived all my life without your love—I felt it always, and I understand why now—but if you hate me I must die. I cannot do what I know is wrong, even for you—but pity me, forgive me, do not hate me. For I have nothing now to love save you, papa, not even a memory. I used to be so happy in thinking of my mother, but now . . . . . . Oh! what shall I do? what shall I do? Yet you must have loved her once, though you have never cared for her child; for her sake will you not take pity on me? Yes, yes, you will listen to me, surely, if in my mother's name I implore you to have mercy on me."

She clasped his knees more tightly, and looked up beseechingly into his face with eyes blinded with tears. But in a moment more she felt herself roughly thrust away, while, pronounced in such tones of bitter concentrated rage as seemed to freeze her blood, there rang in her ears the words:

"Your mother!"

Hardly knowing whether she were awake or the sport of a fearful dream every moment assuming some new and more horribly grotesque shape, she sank down on the spot where she had been thus spurned, in a speechless stupor of despair.

Meanwhile Mr. Fleming, with quick hurried step, strode up and down the room, as though under the influence of some all-mastering excitement. Presently he grew calmer, and, approaching the passive form that still remained mute and prostrate where he had left it, said in a subdued voice:

"I forgot myself just now, Maud, and I am sorry for it, but you provoked me beyond endurance. The fault has been mine, however, for harassing you with my plans for the future at a time of sudden grief and excitement, when I ought to have known that you were hardly yourself."

He passed his arm gently round her waist, and assisted her to her feet.

" Get to bed and to sleep as quickly as you can; you want rest, and you shall have it before we think of anything else. In the mean time let all that has passed between us to-night be as if it had never been; forget that I treated you so harshly just now, as I will forget that you threatened me with infamy. We will consult again on the future to-morrow morning, when I doubt not that time and reflection will have brought you to a more fitting sense of your duty."

She made an effort to speak; stupified as she

was, she retained self-consciousness enough to know that the change which her father apparently still expected to bring about in her resolution could never take place; but ere her parched lips could articulate a word he had resumed authoritatively :

" Not another syllable to-night — I will take your answer in the morning, and not before. Go to your room ; at this hour the servants must be at supper, so you run no risk of being met. Goodnight, and forget how far I suffered anger to carry me."

He pressed his cold lips formally on her forehead, and led her unresistingly towards the door. She felt that it was of no use to argue further with him that night, even if strength to brave his wrath had still remained to her, and she passed out of the room without a word more.

For some moments she stood as one paralysed, then made a few staggering steps forward towards the staircase. But as she crossed the hall, a faint breath of soft summer-night air, wafted through the open back-door that led into the grounds, made her turn her head, and she saw the grassy slopes and nodding trees without bathed in a liquid flood of moonbeams, shining full upon them with a gentle chastened radiance which made the artificial lights burning in the hall look dismal and funereal in comparison. As she gazed, an instinctive yearning told her that in communion with the trees and the moonlight and the cool evening breeze she would find elements of consolation which she might seek in vain in the gloomy solitude of her chamber; and, yielding to an irresistible impulse, she glided forth into the pale sea of brightness, as eagerly as though she hoped to find in its mild influence oblivion for the cares which pressed with weight so crushing upon her soul.

CHAPTER IV.

BY THE RIVER.

AY, she could breathe more freely here, under the broad vault of the silent moonlit sky, with the evening air playing in fitful ripples round her hot temples. She turned her face in the direction of the faintly stirring breezes, and strained back the hair from her forehead that she might lose none of their fresh fragrant breath. If only they had dealt with her a little more roughly! if only they could have come charged with cold reviving rain-drops, or, better still, with keen driving snow! for her brow burned as fiercely and her pulses beat as fast and painfully as though she were being consumed by a raging fever. While she stood thus, gazing into the pale luminous haze of the moon-light, and longing for an Arctic blast to sweep through the languid summer atmosphere, her eye was suddenly arrested by the glittering reflection of the moon's rays in the shifting waters which washed the base of the slopes of sward and woodland that lay stretched before her. Even as the parched traveller in the desert is inspired with redoubled energy by a far-off glimpse of the green-shining oasis, so did Maud gather new strength from the sight of yonder liquid gleam; and with quick impatient step she hurried downward by the shortest path, intent on refreshing her throbbing brow and burning hands in the cool clear current.

Temptingly cool and clear indeed the river looked when she reached it, and gazed with her hot tear-stained eyes into its eddying depths. She hastened to a point where, as she knew, the turf-covered shore was a little worn down by the chafing of the stream, so that the water rose almost to a level with the grass. Here, kneeling down, she plunged her hands and arms in the darkly gleaming flood, and laved it up on her flushed brow and cheeks, almost revelling in the revivifying influence of the hour and the spot. Cooled by the exhalations of the water, the wind blew more freshly here than elsewhere, in spite of the obstructions offered by the tangled foliage of the trees and shrubs that grew thickly around. Then the river itself looked so dark and cold beneath the night sky, notwithstanding the glitter of the moonlight, which indeed only served more vividly to suggest the depth of that troubled mass of water which the penetrating rays failed to fathom.　Both in the fretting motion of the tiny waves that broke splashingly under the black shadow of the bank, and yet more perhaps in the silent whirl of the mysterious glassy circles into which the water here and there formed itself a little way from the shore, the wearied eye and heart found a sense of coolness and refreshment.

But the gradual calming down of the fever which for a while had taken possession of her brought to Maud not a cessation, only a change, of torment.　She forgot the painful throbbing at her temples, the convulsive tightening at her chest, the consuming fire in her brain, to remember nothing but her misery and her degradation.　The friendly moonlit river, with its fresh breezes and its splashing wavelets and its smooth eddies, had exhausted its restoring influences on her now; and with a long quivering breath of despairing anguish she laid her head heavily on the ground, burying her face in the tall dew-beaded grass.

A strange experience it was, this first attempt at familiarising herself with the disgrace and wretchedness which must henceforth be her lot —so strange that more than once she would have believed the whole thing a ghastly dream, if the damp grass and hard unyielding ground, which she desperately clutched at with her fingers in the vain hope of finding them other than they were, had not reminded her all too well how she came to be lying there instead of on her usual bed in the pleasant little chamber set apart for the mistress of Carleton Grange. In the intervals during which she was able to grasp the full significance of what had passed that evening, it seemed to her as though the best part of herself had been utterly blotted out and annihilated, and nothing left behind save the capability of feeling pain. It was as though the sense of her own personality—that sense which distinguishes thinking, reasoning life from mere sentient existence—had been rudely torn away from her, leaving her whole being a dull aching void. It was not only that she was no longer Maud Fleming, owner of Carleton Grange; the loss of a mere external identity would have troubled her little if with it she had not lost hopes, memories, and beliefs which had constituted an identity far dearer to her than that conferred by the right to bear a certain name and to enjoy certain property. But in ceasing to be Maud Fleming she had almost ceased to be everything that but a few hours ago she had been. The whole fabric of her being, in the past, the present, and the future, in its relations internal and external, had been shaken to the very foundation. She had learned that she, who had never consciously

breathed aught other than an atmosphere of purity
and innocence, was what she had formerly blushed
to think that any should be, the offspring of shame
and sin ; her self-respect was gone from her ; and
even the garnered-up memories of past joys were
transmuted from precious treasure into worthless
trash, as witch-given gold in the tales of our childhood turns to dead leaves under the most watchful
guardianship.   A glamour had been before her
eyes all her life, and now that it was taken off she
almost hated the happiness of her youth as having
been imposed on her under false pretences.

Then not only had she abruptly awakened from
her golden dreams to the sense of her own abase-
ment, but to that of her father also—that father to
whom all her life long she had looked up with
loving reverence, and whom she now discovered to
have been steeped in fraud and falsehood ever
since she had known him. Her love had been
thrown away and squandered even as her veneration, for he had responded to the one as little as
he had deserved the other. Yes, she saw it all
now.   The coldness with which he had ever
treated her, and which she had deemed a mere
mask to feelings that he was too proud and reserved to show, was but the natural expression
of indifference, perhaps of actual dislike. How,
indeed, could he have loved her even had he tried

—her whose presence must have been a perpetual reminder to him of an unexpiated, still enduring crime?

She might yet not have felt so totally lost and hopeless, so totally severed from her former self, could she still have fostered the bright ideal which her yearning heart had made for itself of the mother whom, as she had hitherto believed, she had never seen—save, indeed, as she had fondly hoped, in dreams. In all the small troubles of her childhood and her girlhood, she had found comfort in the thought that that gentle spirit might even then be looking down upon her, watching her with compassionate helpful love as a guardian angel. But now, in this time of cruel soul-killing anguish, the sweet gracious image had faded away from before her mind's eye, and she was left absolutely desolate and alone. Now, when she sought to invoke the cherished name of mother, there rose before her a dark face—beautiful, but bearing all too deep traces of the care that sin leaves in its wake—a face suiting so ill with the attributes of perfect purity and goodness which under that name she had hitherto loved to worship, that, strive as she would, she could not make it welcome. She could feel no love, no reverence, for the memory of that strange dark-eyed woman whom she had seen at Laviston, and who, as she understood but too well, must have been her mother. Nay, now that she knew how fallen and guilty that woman had been, she could only think of her with a shrinking which made her shudder anew at her own impiety when she remembered that it was her mother whom she thus condemned — her mother, whose fond endearments and caresses, though long ago forgotten, had probably given her that conception of the strength and beauty of maternal love which had caused her to turn so longingly towards the ideal mother of her dreams. She hated herself for her unnatural obduracy, but the tender reverential homage of a child she could not bring to the memory of that poor sinner whom she yet so deeply compassionated. She could only pray that God might forgive her unfilial hardness of heart in consideration of her utter misery.

Utter misery indeed—misery which penetrated the inmost recesses of her being. For it had been ordained that the blow should fall at the time when she was most vulnerable to it — at the time when a pure and innocent love had taken possession of her heart, giving her an additional stake in that existence which had been suddenly made worthless to her. A short while since, before she loved Philip Ormond and knew that she was loved by him, she would doubtless have suffered as much as she now did in the discovery of her father's guilt and her mother's frailty, and in the loss of self-respect which the knowledge of these inflicted on her; but she would have recked comparatively little of what others might say or think. Now, however, some of the sharpest of her pangs were caused by the contemplation of that exposure of her own and her parents' shame which must shortly take place before the eyes of Philip Ormond and the world in which Philip Ormond lived. With a morbid vividness of imagination that would not suffer her to spare herself the pain of a single detail which could give additional effect to the picture, she strove to realise the manner in which the tidings would probably be first imparted to him, the manner in which he would receive them. According to what he had told her of his plans in those few oft-conned words which she had heard as she parted from him at the schoolmaster's door, he must have been in London since the previous day; he would doubtless be in London still when the secret which it almost maddened her to think of should reach his ears. How and from whom would he hear it first, she wondered; and would the teller most incline to execrate the guilt of which she was the representative and the instrument, or to commiserate the wretchedness with which it overwhelmed her?

But it mattered not. Even if the first narrator were merciful, others would not be so; others would assail her own and her father's name with thousands of bitter, perhaps unjust, reproaches, not one of which on his return could fail to come to Philip Ormond's ears. Alas! how she shuddered now to think of that return to which but a few hours since she had looked forward with such eagerness! For ere his return her misery would be consummated, the whole world ringing with the tale of her disgrace and of the guilt of the father she had been so proud of, and she herself cast off by that father in wrath and hatred.

Cast off by her father! Surely this was worst of all. At a moment when the very ground seemed to have given way under her feet, to be spurned in anger by the only creature whom she might have hoped to find still left to her to cling to in the general ruin! But after what she had heard that evening, she knew that her father never would forgive her if she were instrumental to the publication of his fraud; and, indeed, when she thought of the load of obloquy which would thus be drawn upon him by her act, it seemed only fitting that he should hate her as she must hate herself for such a breach of filial duty. Was not the betrayal of a father a crime abhorred by nature itself? Yet how surrender the profits of his guilt unless that guilt were to be made known? and how keep the profits of that guilt without sin? And again there broke from her tortured breast that wild moan of impotent despair—"What shall I do? what shall I do?" Ay indeed, what should she do to escape from a dilemma each alternative of which was fraught with consequences so dire?

"What shall I do? what shall I do?"

And then the wail of anguish died away, and she lay still and prostrate on the dank grass, half hoping that the powers of surrounding nature might take pity on her misery and find a voice to answer her. But vainly she listened for spoken response; all was hushed and silent save for the stirring of the wind among the trees and the gurgling ripple of the river as its waters coursed towards the far-off sea.

CHAPTER V.

THE WAY POINTED OUT.

PRESENTLY she raised her head, and sat up to look at the dark moonlight-tipped waves with an expression of suddenly awakened interest and comprehension. No articulate sound had met her listening ear, and yet had an answer been obtained, clear and intelligible as though conveyed in the plainest human speech. Yes, those gurgling waves had told her what to do—had spoken wise and friendly counsel, which, could she but have resolution to follow it, would quickly end her troubles. Once underneath that bright surface on which the moonbeams were disporting themselves so joyously, and shame and sorrow would have ceased to be. Yonder, through those glancing ripples, was the way of escape for which she had sought—yonder, in the still depths they masked, the sure and hospitable refuge for which she longed. One bold step forward among those music-making waters would reconcile for ever the keeping of her father's secret with the restoration of Sir Arthur Ormond's rights, would give Carleton Grange to its new owner without need of explaining that the real Maud Fleming had died fifteen years ago, would set her free from all obligation to unveil before Philip Ormond's eyes her father's crime and her own ignominy. Strange that an expedient so simple and so certain had not occurred to her before; strange that the kindly call of invitation should have sounded in her ears so long in vain. Was it not the most natural thing in the world that she, so grief-laden and shame-stricken as she was, should seek rest in those clear tempting depths? Must not Providence itself have destined them as the asylum of those for whom life had lost its happiness and its hope?

But still she lingered on the brink, in spite of her yearning wish to be at rest, held back by a strange mysterious influence whose power she felt without being able to analyse its nature. Could it be cowardice, she asked herself, that made her thus delay obedience to that loving summons repeated by each wavelet as it broke against the shore? But no, how could that be? for what had she to fear? Surely not the giving up of a life which had become a mere weariness to the spirit—a life from which she pined to be free

as from a burden too heavy to be borne. Surely
not either the cold embrace of the friendly waters
as they should close around her and above her,
for did she not long to feel the cool yielding
fluid undulate about her? did she not desire
to sink down among those silvery ripples, as she
had sometimes desired, when worn out with lassi-
tude, to sink down upon her bed? And she
could not doubt that she would find the refuge
which they offered as pleasant and hospitable
as it looked. Had she not been told of persons
who, brought to shore when life was all but
extinct, had on their recovery declared their
sensations as consciousness departed from them
to have been the most pleasurable they had
ever known? She remembered to have heard
of a young man, thrown into the water by the
upsetting of a boat, who had told those who
rescued him that, when the first mechanical
struggles for breath were over, he had dreamed
of falling asleep on a bank of roses. Though, on
the other hand, to be sure, a woman she had
lately read of had described experiences of a
very different kind; but then, that being a case
of attempted suicide . . . . .

Suicide! As the course of her meditations
brought her to this point, her heart bounded
painfully, and she recoiled a few steps backwards

from the stream which an instant before she had regarded so longingly. Suicide! did not that word designate the act by which she had just now proposed to escape from the ills of her lot? and had she not always been taught, had she not always felt, that suicide—self-murder— was a sin? She stood for a moment dumb with horror, hardly daring to believe that in the very madness of despair she could have actually contemplated the deed expressed by those evil-sounding syllables.

When by degrees she realised how near she had been to charging her soul with that guilt which allows of no repentance and no expiation, she turned affrighted from the scene of temptation, and, hurrying along an upward-leading path, never stopped till she had reache such a distance from the river that its siren-like murmur was overpowered by the sighing of the wind among the intervening verdure. At last she sank down amid the moss-grown roots of one of those old trees she had loved so well, and, burying her face in her hands, gave herself up to the bitterness of a sorrow hopeless, not only of being comforted, but even of being put to rest.

For some time she remained absorbed in a torturing self-introspection which made all a blank to her save the miserable world of her own thoughts. Then gradually she became aware that either in imagination or reality she heard a sound of distant but ever nearer-coming voices. Rousing herself somewhat from the dull apathy of her despair, she raised her head to discover if her retreat were threatened with intrusion, when her attention was arrested by the unwonted appearance of lights flickering among the trees in front of her, as though ascending from the neighbourhood of the river. She waited long enough to ascertain that they seemed to be moving in her direction, and then sprang to her feet and turned to fly, caring not whither so that she could but avoid for the present letting any human eye look upon her in the abjectness of her misery. Scarcely, however, had she made a step when she was brought to a stand by hearing a shout raised in the quarter from which the lights were approaching.

"Miss Fleming—Miss Maud—where are you?"

She tried to answer, but her dry lips refused to articulate, and in the next moment she was glad she had not betrayed herself. To be seen by any one just now was more than she could bear; fortunately it was impossible that, at the distance at which she still found herself from the advancing lights, she could as yet have been either seen or heard. But who could it be that was thus seeking her, and wherefore? And then, as the same cry was again raised, more than one voice joining in it, she remembered that it must now be not far from midnight, and that her absence from her chamber and from the house at such an hour must naturally have led to an alarm and a search.

Well, she must go in now; there was no choice since it had been discovered that she was missing. But still, if she could, she would fain avoid the torture of confronting for that night the curious eyes that would be ready to probe her grief and shame to the very quick. Thus resolving, she flew along under the shadow of the trees towards a path which she knew to be, from that part of the grounds, the nearest way to the Grange, and which, having found it, she threaded with trembling haste, bent on gaining the house unobserved and on locking herself in her room till the morning.

The repeated shouts of the party of searchers returning from the river-side were already growing faint in her ears, and she was beginning to breathe more freely in the certainty of being beyond reach of their pursuit, when all at once there appeared before her, a few yards further on in the narrow path along which she was hastening, a yellow strip of light which she knew to be the glare of a lantern. She came to an abrupt, terrified halt ; and then she heard on the gravel the sound of footsteps, apparently those of two persons, while the reflection cast by the light on the ground drew nearer and nearer, defining itself sharply amid the shadow made by the surrounding masses of foliage· Her first impulse was to plunge into the thicket that skirted the path on one side, but through its long dark glades she still saw moving hither and thither the lights whose unexpected appearance had originally startled her, and, affrighted and irresolute, she looked around for some safer refuge. But on her other hand ran a thick hedge through which it was impossible that she should make her way. Finding her retreat thus barred on either side, she turned like a hunted deer from the advancing rays, and, just as they were about to fall on the hem of her dress, she glided from the spot where she had been momentarily arrested, and sped noiselessly down the narrow way with even greater haste than that with which she had just before been ascending it. A few seconds brought her close to a summer-house which stood hard by the path, though with its entrance turned round so as to command the most picturesque view of the river—the same summer-house whence she had peacefully watched the sunset a few hours before. Here she stopped for an instant and looked round. The light was still following, accompanied by the steady tramp of footsteps, and without further consideration she gave way to the instinct of terror, flew round to the familiar door, and threw herself panting on the bench inside.

Scarcely had she had time to draw a few troubled breaths in her place of refuge, when she regretted having chosen it. What more likely than that she should be sought here—here where all the household knew that she loved to come and sit, sometimes for hours? She started up in dismay, and was about to pass out, when the sound of voices, borne through the half-open casement looking on the path she had left, warned her that those whom she strove to avoid were close at hand, and that any attempt to cross the moonlit space in front of the summer-house must be followed by instant detection. So with beating heart she stood still, and awaited what fate might be in store for her.

Yes, sure enough the unconscious pursuers were close upon her, so close that had they listened they might almost have heard the throbbing of her pulses; and, more ominous still, they had made a pause under the very walls of her retreat. She held her breath in an agony of fear, thinking that the next second would bring them before the door, when all at once she heard a voice, still sounding from the path behind.

"'Taint no use—I've been in there already—'twas the first place where I thought of looking, and I've been over all the grounds pretty nigh now. Better let's go and find some of the others, and see if they've come upon aught."

The voice was that of old Timothy the groom, and immediately another responded which Maud recognised as belonging to Mr. Rowley, the pompous butler.

"Stop just one moment, till I get my breath again—you forget that I am not used to such violent exercise. What a dreadful thing, Timothy, to be sure!"

"Ah! it's a bad job," said Timothy with a groan. "She wur the sweetest critter as ever I had to do with."

"In the midst of death we are in life," said Mr. Rowley solemnly—"at least I mean the reverse, but it comes to the same thing. Though I can't but hope it may turn out she have only dropped asleep somewheres or other in the grounds, for after all one don't hear of such accidents happening often."

"Dropped asleep!" repeated Timothy in accents of grim contempt, almost forgetting the deference due to Mr. Rowley's elevated social status.

" Dropped asleep since eight o'clock, which I seed her leave the house then with my own eyes ! And with a dozen people hunting and bawling after her for the last half-hour ! It ain't a lively skittish young thing like her as 'ud drop asleep and stay asleep at that rate."

" It is surprising how sound people may sleep at times though, especially after dinner," said Mr. Rowley axiomatically. " It was only last Tuesday as ever was—that day the port was bottled, you know . . . . Still, as you say, perhaps he cases may be different. But Timothy, are you sure the river is so deep as all that near the edges ?"

Timothy groaned again.

" It shows you ain't been born and bred here as I have, Mr. Rowley, or you wouldn't ask. I could show you a dozen places where you'd be out of your depth with a single step off dry land, and even where it ain't deep it runs so strong that if you didn't look sharp you might be drawed away under water in no time, and under ground too perhaps. They say the bottom's all over with holes reaching nobody knows where, so that if you was once to be sucked into one of 'em you'd be drowned and buried too, and it 'ud never be so much as knowed what had come to you."

"What a horrible thing to think of!" said Mr. Rowley, in dismayed tones.

"Ain't it?" said Timothy with a shudder. "Poor innocent young critter — it makes me come all over quite sick like only to talk of it. And her well-nigh a stranger in these parts too, and never to have been told p'raps what a place it was."

"An awful visitation indeed, but mysterious are the ways of Providence. Such things must happen sometimes, in order to be a warning to those that remain to live in a constant state of preparation for being took off. And likewise to be very careful about walking too near the edge of rivers and such like, though for my part I don't think I ever was given to be rash in that line, for I never could abide water. But look, there are the others, down there where you see the lights among the trees. We may as well join them, for if it is as you say, there is nothing to be got by separating, besides which it is very dull to be so long by ourselves in such a lonely place. Lead on, Timothy."

"Very well, sir. Poor young lady—poor young lady!"

And immediately the sound of retreating footsteps was heard, mingled with an accompaniment of sighs and lamentations from Timothy, which in a few minutes died away in the distance, leaving everything hushed and quiet as before.

But still Maud remained transfixed to the spot, unable for a while to shake off the strange impression made upon her by what she had heard. For, as she followed the course of the conversation, it had almost seemed to her that she must surely have availed herself of that easy and pleasant method of escape which the compassionately murmuring waters had suggested, and that now, as a disembodied spirit, she listened to the first conjectures which her disappearance raised among those left behind. How smoothly and naturally everything seemed to work! Already the theory was accepted, that she had sunk, never to rise again, beneath that glittering surface which had tempted her so sorely — accepted readily and at once, without any inquiry into the possible motives which might have actuated her, without any questions raised which could injure or embarrass her father, without a suggestion of aught that could hurt her in the estimation of Philip Ormond. Ah! if it had indeed been as they thought — if an accidental slip, the giving way of a sod of turf on the brink, had been the means of consigning her without guilt on her own part to the kindly shelter of the waves, or, better still, of one of those dark mysterious cavities over which they rolled! But alas! it had not been so ordained, and she lived still to suffer the world's obloquy, and Philip

Ormond's scorn, and, worse than all, her father's curse.

All at once a ray of something like hope illumined the blackness of her despair. An idea had flashed upon her which showed a new and heretofore unthought-of way, not indeed out of her sorrow, but peradventure out of its lowest depths. For some minutes longer she stood, wrapt in thought ; then, with the quick movement of one who has no time to lose, she caught up from the ground on which they had fallen the hat and shawl she had cast aside in that same summer-house a few hours before, threw them hastily on, and, thus equipped, sallied forth with firm decided step into the moonlight.

But not now did she take her way towards the house, nor yet either in the direction of the river. A few steps further down the path along which she had lately fled brought her to a trim balustraded walk, leading through that part of the grounds which was laid out in artificial terraces. Into this she struck without hesitation, and journeyed steadily along it, her face being now turned towards the wall which bounded the park in the direction of Hernebridge. There, as she remembered, was the door through which she and Josephine had passed on the day when she had found the schoolmaster's nephew in the snow, and through which she had resolved to pass for the last time that night. Whither to betake herself afterwards she as yet knew not; but thus far she had decided, that never again would she enter the home which was no longer hers, that never again would she let herself be seen or heard of by any of those among whom she had lived. They thought her dead—let them think so still; and thus, without the guilt of self-murder, would that tangled skein be cut which she could not unravel; thus would Sir Arthur Ormond be restored to his rights, and yet Gilbert Fleming's secret still be kept. What would become of herself she could not foresee, but neither dids he care, if only with a clear conscience she could draw the veil over her father's guilt.

She had not, however, made many steps in this new path, when she was almost turned from her purpose by the sound of a wailing voice borne towards her by the wind — the voice of a trusty friend whom, as she now confessed to herself with shame, she had forgotten in the extremity of her sorrow. She stopped, full of compunction, and looked round, half inclined to cry aloud on the name of Josephine and to fly back for refuge to those faithful arms which she knew would be ready to close on her so lovingly. But she saw lights approaching from behind by a lower terrace running parallel with that on which she

stood, and checked herself, still instinctively shrinking from laying bare her misery to the public gaze.
Nearer and nearer meanwhile with the advancing
lights sounded the tones of that familiar voice, and
presently Josephine's kind homely face, convulsed
with grief, became visible among a group of
servants and others passing along the terrace
below.

At the sight of it Maud was fairly overcome,
and would surely have betrayed herself had not
her eyes just then fallen upon another face that
appeared behind — pale, indeed, and bearing
traces of deep agitation, but with so little in its
expression of the passionate sorrow which depicted
itself in Josephine's that a chill came over her
heart, and she was silent. It was her father's
face, and when she looked she could not but
remember that he had never loved her, and that to
him her disappearance offered a promise of escape
from ignominy. She was silent, therefore, and,
cowering down to hide herself from the bearers of
the lights below, watched the approaching party
between the stone columns of the balustrade.

Josephine was sobbing violently, and Mr. Rowley was administering consolation with his usual
unctuousness of manner.

"It is a dreadful trial, mam'selle, but it has
been sent for our good, and it is our duty to accept

it as such, besides which we're only just now going to look through the grounds t'other side the house, and until we've been everywhere, you know, we can't tell but what it's all right after all."

"And this brooch — what say you then of this brooch?" panted forth Josephine between her sobs. "Is it not that I have found it myself on the border of the water? Ah! my child, my darling, my angel, I know what is arrived. This river—this frightful river" .   .   .   .   .

She stopped, choked by her tears, and Maud, raising her hand to her collar, missed a brooch which she was accustomed to wear there ; doubtless it had fallen out as she lay in her agony by the river-side.

"She carried it this evening; I gave it to her when she was making her toilet. Ah ! why have I not crushed it under the foot, since it was going to kill my child ? I see all — it is fallen — she has wished to find it — the foot slipped her — Ah ! I will die of grief."

There was a new storm of sobs, and when their violence had again somewhat calmed, the little group had passed on so far beyond her that Maud could no longer distinguish a word. She was glad that it was so, for already her resolution had been put to a sore trial — a trial which she would never have been able to withstand but that the emotions

raised by Josephine's distress had been kept in
check by the cold silence and stony rigidity of
expression preserved by Mr. Fleming. *He* would
not die of grief for her loss, and why should she
falter in the execution of a plan which would save
him from the infamy he dreaded?

She waited until the lights, having reached a
point where several paths met, made an upward
sweep towards those higher parts of the grounds
which lay near the house, leaving her free to continue her journey without fear of further interruption. Then swiftly she sped onwards, and in a few
minutes there might have been seen, gliding along
the narrow sunken way which ran outside the
wall of Carleton Park, a graceful girlish form,
moving quickly yet stealthily, as though fearing
detection, towards the path that led over the hill
to Hernebridge. It was the reputed mistress of
Carleton Grange, who had left her home and all
that she had hitherto counted hers, and was
timorously making her first solitary plunge into a
world of which she knew nothing save that it was
scarcely likely to deal gently with an unknown
and nameless stranger.

CHAPTER VI.

OVERTAKEN.

AT first she could only urge herself forward in blind unreasoning terror, careless whither she shaped her course so that only every step should increase the distance between her and those whom she knew to be seeking her. But presently, as she reached the top of the bare hill, and, looking round, saw by the aid of the moonlight that no one was on her track, the wild excitement of her pulses calmed down, and she began to understand that it was necessary to decide on a plan of action in order to make good the escape of which as yet she had only completed the first and easiest stage. It was nothing to have penetrated unobserved beyond the walls inclosing her home if she could not succeed, first, in making her departure from the neighbourhood with equal secresy, and, next, in finding her way to some asylum where all traces of her would for ever be lost.

As she pondered what place would offer the

surest refuge, the idea of London naturally presented itself. Thanks to the theory by which, as
she had heard, her disappearance was accounted for
at home, she had little to fear from pursuit if she
could but avoid incurring suspicion among those
with whom she might in future be brought into
contact ; and what place where the affairs of
a lonely and friendless stranger were more safe
from discussion than in the busy world of London ?
There, too, she would be far more likely than elsewhere to find means of making a livelihood by
teaching, or, in default of teaching, by the labour
of her hands, though indeed she was too much absorbed in the problem how to secure her flight
from discovery to give more than a momentary
thought to any remoter considerations.

Yet though her difficulties were so far smoothed
that she had now a definite object in view, a
definite place of destination if possible to attain,
enough remained to render her final success very
problematical. If London were once reached all
would comparatively be well, but in the meanwhile she knew not how or where to launch herself
on her journey thither. Want of money fortunately
did not for the present constitute one of her
embarrassments, as her purse contained a pound or
two which would suffice for travelling expenses,
while the sale of her watch and a few trinkets she

had about her would for a time provide her with the necessaries of life. But how to get herself started on her way to London? here was the difficulty. She could not present herself at the Hernebridge railway station, where she was known to every official about the place. On the other hand, it seemed almost equally out of the question that, exhausted as she was by a day and night of cruel excitement, she should be able to drag herself on to the next station, a distance of some seven or eight miles, without a delay that must cause the total failure of her project; for if day dawned and found her still in the neighbourhood of Hernebridge, detection was inevitable. And yet, hopeless as it looked, the attempt must be made. Happily, if she could but reach that next station before her disappearance should be the theme of general remark, she might hope to find no opposition offered there to her escape; for it was larger and busier than that of Hernebridge, and, in consequence of her comparatively recent arrival from a distant part of the country, Maud was personally little known beyond the limits of her own immediate neighbourhood.

By the time she had thus matured her plans, she had descended the hill on the Hernebridge side, and had reached the point where the footpath she had hitherto followed diverged into the highway, just beyond the most populous part of the village. She hesitated a moment before venturing to emerge into the road, still and deserted though it was ; but it was the only way she knew of to her destination, and no doubt the inmates of the few straggling houses that were yet to be passed before Hernebridge should be left behind were long ago asleep, according to the wont of those punctual and early-rising villagers. Timidly and cautiously, then, she stole into the road and glided watchfully along, ready to seek shelter in the friendly shadow of the clumps of trees which here and there skirted it, in case there should appear to be any other passer-by at hand than herself.

But no, all was profoundly still; the whole living world appeared to be at rest. It seemed almost unnatural to see the familiar place under so unfamiliar an aspect—the stretches of hedgerow and thicket and orchard-wall which intervened between one isolated homestead and another sleeping in the calm pale light of the summer night, and the houses themselves, which she had never yet passed without bringing signs of life to the doors and windows of some of them, closely sealed at every outlet, and as hushed as though a spell of silence were laid on them. Strange to think of those who slept peacefully on the other side of the dark panes on which the moonlight was shining, unconscious that within a few yards of where they lay she whom they deemed so highly placed by fortune was toiling on her lonely way an outcast and a fugitive, bound on a journey that was to withdraw her from their ken for ever.

And what a journey it was! so painful and laborious in the exhausted state of her physical powers that she knew not how she should be able to accomplish it. Her tremulous limbs almost refused to carry her, and every step was an effort which only a strong exertion of will could have rendered possible. But still she braced up her will to the task, remembering that if weakly she gave way and turned homewards a yet more terrible ordeal would await her—the encountering of her father's curse. So she struggled onward, though ever with increasing difficulty, and with an increasing sense of discouragement as she found how slow and laboured was her progress. Already it seemed an age since she had stolen through the little door in the park wall on to the hill-side, and yet she was only now passing fairly out of Hernebridge. For there, the last of the straggling series of wayside dwellings which terminated it in this direction, stood a little white house which she recognised as the schoolmaster's—that house in whose homely parlour she had first seen Philip Ormond, that house before whose gate she had seen him last, and heard him speak words which it thrilled her heart even to remember.

A fond longing glance she cast towards its narrow unpretending windows, and then she saw that in one of them a light was visible through the drawn blind. She recollected having heard that the schoolmaster was wont to sit up late in company with his books or his violin, and quickened her pace as she passed by. But she slackened it again as soon as she had got beyond that part of the road directly overlooked by the windows, and gazed back at the gleaming light with sad lingering look, as though taking the last farewell of a friend. And as a friend indeed she could not help regarding that solitary ray, showing her as it did that among so many sleepers there was one waking creature still left capable of being moved by sympathy, one human being in whose neighbourhood so long as she remained she need not feel herself quite alone. Not for the world would she have had Nathaniel know that she had just passed his door, and in plight so wretched; and yet, with a strange inconsistency, she found comfort in the idea that he watched yonder, so near her that a single cry might bring him to her side. And he was one surely from whom, if from none other, she might hope to find some tenderness, some compassion for her misery. For, as she took a dreary pleasure in remembering, she had established a claim on his good-will—a claim which he had not been slow in acknowledging ; and something told her that a friendship once professed by the school-master must be sincere and not easily shaken by adversity. Ay, perhaps even the whole story of her father's falsehood and her own unwitting im-posture, could it be made known behind that dimly-lighted white blind, would excite sympathy and pity rather than any harsher feeling.

But the precious moments were flying on. She must bid farewell to yonder friendly light, and, at any cost of pain and suffering, force her fainting limbs to carry her beyond the reach alike of the compassion and the contempt of those who had hitherto constituted her world. One last look she gave, and in a moment more the schoolmaster's house was lost to sight behind a bend in the road ; the companionable ray had ceased to beam upon her, and she was alone. Alone—with no sign of human life to be descried far or near, with no sound to break the funereal silence of the hour, save the faltering and ever more slowly recurring fall of her own footsteps.

Wearily and more wearily she toiled on, her powers of mind and body becoming as it were numb with exhaustion, when all at once a sharp thrill of terror ran through her which roused them even as they seemed to be giving way. Was it fancy, was it an echo, or did she in truth hear, mingled with the sound of her own footsteps, that of others following in the distance? She turned round and paused to listen. Nothing was visible save a long track of moonlit road, bounded by the curve which had hidden the schoolmaster's house from her view; but still from afar she heard a sound as of a quick irregular stride, faint indeed, yet falling ever more distinctly on her ear. Terrified she looked round for the means of concealment, but she found that none such were at hand, having reached a part of the road which for some way both before and behind was bare of trees and skirted on each side by a tall impenetrable hedge. Meanwhile the heavy fitful tramp behind grew plainer and plainer still, and, finding that no other way of escape was open, she urged her tottering steps forward at their utmost speed.

But despite her desperate efforts to advance, she heard that rapid stride advancing more quickly still. On she went, as one in a hideous dream, but ever nearer and nearer came the pursuer, till she almost fancied that she heard the sound of his breathing. Strange that there had been no acceleration of his pace since he had come thus close upon her; was he amusing himself with her impotent endeavours to escape, or was it possible that he had not yet discovered how nearly he had overtaken her? She longed to look round, but through very cowardice dared not, and still pressed forward.

Presently an exclamation of surprise sounded at her ear, and she heard her name ejaculated by a voice which she knew, but did not immediately recognise. She made a sudden halt, and, trembling in every fibre, turned her head. But scarcely had she done so when the tension of her nerves all at once relaxed, and a burst of tears came to the relief of her overcharged heart. For yonder, unless her eyes deceived her, instead of a triumphant pursuer who would drag her home in view of all the gossips and scandal-mongers of the village, was a friend who would surely listen to her ere he condemned her and her father to public shame—the friend in whose sympathy she believed before, and more than ever believed now that she saw his honest homely face looking at her so wonderingly yet kindly in the moonlight— Nathaniel Digges, the poor lame schoolmaster.

CHAPTER VII.

NATHANIEL CONSPIRING.

IT was indeed Nathaniel Digges, who had just put
away his books and his violin and come forth
for the midnight walk with which it was his
custom to recruit himself after the labours of the
day. Hardly believing his eyes, he gazed in infinite astonishment on Maud, whom, with his habi-
tual absence of mind, he had altogether failed to
notice till his usual swift stride had brought him
close up to her, and whose wild outburst of passionate grief now filled him with as much bewilderment as though he had hitherto held her
a celestial being beyond the power of care or
sorrow to touch.

Heedless of his surprise, Maud wept on, so
violently agitated that for a while she could not
articulate.

"Save me!" she panted forth at last, putting
her trembling hands imploringly together. " Oh!

you will be my friend, you will save me, will you not?"

The ground seemed to heave beneath her as she spoke, and, giddy and fainting, she would have fallen had she not caught at Nathaniel's arm for support.

"Merciful Heaven! what can have happened?" he exclaimed, his face almost as pale as her own. "You are ill, Miss Fleming—very, very ill!"

"No, no, I am not ill—only so glad to see you. You will save me, you will help me, is it not so? Say that you will; for mercy's sake say that you will."

She looked eagerly into his face, and her fingers tightened convulsively round his arm.

"Oh! Miss Fleming, don't you know I would give anything in the world to be able to serve you? Only tell me what I had best do. Shall I run to the Grange and get them to send the carriage for you, or do you think, with my arm, you are strong enough to walk home?"

She recoiled from him in terror.

"Home!" she cried, shudderingly, "you would take me home!"

Then, remembering that he knew nothing yet of the reason why he found her thus a lonely wanderer, she added faintly:

"I have no home now. I can never go back."

Nathaniel looked in mute amazement.

"You think me very wicked, I know. I should have thought so too once of any girl I found running away from home."

But indeed Nathaniel had been thinking nothing of the kind. The notion of Maud Fleming doing anything wrong was so utterly inconsistent with all his ideas of her that the strongest circumstantial evidence would have failed even to suggest it to him.

"I don't know what you mean," he answered at last. "Surely I must be dreaming or going mad, for I cannot understand a word you say."

"You will understand soon — I will explain . . . . . Oh! bear with me patiently, for I am very, very miserable."

She sank down, in a flood of tears, on a bank by the wayside, while Nathaniel knelt by her, stunned by the spectacle of her grief.

"I would trust no one except you," she faltered. "But you have always been my friend, I am sure."

"Yes, yes," cried Nathaniel, flushing with sudden pleasure at the words. "I would give my life to do you service, Miss Fleming—so far I deserve what you have said. You may trust me, indeed you may."

"And I will, I will, and am almost glad that I have been forced to it. I think I may be happier for feeling that I am not left quite alone to bear the weight of such a secret; and I know not how it is, Mr. Digges, but it seems to me that you are the one person in the world whom I need not fear to see look coldly on me when I tell it."

" Look coldly on you! Oh! Miss Fleming!"

" I believe I should have come to you of my own accord to ask your help, if only my secret had been altogether mine. But it was not, it is not; and were it not that telling you is the only way to save him, you should know nothing even now.   You are not angry with me for saying so?"

" Miss Fleming! how can you think of such a thing? what can you take me for?"

" You are so kind to me!" she murmured. " Oh! if only you would promise to be as kind to those I love! if only you would promise not to judge too harshly of papa. Poor papa! he has suffered so much, and we have not felt what it is to be tempted as he was. Will you promise, Mr. Digges, for my sake?"

" I do not know what there is that for your sake I would not try," said Nathaniel in a stifled voice.

Maud was satisfied with the response, and, having thus prepared the way for her story, briefly put the astounded schoolmaster in possession of those circumstances relating to the past which had been recounted to her that evening, and also of the resolution which she had formed with regard to the future.

With dumb horror and amazement Nathaniel listened, at first hardly understanding what he heard, but gradually, as the recital went on, waking up to such a comprehension of its meaning as seemed to make his very pulses stand still. Had the narrator been any other than Maud Fleming's self, he could have taken refuge in doubt and unbelief; he would have held the whole tale as the hideous invention, if not of malice, at least of madness. But Maud herself was the speaker—Maud who in his imagination had ever been so exalted above the infirmities of ordinary human nature, that what in others he would have set down as the raving of delirium he could not but instinctively accept from her as absolute indubitable truth.

She ceased, and there was a long pause, during which Nathaniel, conscious of nothing save the dread impression of the revelation he had heard, gazed before him into vacancy as one walking in his sleep. Meanwhile Maud, uncertain what construction to place on his silence, fixed her eyes on him with an expression of intense anxiety.

"You will help me, will you not?" she said at last in imploring tones. "You said before that you were ready to serve me, and you will not retract now that you know what I am—oh no! You are too good, too generous for that, surely. Oh! Mr. Digges, won't you answer me? Say that you will help me; the whole world must find it out else, and he will hate me for ever."

She stretched forth her hands as though praying for mercy. Nathaniel looked round, and then she saw that at least she had no harshness or contempt to fear from him, for the moonlight showed tears glistening on his face, which, as it turned towards her, wore an expression of infinite sorrow and compassion. And when he spoke, it was in tones of entreaty as anxious and beseeching as her own —tones rather befitting the humblest of petitioners than one whom she regarded as the arbiter of her destiny.

"Miss Fleming, consider—for Heaven's sake consider. Better a thousand times that everything should be told than such a sacrifice—of your own happiness, of the happiness of all who have learned to . . . . . that is, of all who know anything about you. Think of yourself— what would you do cast alone on the world? Miss Fleming, consider again; it cannot, must not be. You want to sacrifice yourself utterly to another, and he does not deserve it, he does not deserve " . . . .

"Oh! hush, hush, if you have any pity, or you will make me hate myself for having told you. Besides, you are mistaken; it is not the sacrifice you think. It is best for him that I should go and never be heard of more, but it is best for me too. Why should I stay to be despised and pointed at?"

"They would not dare!" cried Nathaniel, clenching his fist with excitement. "If I only thought such wretches were to be found anywhere . . . . But thank Heaven, I don't believe they exist. And if they do, if they do, so much the worse for them, for they will not be long of learning what honest people think of their villany."

Maud shook her head sadly.

"I shall never be able to thank you enough for all your kindness, but I know the world is not like you. Oh! Mr. Digges," she went on with a new outburst of passionate entreaty, "if indeed you can feel friendship for me after what you have heard, if indeed you do not despise me as the rest will, have mercy on me, and help me from this place. If I stay it will only be for my own misery and that of others. I make no sacrifice; after what I have suffered I long to be away, never to return, never to see again a face that I have known here."

Nathaniel sighed deeply.

"It is only natural, I suppose," he said after a pause. "But for your own sake, Miss Fleming, will you not consider? You have not thought of the trials, the hardships, that you might have to meet."

"The more of them the better; they would perhaps now and then enable me to forget. Help me, help me, if you have any touch of pity or friendship for such as I am."

He looked at her with a face of agonised perplexity.

"Do not ask me—I entreat you, do not ask me."

"But I will ask you; I will ask you, and I will not cease asking till I have obtained. You are my only friend, and if you do not help me there is none other that I can look to. Promise me that you will, promise that you will."

What was Nathaniel to do—he who, ever since he had known her, had looked up to Maud as a bright being to be worshipped at a distance with reverential homage? And now she was pleading before him a stricken suppliant, pleading as for dear life—she whose lightest wish it would hitherto have been his pride and joy to gratify. He did the only thing which under the circumstances it was possible for him to do. He yielded

—unwillingly, and yet with the same undoubting submission as though the sweet voice that rang with appealing desperation in his ears had been proclaiming with iron tongue the dictates of Fate.

"I promise," he said hoarsely. "But oh! Miss Fleming, is it not a mistake?"

No sooner had he spoken than she started up from the bank where she had been resting, and motioned to him impatiently.

"Quick, quick—I must go at once—there is no time to lose. Is this the nearest way to Ellington?"

It was Ellington station whither she had been bound when she was overtaken by Nathaniel.

"Yes. But surely—Ellington—why, it is seven miles—you can never think of walking so far to-night."

"I must, I must—how else shall I get to London? And I have to be far on my way thither before sunrise, or I am lost. The night train to London stops at Ellington, does it not?"

"At ten minutes before two, I think. But, Miss Fleming"—added the schoolmaster, with evident relief, while he consulted a ponderous silver watch which he always carried about him—"you cannot be there in time—indeed, indeed you cannot. It is twenty minutes to one now; there is no use in thinking of such a thing."

Maud clasped her hands in agony.

"What will become of me? If they find me here in the morning I must die or go mad—I cannot live to betray him, I know I cannot. Oh! Mr. Digges, you promised to help me—will you not keep your word?"

The sight of her anguish—still more, perhaps, a sudden fear which thrilled through him as she spoke, lest the defeat of an object on which her mind was set with such frantic tenacity might indeed be dangerous to her life or her reason—shook Nathaniel to the heart's core. The satisfaction which he had felt on discovering how formidable an obstacle was interposed to the execution of her purpose by the lateness of the hour died away, and was succeeded by something like dismay; and desperately he racked his brain for the means of fulfilling the promise which she claimed so urgently.

"If there was such a thing to be got as a carriage, or a cart even, we might do it," he said meditatively. "I'm a tolerable hand at driving, and know all the short cuts. But at this hour of night . . . Oh! Miss Fleming, you must give up the attempt, you must indeed. It is impossible, quite impossible."

"No, no, no. Something surely can be found to take us. Think again, Mr. Digges, think again."

"There's Farmer Spratt's gig—we might have that if it were day-time, I dare say. But I could never ask him to lend it me at night, you know."

"Oh! do, do—for the love of Heaven do. I have nobody to help me but you."

Now Nathaniel had ever been one of the most unready and uninventive of men, easily deceived, but utterly unskilled in deceiving—in short, so absolutely devoid of guile that any one who knew him would have pronounced him the last person in the world to apply to in a case requiring the smallest exercise of the intriguing faculties. But even as in the ornithological kingdom we sometimes see the most simple and foolish of fowls animated by a sudden ray of sagacity in a time of extreme peril, especially if that peril threaten their tender nestlings, so Nathaniel, in his intense anxiety to serve the fair young creature who cast herself so helplessly on his aid, found himself all at once inspired with a genius he had never known before.

"If I were to say that I had an appointment to meet some one at the railway," he mused—"a friend travelling by the night train, I could tell them—and that there were some things I had promised to take to him . . . . I might say *him*, you know," he added triumphantly, struck with the brightness of the idea.

"Yes, yes," cried Maud breathlessly. "Oh! that will do, I am sure."

"It's lucky the night train don't stop at Hernebridge," went on Nathaniel, "so that they won't wonder at my not going to the station here. And wait a bit, Miss Fleming," he continued, stimulated to fresh efforts of imagination by finding that his plan met with her approval—"I dare say I might manage to make them think I had only just found out about its not calling here, and that would explain my wanting the gig all of a sudden in the middle of the night, you see. But anyhow I don't suppose they would stop to ask questions —I don't fancy much any one about the place would take it into their heads I was likely to have anything to do with a secret."

"Never, never, I am certain of it. Only ask them, you will find they will let you have anything you want."

"I hope so," said Nathaniel nervously. "There's old Mrs. Slade, the housekeeper, who takes the keys of everything to bed with her—she is noted for being cross, but she has always been very good-natured with me considering, and if she would but throw the key of the stable to me out of the window I could manage the harnessing and all that myself. She will scold a good deal, I dare say, but of course I shan't mind that."

"Oh! make haste, Mr. Digges, make haste, please."

"I will run this minute—this minute"—said Nathaniel resolutely, swallowing down the terrors suggested by the name of Mrs. Slade. "And in the mean time you will do me the honour of resting in my house, will you not? Jemima and all of them are in bed hours ago, so that you have nothing to be afraid of."

It was necessary that she should wait somewhere, and, Nathaniel's cottage being on the way to Farmer Spratt's, Maud had no choice but to allow herself to be conducted thither. And now followed a long weary period of waiting, during which, unable to touch the food with which Nathaniel's unwonted thoughtfulness had ·abundantly supplied her, she sat counting the minutes of his absence, and wondering whether after all her project was destined to failure, and how she should meet failure if it came. At last, as she was beginning to despair, the door was pushed softly open, and the schoolmaster's lank figure appeared on the threshold.

"All right," he whispered almost exultingly, as he made his way forward on tip-toe into the room; "I've got it waiting for us round the corner. I'm sorry I've been so long, but I thought I was never going to make them hear, and when at last I managed to wake up Mrs. Slade, she was crosser than I had ever known her. But it's all right now, and old Simple Simon—that's the horse—seems quite pleased to let me drive him."

She rose, and impatiently sought to hurry from the house, but Nathaniel detained her.

" One minute, Miss Fleming, if you please. I have just been thinking that it would be better, in case you should run any risk of being recognised ". . . . .

As he spoke, he hastened to a chest in a corner of the room, and, opening it, produced a large shawl and a long thick veil.

"They belonged to my poor mother—she used to go to church in them on Sundays," he said, looking at them fondly. "I never thought to see them worn again, but if you wouldn't mind putting them on, Miss Fleming, I should feel all the happier in thinking that they had been of use to you."

Strange how fast the capacity of scheming was developing in the bosom of the once simple-minded pedagogue! Who of all his neighbours would have dreamed of Nathaniel Digges recommending the expediency of a disguise?

Maud, however, did not stop to moralise thus, but, appreciating at once the value of Nathaniel's suggestion, eagerly availed herself of it. In a minute more her slender figure was completely concealed by the massive folds of the shawl, while her face was no less effectually hidden by the thick veil—the schoolmaster assisting her with the arrangement of them as tenderly, if not as skilfully, as a mother who adds the last touches to the toilet of a favourite child.

Still a few seconds more had Maud to restrain her impatience, while Nathaniel went to his desk and took thence something which jingled as he wrapped it up carefully in a piece of paper. Then slipping a small packet into his waistcoat pocket, he declared himself ready, and they hurried forth without further loss of time. The patient steed of Farmer Spratt was standing tractably on the spot where he had been fastened, a few yards from the house by the lonely wayside; and, Maud having taken her seat in the gig, the capacious hood of which the wary Nathaniel drew up to its full extent so as thoroughly to screen her from the observation of any chance passer-by, the school-master sprang up to her side, seized the reins, and started Simple Simon at full trot towards Ellington.

For some time no word was spoken either by Maud or her companion, both being engrossed in their own thoughts. At last, their journey being more than half accomplished, Nathaniel broke silence.

"I have meant it all for the best, but God grant I am not doing you a cruel wrong. You so young and delicately brought up, and to be cast adrift on the world! Oh! Miss Fleming, forgive me, but have you thought of what is before you, have you thought of how to meet it?"

"I have hardly had time yet," faltered Maud. "But in London there are so many opportunities, and a trifle will do for me to live upon. I know enough to be able to teach, I think, and I shall be content with so little that I shall surely find some one willing to give me employment."

Nathaniel fixed his eyes on her, his breast swelling with painful emotion. She was so young, so tender, so ignorant of the difficulties of that rough up-hill fight to which the world dooms those who have their own way to make in it. He remembered how hard the battle of life had been for himself, and his heart ached as he thought of her waging it alone and unaided. Unaided, for alas! what could he do—the poor Hernebridge schoolmaster, already staggering under the self-imposed burden of maintaining his sister's family—what could he do that could appreciably temper the violence of the change from a lot of dignity and wealth to one of obscurity and poverty? He heaved a deep sigh; never had he so much regretted the scantiness of his means as now—not even when he had been distressed by the thought of Jemima's neglected education and premature acquaintance with household cares.

Maud looked at him inquiringly, not knowing how to interpret his silence.

"You think, then," she timidly said at length, "I shall not find anybody willing to let me teach their children? Well, I must be content at first with some other employment — sewing or fancy-work — that is all. To be sure, there are so many governesses, and I suppose it will be very much against me not being able to produce references, or even to name any one I have formerly known. I had not thought of that."

Nathaniel had not thought of it either, and his blood boiled with indignation as he pictured to himself the insults and mortifications which she must meet with if, as an unknown stranger, she had to seek a livelihood in a calling in which competition is so fierce and formidable even for those who have every advantage that testimonials and recommendations can confer. But, thank Heaven, so far at least it would possibly be in his power to help her, that he might shield her from the humiliations which must fall to the share of utter friend-lessness. If he was too poor to spare her the necessity of earning her bread by her own toil, he was at all events enough known and respected within the limits of a tolerably wide circle to have some chance of being able indirectly to introduce her to sufficient means of self-support. And then, as he rapidly passed in mental review the various occasions on which, had he chosen, he might have been able to procure a governess's situation for any one desirous of obtaining it, it flashed across his recollection that such an opportunity had occurred very lately — so lately that for aught he knew it might still be open to him to avail himself of it. He described an excited flourish of the lash about Simple Simon's ears which imparted new vigour to the movements of that estimable animal, and, having thus secured an interval of repose for his whip hand, said shyly :

" I don't know whether the chance has gone by now, but three or four weeks ago I was asked if I could recommend — that is, if I knew (you see sometimes it happens I am in the way of hearing of such things) — a young lady suitable for — willing to undertake the duties — of — of — of governess, in fact. I can't bear thinking of your having to do such a thing, Miss Fleming, but as it must be, I know you will excuse me for taking the liberty of speaking of it ; and it is so highly important that if you do accept such a post you should find yourself as happy and comfortable as possible " . . . .

"Mr. Digges!" remonstrated Maud. "Surely you know I should be only too thankful if you can but help me to find a shelter to my head."

"Such employment is not worthy of you for an instant, of course," persisted Nathaniel, "but I think perhaps that in this particular family you might find it less unsuitable than in most others. There is only one pupil, thirteen years old, and I should think the terms would be tolerably good; and though I don't know anything about the family myself, I am sure they must be nice people or else they would not have anything to do with the person who wrote to me about them, and who is one of the best, kindest, most considerate . . but never mind that just now. What do you think, Miss Fleming? Would you wish me to write and see about it? I will directly I get home, if you fancy there is any chance of your liking such an arrangement. Though of course I know it is infinitely beneath you."

"Oh! do, please do. How am I ever to thank you for such kindness? But — but — they live a long way off, I hope? I must not remain anywhere near here, you know."

"A very long way off," said Nathaniel with a sigh. "Quite in the North country."

"That will do — nobody knows me there. Oh! if only we find the situation still open!"

"I dare say it may be. It can't be much more than a fortnight since I wrote to—to the person who applied to me about it, to say I didn't know of anybody just then likely to suit — to accept the responsibilities, I mean — and that was almost immediately after I heard of it first. And the lady was not wanted till after the Midsummer holidays, so there was no need to engage her at once."

"Then I may have a chance, perhaps. When do you think you will be able to let me know ?"

"In three or four days at most, I don't doubt. All I can say is, you may depend on me for not losing an instant."

"I shall so long for your letter," sighed Maud. "Not only to learn what I have to expect for myself — but I shall be so anxious to hear — to have news of . . . Oh ! Mr. Digges, you will promise to tell me something of what goes on at home ? "

He promised, as indeed he would have promised anything that she asked him.

"And — and about papa," she went on through her tears. "I must know how he is, how he bears . . . . You will be sure to tell me everything about him ? Don't be afraid of grieving me ; even bad news I must have. I could endure it better than the thought that anything had happened to him and that it was being concealed from me. But you will always write if anything is wrong, won't you—always, always? I am never to see him again, but for all that I can never leave off loving him."

A violent sob burst from her as she spoke, but Nathaniel soothed her with the assurance that he would in all things do as she desired.

"Oh! Mr. Digges, what should I have done without you? Surely Heaven is merciful after all. When I found that I must give up papa, I felt as though I were alone against all the world, and yet how mistaken I was! For no father could have done more for his child than you have done for me to-night, and believe me, believe me, no child could be more grateful than I am."

She sighed, thinking how much more tenderness and sympathy she had met with from a comparative stranger than from the father on whom she had lavished her affections ever since she could remember. And Nathaniel sighed too, very sadly and rather bitterly — why he could hardly have explained even to himself, for he knew well that he ought to have been penetrated with joy at receiving such an assurance of regard and gratitude from one whose regard and gratitude he would have given everything in the world to obtain. He did not speak for some minutes, and when he did it was not to respond to Maud's warm expression of feeling, but only to give her the address of a lodging-house where he had put up when he had gone to London to superintend the settlement of his sister's affairs, and where the use of his name would secure her a welcome.

By the time he had completed his instructions, and thus, as far as in him lay, smoothed for her the difficulties of the more immediate future, Simple Simon had accomplished his task and brought them in safety to the Ellington station. Here they found a rather more than usual number of passengers and packages waiting to be taken up, occasioning an amount of bustle and confusion in the midst of which there was no time for inquisitive officials to bestow attention on Nathaniel and his companion. Thus everything favoured the scheme which she had so boldly planned, and which he had so craftily helped her to execute; and yet Nathaniel was almost sorry that it was so. He had succeeded — but succeeded in what? In giving effect to a project which would deprive him for ever of the sight of that bright gracious being whose presence in Hernebridge had been as sunshine in his eyes. He looked at her as she bent forward to speak to him at the window of the railway carriage, the thick veil just so far lifted from her face that he could see by the light of the station lamps the quivering of her sweet, delicately moulded mouth; and he wondered how he could ever have been persuaded to let her go from him. But it was too late now, for the whistle of the guard sounded shrilly in his ears, threatening that another moment would bear her from him for ever.

"Good bye," she said, putting her little trembling hand trustfully into his. "Good bye, and may Heaven reward you for all that you have done for me. I can never forget you or cease to pray God to bless you—never if I lived a thousand years."

Alas! and could he ever forget her, ever forbear being haunted by the recollection of the hours he had spent in her presence, making all else in life look stale and dull in comparison? But he could not trust himself to speak a tenth part of what he felt.

"Good bye — pray Heaven that in my weakness I have done you no wrong. But you would have it so, and what could I do? Allow me, I think you dropped this."

The train had begun to move, and he threw into the carriage a small packet which he had made a feint of lifting off the ground, and which she found on her lap when it was already too late to tell him he had made a mistake. But presently she saw

that it had been no mistake after all, for on opening it she discovered, done up in an old letter
addressed to Nathaniel, a tiny pile of money —
two or three gold pieces and a number of loose
silver coins — and tears sprang afresh to her eyes
as she understood the artifice.

Surely the schoolmaster had that evening made
astounding progress in the unwonted ways of
cunning and duplicity.

CHAPTER VIII.

THE TELLING OF THE TIDINGS.

LITTLE guessed Maud, as she sat watching the dim outlines of trees and hills and sleeping villages which for the next few hours flew past her, that on the same iron road along which she sped there travelled that same night towards the home she was forsaking he whose return to it she had but lately anticipated with happy eager long'ing — he whose image still haunted her heart, though no more to warm it with hope and joy. Yet so it was. Each thinking of the other, Maud and Philip Ormond had met and passed on the way, unwarned by any instinct of sympathy, and as unconscious of the close personal proximity into which they were thus momentarily brought as of the infinite gulf which separated the rose-coloured waking dreams of the one from the blank dreary misery of the other.

For Philip was that night almost as intensely hopeful and happy as Maud was despairing and wretched. The business which he had gone to London to manage for his father had taken an altogether unlooked-for turn, which not only set him free far sooner than he had anticipated, but was sure to put the old baronet into a state of elation and good-humour highly favourable to the success of Philip's own cause. Immediately on his arrival in London, having two or three vacant hours before it was time to keep an appointment made with his father's lawyers, he had set himself to inspect a boxful of supplementary papers which Sir Arthur, determined that his advisers should not go wrong for want of materials, had been raking together for the last few days from odd holes and corners, little heeding whether they were relevant or irrelevant to the case in hand. Among these Philip found a deed which, in consequence of a mistake in the docketing, had hitherto escaped attention, but which on examination seemed to him a decisive confirmation of his father's claims, of the legality of which he had never yet been absolutely clear. This view he had the satisfaction of finding shared, not only by Sir Arthur's lawyers, but by those of the opposite side, who, on learning the discovery which had been made, agreed that to bring the matter to trial would only be to subject their clients to a worse than useless expense. The case thus virtually settled, there was no reason why Philip should remain longer in London, especially as he felt himself drawn homewards by the strongest of all possible attractions. Such was his haste to be once more near Maud, and to open that suit on whose result he felt that the happiness of his life was staked, that — the surrender of the opposite party not being announced till towards the close of his second day in town — he decided on travelling home by the night train from London, so that the following morning might find him ready to demand his father's consent to his wooing.

Hernebridge was not deemed a sufficiently important station to be touched at by the night trains, and Philip was consequently subjected to considerable delay on the way, waiting for a train which should take him on to his destination. In spite, therefore, of his despatch in leaving London, he did not find himself entering Hernebridge station till nearly seven in the morning. A dull cheerless morning it was, such as we sometimes see interpolated between spells of bright summer weather as though to make them more precious by force of contrast — with cold grey sky overhead, and long boisterous gusts of wind sweeping over the surface of the earth. Philip, however, was too much under the impression of those ecstatic visions of love and joy in which he had been indulging during the night to be conscious of any depressing influence in the leaden sky or ungenial atmosphere; and as the train came to a standstill at the tiny station, he looked forth at the familiar objects which met his eye from the carriage window with more friendship and kindness than he had ever felt towards them before on returning after the longest absence. But, as he looked, it struck him, in a hazy doubtful kind of way, that there was something unwonted about the place — what he could not exactly define. Perhaps he had been more accustomed to see it in sunshine than on a bleak grey morning such as this; or, more likely, perhaps he had never before arrived at it so early in the day, when the porters and other officials appeared scarcely waked up to their duties, and for the most part seemed disposed to stand about talking either to each other or to such of the public as were willing to enter into conversation with them, rather than to perform the fatiguing and apparently purposeless feats of agility which they usually went through on the advent of a train. Whatever it might be, something there was which appeared to Philip strange and unaccustomed about the aspect of Hernebridge station that morning.

After an instant's delay spent in reconnoitring the scene from the carriage window, he alighted, and, having succeeded with a little difficulty in attracting the notice of one of the usually ready attendants, he placed his baggage in that functionary's charge, with instructions to send it after him to Ormond Hall. Even while he was speaking he could not help being struck with the man's odd, pre-occupied air; but his directions being so simple as hardly to admit the possibility of mistake, he did not think it necessary to reiterate them, and was about to hurry away towards Ormondsbury when he was arrested by the porter asking respectfully, with a touch of his hat:

"I beg your pardon, sir, but I suppose you have not heard the news?"

"News! what news?" demanded Philip, pausing a little impatiently in the expectation of being treated to some dull piece of village gossip.

"Poor Miss Fleming, sir. Such a dreadful thing, to be sure!"

Miss Fleming! Philip was by nature reserved and undemonstrative where his deeper feelings were concerned, and no sound escaped him when he heard the name of Maud thus mentioned. But a sharp pain shot through his heart as though it were contracted by a sudden spasm, and its pulsations seemed to cease while he listened for what should come next.

The man was too intent on the disclosure of his

tidings—the best of us are not above the weakness of enjoying the importance conferred by having weighty news to communicate — to notice the deadly pallor which had all at once overspread Philip Ormond's face ; and he went on :

"Yes, it's the worst job that ever was heard of about these parts, sir. Though she ain't the first either by long chalks that that there river's got to answer for."

The river! A mist swam before Philip's eyes, and the ground swayed to and fro beneath his feet.

"But somehow it seems to give one more of a turn to think of it happening to such a one as her —with everything you could name to make her happy, and so much liked through all the neighbourhood as she was too."

Was! The little station and everything in it seemed to fly round in a wildly fluctuating circle of which Philip was the centre.

"I've seen a good deal of trouble, sir, in my time, but I don't know as ever I was took more aback by bad news than when one of my mates came up to me this morning, and said as how Miss Fleming was drowned."

He had almost known this word was coming, and yet, when it did come, it smote on his heart so fiercely that he had nearly reeled with the pain, while from his lips broke a slight sound as of a suppressed groan.

"Yes, I was sure you'd be shocked to hear of it, sir. But there can be no doubt about it, I'm sorry to say. She was last seen alive about eight o'clock last night, going out for a walk in the grounds by herself, and they've never set eyes on her from then till now. They know she was down at the river, though, for they found a brooch, or summat like that, close on the water-side, no doubt just where she slipped in, poor young thing. And I don't need to tell you what the river is, sir; you've lived too long beside it not to be pretty well up to its ways. I'm afeard it's a chance if they ever so much as find her to read service over, for they've been dragging all morning— at the place where it must have happened, and ever so far below—but they ain't done a bit of good yet. It's a bad job altogether, ain't it, sir? All right, Bill, I'm a coming."

And with a final hasty touch of his hat the man bustled away to assist a comrade in the management of a cumbrous bale of goods.

Mechanically and involuntarily, as one stunned, Philip staggered away from the spot, unconscious of where he was or whither he went, until in a few minutes he gradually awoke from his first state of dreamy stupor and found that, having cleared the station and passed the straggling succession of farmsteads and isolated cottages which lay between it and the village, he was just entering Hernebridge proper. There was something in the aspect of the familiar things he saw around him— the shops and houses the order of which he knew by heart, with every one of whose inmates he had been more or less acquainted since boyhood— which had the effect, not only of rousing him to a renewed sense of the present, but of making what had just passed look more unreal and dream-like than ever. In the midst of these well-known every-day scenes, calling up none but ordinary commonplace associations, it seemed impossible to believe in the reality of so hideous a catastrophe as that the idea of which had struck a chill through his blood. The mere fact that here was standing the baker's shop where he had bought rancid pastry when he was a boy, and there the haberdasher's from which an inflated circular had been annually issued ever since he could remember, was so grotesquely inconsistent with the black horror of those tidings he had just heard, or dreamed of hearing, that for a moment it appeared to give them definitively the lie. Yes, he had been under the spell of some ghastly delusion, and now he had awakened to the real tangible world again—that world the very vulgarity and grossness of which would surely seem to be a guarantee that its tragedies shall never pass a certain limit of terror or pathos. And forgetting of what a mass of incongruities human life is made up—how the coarse and the refined, the prosaic and the ideal, the horrible and the ludicrous, the mournful and the joyous, not only touch but mix and blend with each other—he momentarily succeeded in half persuading himself that he had been deceived by some strange freak of fancy into believing what he believed a while ago, and that in reality all must be well.

But as he was thus beginning to find comfort in contemplating the familiar village street he had known since childhood, he gradually became vaguely aware of something abnormal in its aspect which thrilled his heart with terror. Surely it was strange, in that ordinarily brisk little country place, whose inhabitants were wont to commence the business of the day long before that hour, to see the blinds of so many windows still drawn, so many shops with shutters still wholly or partially closed. More strange, inasmuch as other signs of life were there in even greater abundance than usual. Knots of people were standing about in the street and at the doors talking, rather as he remembered to have seen them on the afternoons of Sundays and holidays than in the early part of a working-day. He paused—arrested by a shivering fear of what he might hear if he went on and attempted to make his way through yonder groups of idlers, among whom there would be sure to be some prating fellow, more forward than the rest, who would accost him and tell him whatever of importance had occurred during his absence. As he stood thus, his attention was attracted by a faint grating noise proceeding from a house opposite to him, one of the few in which, as he had observed an instant before, the inmates had not omitted to draw up the blinds that morning. And now, when he looked, he saw that one after another they were being lowered again.

Trifling as the incident was, it seemed to him to convey a death-warrant to happiness and love. The last struggles of rebellious hope, refusing to believe tidings which threatened to annihilate its existence for ever, died away within him; and what a few instants ago had seemed too terrible to be aught other than a fearful hallucination stood forth now in all its grim proportions as an actual waking fact—only invested with a new and hideous realism by the triteness and vulgarity of the every-day sights and sounds that surrounded him. He believed now, and knew that he believed, and with belief it seemed as though a darkness blacker than night took possession of his soul.

He could not run the gauntlet of the inquisitive eyes that would be turned on him if he passed along the village street. As a wounded animal seeks a solitary place where it may lie in its death agonies unheeded and undisturbed, he looked about him for a way by which he might escape to be alone with his despair. A few yards further on, just before coming to the first of a row of consecutive shops and houses in front of which the loiterers were mostly congregated, there was a gate by the roadside which opened into the fields. Towards this he made his way, accelerating his pace as he approached it to avoid being accosted by a couple of old village crones who stood hard by under the shelter of the hedge, one of them apparently attempting to explain something to her deafer companion, who was listening with her hands raised to do duty as a natural ear-trumpet. But they were too intent on communicating and receiving the news to take any heed of Philip, and uninterrupted he reached the gate and passed through it into the field beyond. As he passed, there came wafted to his ear four words spoken by a shrill cracked voice—the words, "Drowned in the river."

Drowned in the river! On he went, through

billowy furrows of long wind-swept grass, over broad exposed slopes where the blasts blew more fiercely than elsewhere—yet seeing nothing of the bleak landscape and grey sunless sky that stretched around him and above him, hearing nothing of the wailing whistle of the wind about his head, his whole faculties absorbed in listening to the echoes which that shrill cracked voice had raised in his brain. "Drowned in the river, drowned in the river"—such was the refrain which rang ever in his ears until it seemed as though the syllables were losing their meaning and degenerating into mere empty jargon. Still he went forward, and still the shrill cracked voice monotonously sounded on, making itself heard above sobbing winds and surging grass, and ever dinning into him the words, "Drowned in the river."

He knew not whither his steps were tending; indeed he scarcely knew whither they had already brought him. The very face of nature was changed as seen through his changed mental atmosphere, and each object that his eyes rested on, though he was conscious that it had been always there, looked as unfamiliar as if he met with it in a new land or a new world. On then he aimlessly wandered, until, with a sudden painful swelling of his heart, he found himself standing by the side of running water, and recognised that river of which the shrill cracked voice at his ear was still discoursing.

Ay, there it was, with the sullen grey sky overhead reflected brokenly in its tumbling storm-troubled waters — tumbling and storm-troubled except where, here and there, they eddied round in smooth glassy circles on the even surface of which the blast beat in vain. There it was, its green fringes of long rank grass wet with spray, and its clear dark waves swept by the pendant boughs of the Ormondsbury trees, from which ever and anon a leaf or twig was prematurely torn by a passing gust and went rushing wildly down the current. There it was, covering with its restless waters, as with a funereal pall, all that was mortal of the best, the fairest . . . . .

Strange, the conflict of feelings which the sight of that fatal river stirred in Philip's heart. He hated it, for it had robbed him of a treasure dearer than his life; and yet he loved it too, for had it not been the last object looked on by Maud's living eyes? Did it not even now hold in its mysterious depths the form of her whose presence had been to him as a foretaste of Paradise? Standing by its brink, within sound of the gurgling music of its waves, he felt himself brought nearer to her whom he believed to be resting beneath its surface ; and gradually the sensation of blank stony horror which had seized him when first he heard of her fate—such a sensation as, long continued, must be destructive to either reason or life—gave way to a grief as poignant indeed as any he had yet felt, but more natural and endurable. It seemed to him as if the pure loving spirit that in its fair shrine of flesh he had so worshipped must have risen up from the waters which had set it free from earthly bondage, and hovered round him even then to instil peace and comfort into his heart.

Why should it not be so? Surely it was natural to believe that the liberated soul should seek to return with a message of hope and consolation to those with whom in life it had been most closely linked. And what bonds more sacred, more indissoluble, than those which had united Maud Fleming and himself? What though their love had not yet been crowned by marriage, what though none save themselves had known of its existence? It could not be more deep, more enduring, nor give him a better right to mourn her, if it had been trumpeted to all mankind. He knew how strong and earnest his own love had been ; and as for hers, could he ever doubt the expression of that candid truthful face which had glowed beneath his gaze the other day as he held her hand by the wayside? Ay, she was his, as much as his though she had been his wedded wife; and the world should soon know that it was so. Let his father be as proud and unforgiving as he pleased, let Lady Rosamond think what she would, they and all who had to do with him should learn ere long that he had loved Maud Fleming, that he loved her still, and held his love the highest glory of his life. A kind of bitter satisfaction there was in the thought that he might proclaim it now in the hearing of all men, with no need of asking sanction from her father or his own; that at least it was open to him to pay this tribute to her memory, of declaring he had held her—her, the daughter of the man his father despised—in greater honour and reverence than any-living mortal. She had been bound to him, and still was, by the dearest of all ties; and all the world should learn and acknowledge it—none should again dare to speak of her to him as that man at the station had done a while ago, as of a stranger whose fate touched him no more closely than the rest. They should know that he mourned her as none other could or did; that the tidings which had been as untenderly revealed to him as though they concerned him not had planted in his heart the bitterness of death.

He roamed dreamily on, thus communing sadly

with himself, until, on rounding a point where the shore gathered itself up into a steep wooded knoll, he was startled by coming on a group of men standing by the river-side, occupied, as he shudderingly perceived, in dragging the water with long fantastically fanged hooks. The sight, with its horrible suggestiveness, made him grow faint and giddy, and he was turning hastily from the spot, when his eye was caught by the figure of a gentleman who stood a little behind, apparently directing the search. Philip recognised him at once. It was Mr. Fleming—he whom he had hoped one day to call the father of his wife. With a sudden accession of interest Philip gazed at him; he was pale and haggard, looking ten years older than his wont, and so absorbed in meditation as he fixed his eyes moodily on the river that a younger gentleman standing by his side, whom Philip did not know, appeared to have some difficulty in obtaining an answer to an occasional remark. As he looked, Philip's heart overflowed with a rush of quick warm sympathy for one with whom he was thus united in a common grief; and, yielding to an uncontrollable impulse, he went up abruptly, and, putting out his hand, said in a hoarse broken voice:

"Mr. Fleming!"

Mr. Fleming looked at him with evident perplexity, and the proffered hand of friendship remained unaccepted.

"You do not know me, Mr. Fleming? I am Philip Ormond."

The name of Ormond—of the neighbours who had consistently slighted him and were now to be the owners of the estate he had sinned so deeply to make virtually his own—grated harshly on Mr. Fleming's ear, awakening even in such a moment all the bitterer feelings of his nature. He knew not and guessed not the sentiments harboured towards him by the young man who thus unexpectedly accosted him as a friend; and it almost seemed to him that Philip Ormond, the correspondent and ally of Lady Rosamond Carleton, could only have approached him at such a time the better to enjoy the spectacle of his downfall. Coldly therefore, with a stiff ceremonious bow, he turned away from the extended hand, and moved a few steps from the spot to speak to one of the men busied at the river-side.

Meanwhile the gentleman who was Mr. Fleming's companion looked at Philip with a strange expression of what might have been taken for mingled triumph and dislike. But Philip did not notice it, and, disappointed and wounded, was about to withdraw, when he heard a voice say close at his ear :

"I am sorry your kind sympathy should have met with a reception so little worthy of it. But I am sure I may appeal to your good feeling to make every allowance for poor Fleming; he hardly knows what he is about to-day, and no wonder."

Philip had no words to answer, and the stranger continued:

"I see you feel for us, Mr. Ormond, and I am sincerely grateful to you. It is a terrible trial, one which would have almost prostrated me even had my acquaintance with the family been only of an ordinary character, and you may imagine that, circumstances being as they are . . . . But perhaps you do not know the relation in which I had the happiness to stand to Miss Fleming. We were engaged to be married in a few weeks, and in losing her I have lost all that made life precious to me."

The voice ceased, and Philip stood mute and motionless as one changed to stone. One glance he cast towards Mr. Fleming, almost expecting to see him turn round upon the speaker and denounce his assertion as a falsehood and a calumny. But though Mr. Fleming stood near enough to hear every word that had been said, no contradiction came; and, after a pause of suspense during which every faculty of mind and body seemed to be held in abeyance, Philip recovered the power of motion, and with a stifled groan staggered away from the spot.

Mockingly and malignantly Francis Godfrey looked after him as he went, well satisfied with the effect of his words. He had hated Philip Ormond ever since hearing the story of his rescue of Maud related in Maud's presence, divining, with the intuitive shrewdness of a jealous and suspicious nature, that her evident embarrassment on that occasion was the proof of a feeling which he knew that he, Francis Godfrey, had not succeeded in awakening. And now that Maud had escaped him, he hated Philip Ormond more than ever, ascribing her refusal of his suit, and all the consequences which had followed, to her preference for his rival. But he was revenged on that rival now, and he felt almost content.

Revenged! ay, surely he was revenged—revenged by the infliction of a blow more heavy and crushing than perhaps his shallow nature was capable of imagining. To believe that Maud, while she had seemed so innocently happy in the unmistakable expression of his love, had been all the time bound to another, was to Philip as the annihilation of light and life and hope, either for this world or the next. Maud dead, drowned in the river, had been his Maud still; he could dwell with fond lingering affection on the memory of the bright moments he had spent in her presence, could recall with a thrill of mournful pride and joy the pleasure which the half-made avowal of his feelings towards her had seemed to give, could look forward to a time when death which had parted them should once more bring them together. But Maud the affianced bride of the stranger who had accosted him just now was no longer his—had never been his at all, or the pure truthful being he had fancied her—had been merely invested with her attributes of maidenly perfection by his own excited imagination. He would fain have spurned from him a notion so wildly inconsistent with his ideas of her character as that of her being another's betrothed wife while taking pleasure in the testimony of his love ; but how disbelieve an assertion openly made in the hearing of Maud's own father ? Yet, on the other hand, how disbelieve the mute eloquence, so deeply graven on his memory, of that deep glowing blush and quivering lip which had told him that his love was returned—of those sweet honest eyes and that high clear brow which spoke of a frank and honourable nature ?

The contradiction oppressed and tormented him, driving him almost to madness in the violent alternation of feeling it produced. For he could make no attempt to reconcile ideas so mutually contradictory as those which now chased each other through his brain, and he was consequently the sport of each of them in succession. He could not try to explain to himself how it might come to pass that Maud, without fault of her own, could have given her heart to him and yet be claimed by yonder man as an affianced wife. Now he conjured up her fair innocent face, and forgot the sinister words so lately heard ; now he called to mind that boldly spoken announcement and forgot his faith in Maud. And when it was the stranger's revelation that was uppermost in his thoughts, what blank dreary desolation took possession of his heart! Truly Francis Godfrey was revenged.

For hours he wandered on, in the miserable unrest of a doubting, despairing spirit, until in sheer bodily weariness he was fain to turn his steps homewards. He had hoped to reach his own room without being called on to confront his father; but the servant who admitted him told him that Sir Arthur was in his study, so that he had no choice except to present himself there at once. He entered, and then he found that his father was not alone, but was going through some accounts with his agent—a thin wiry lantern-jawed man, very business-like and respectable, who rose on seeing Philip, and remained standing till invited to sit down again.

"Come in, my dear boy," said Sir Arthur cordially, "come in. I'd get up if I could to clap you on the shoulder and tell you what I think of the way you have managed matters, but this cursed gout . . . . Shake hands, there's a good fellow. I had your telegram yesterday, and have been expecting you to follow ever since. You've a capital legal head, Philip; I hardly gave you credit for it, but after all, these things run in families generally. Didn't I always say they hadn't a leg to stand upon? Sit down, Mr. Hickey, sit down. You're looking a little done up though, my boy; I dare say you found it rather tough work."

Philip muttered something about a long journey, and Sir Arthur went on in more subdued tones:

"I suppose you have heard what has happened here since you left? It's a sad thing, isn't it? I don't know that ever I heard of a sadder."

Sir Arthur's voice trembled a little, and he paused, partly to recover it, partly to give Philip an opportunity of speaking. But Philip never said a word.

" She was so young, poor thing—almost a child,

you know, and such a cruel end! I would give a great deal to have had it otherwise, Philip."

Still Philip said nothing, and Mr. Hickey, whose notions of propriety were probably offended at the idea of letting any observations coming from such a quarter go without response of some kind, took upon himself to answer for him in meek tones:

"I am sure you would, Sir Arthur. A shocking thing indeed! So young, as you say—poor lady."

And the agent sighed in concert with his employer.

"And with such brilliant prospects before her too, if only she had lived to come of age," went on Mr. Hickey, rubbing his hands gently. "It's a fine property to be sure—about the best land, both pasture and arable, that we've got in the county—and thirty thousand pounds' worth of leases to fall in at the end of a matter of five years or so. And to think that now . . . . I know you are the first to deplore the melancholy occasion of such a change of hands, Sir Arthur, but since it was to be, I hope you will allow me to offer you my congratulations on such a property coming to you in preference to anybody else. My best and sincerest congratulations, Sir Arthur, I am sure—and to you too, Mr. Philip. And long life and happiness to enjoy it."

Poor Mr. Hickey! he little guessed how nearly his anxiety to please had at that moment brought upon him the most annihilating rebuff he had ever met with in his life. For, as he spoke, it was on Philip's lips fiercely to bid him hold his tongue, and passionately to declare that Maud Fleming had been his destined wife, that the fatal chance which had brought a new fortune to his father condemned him to life-long despair. But ere the words were uttered, a malignant triumphant face rose up before his mind's eye, a mocking incisive voice rang in his ears, and he was silent. Sir Arthur bowed complacently, and Mr. Hickey never knew the danger he had been in.

And thus it came to pass that Philip Ormond kept his secret.

CHAPTER IX.

IT was a sunny August afternoon, some two or three weeks after the night which had witnessed Maud's flight from Hernebridge, and she was drawing towards the end of a tedious railway journey which she had that day undertaken from London to a far-away county in the North of England. She was on her way to the home of the family of which Nathaniel had spoken to her during the drive to Ellington, and in which, thanks to the schoolmaster's good offices with the friend through whom he had first heard of the situation, it had been settled that she should fill the post of governess. The negotiations had of course been conducted by correspondence, but, so far as she had the means of judging, the engagement was one which, all things considered, she might deem herself particularly fortunate to have obtained. Her employer, Mrs. Arbuthnot, was the comfortably dowered widow of a physician, and lived in the neighbourhood of Grantwick, a small town in the North country, with her three daughters—the two elder ones grown up, and the third, Maud's future pupil, a girl of thirteen. The terms were good and decidedly above the average, and the Arbuthnots were declared by Nathaniel, on the authority of his friend, to be considered especially pleasant people by all who knew them.

An additional element of good fortune was the facility with which the situation had been obtained—the simple recommendation of Nathaniel having been accepted as sufficiently superseding all the usual preliminary inquiries as to qualifications or antecedents. Against all danger of subsequent questioning on this latter point, Nathaniel—with a new flash of the genius which had first inspired him in the hour of Maud's extremest need—had artfully provided by representing that Miss Travers (such was the name by which she was to be henceforth known) had not long before been left an orphan under circumstances so peculiarly distressing that all reference to her former life was in charity to be avoided as calculated to cause cruel and needless pain. Thus her way lay plain and smooth before her, and if she had had no recollections of the past to torment her, she might have found the present happy and hopeful enough.

Even as it was, in the midst of a thousand bitter memories, the mellow rays of the August sunshine, lighting up the country in the neighbourhood of the new home she was approaching, seemed to convey a promise of comparative peace and rest which was very soothing to her after the sufferings of the past few days. The very character of the scenery through which she travelled, not grand nor even particularly picturesque, but simply rural and pleasing—an expanse of green fertile plain here and there diversified either with a newly cut cornfield, a group of clustering gables round a village spire, or a thatched farm-house with cattle grazing near—had in it a suggestion of tranquillity and repose which could not fail to be welcome to one fresh from such an ordeal of torturing excitement as Maud had just passed through. She felt that it was something to be out of the turmoil of London—something to be spared the necessity, which would have been so harassing in the then shattered condition of her nerves, of plunging into the great battle always waging there for the means of subsistence ; and she looked on the peaceful landscape before her almost with the feelings of a storm-tossed voyager entering port.

Then, however painful the memories which constantly haunted her of her former life—that former life from which she was now divided by what seemed an infinite gulf of time—she had at least the satisfaction of knowing that the sacrifice she had made for her father's sake had not been made in vain. Nathaniel had observed his promise of keeping her informed how things went on in the home now no more hers, and she knew that her scheme had been successful—that Sir Arthur Ormond was recognised as lawful owner of the Grange, and yet no breath of suspicion had fallen on her father's fair fame. She knew, too, that Mr. Fleming was well in health, and, though even more sternly gloomy and silent than of yore, had borne his bereavement with an apparent stoicism which had taken the simple villagers at Herne-bridge by surprise—ay, she had guessed it would be so—that Mrs. Nicoll's comfortable embon-point had by no means suffered, and that even Josephine, the only one whom she felt remorse in having left, had at length sobbed and lamented herself into a state of comparative resignation. For further intelligence she searched Nathaniel's letters in vain, Philip Ormond's name not being once mentioned in them. And perhaps, as she admitted to herself, it was better that it should be so. To learn that he was in sadness and sorrow would, she felt, have been a heavy aggravation of her lot, while on the other hand, to be assured of the contrary .   .   . It was better that she should know nothing.   Yes, truly it was better, for could she have suspected how she had been slandered to him, a thorn would have been implanted in her breast which would have robbed her of all power of appreciating the peaceful calm of sunny pasture lands and smiling villages.

Grantwick station was reached in due time, and Maud on alighting was immediately accosted by a buxom little lady, somewhere between forty and fifty years old, with a pleasant face and genial voice, and attired in widow's weeds of a very modified and highly becoming character.

"Miss Travers, I suppose? I am Mrs. Arbuthnot."

Maud made a gesture of assent, and put her hand into that which Mrs. Arbuthnot frankly held out to her.

"I am so pleased to make your acquaintance, Miss Travers, so very much pleased. I hope you have had a pleasant journey, and don't feel much tired. I am quite glad to have got here in time to welcome you. Laura—that is, Miss Arbuthnot—said I need not trouble myself, for you would not expect me; but you would have felt very dull and friendless to arrive and find yourself all alone, would you not? Will you tell me what luggage you have that I may see about it? that again is an affair you would have found it very awkward to manage by yourself."

Maud's luggage—containing the modest outfit with which she had been . obliged to furnish herself in London—was not very cumbersome by reason of weight or bulk, and was soon stowed with herself and her new friend in a rickety fly which went rattling along towards their destination so noisily as to render any attempt at conversation out of the question. They were not long in getting through the streets of the small town, and, after a further drive of half-a-mile or so through a pleasant country road, the fly stopped before Fairlawn Cottage, a pretty little house standing in its own trim though not very extensive grounds—its mini-kin proportions rendered tolerably imposing by the addition of a conservatory projecting into the smooth well-kept lawn in front. Altogether, a neater and more elegant dwelling for people of refined tastes and restricted incomes could not have been desired.

Mrs. Arbuthnot led the way up the gravel walk and through the slightly pretentious stone portico into the house, and, ushering Maud into a pretty drawing-room opening into the conservatory, introduced her to two young ladies who sat at work there.

"Here, my dears, you see I have brought you Miss Travers. She would have been quite lost if I had not gone for her, for the station was busier than usual, and there was only one fly. My daughters, Miss Travers—Miss Arbuthnot and Miss Frederica."

The young ladies—tall and rather elegant-looking girls, aged respectively nineteen and eighteen—rose from their work and shook hands very graciously with the new-comer; and then their mother, opening a door communicating with another room whence proceeded the sound of scales imperfectly executed on an ill-tuned piano, called on her remaining daughter, Cecilia, to come and be introduced.

A girl dressed in a frock which was somewhat short for her years, but otherwise as nice-looking as a girl can be expected to be at the age of twelve or thirteen, the age of female hobbledehoyism, came forward rather sheepishly, and shook hands with Maud as instructed to do by her mother, who explained:

"This is Miss Travers, my dear, the lady who has been kind enough to undertake to teach you. I hope you will do your best to make her task an easy one."

Meanwhile Maud was inwardly congratulating herself on having fallen in with such a family as the Arbuthnots, so thoroughly amiable and warm-hearted. What a benevolent hospitable woman Mrs. Arbuthnot was! and how thoughtful and considerate of her to insist on going to the station to meet the governess! Maud was quite overwhelmed with so much kindness.

" Sit down, Miss Travers, pray, and rest a little before I take you upstairs to your room," said Mrs. Arbuthnot, placing herself on the sofa and motioning Maud to sit beside her. " Now I hope you will understand that in this house you are to feel yourself quite at home. It has always been my opinion that where there is a governess she ought to be treated as one of the family, and I think you will find that I act up to my principles."

" You are very kind," murmured Maud, more oppressed than ever by her grateful appreciation of the lady's good-nature. " I hardly know how to thank you."

" Not at all, not at all, it has always been my way. I should be ashamed of myself if it were otherwise, for I consider the manner some people treat their governesses perfectly disgraceful, really I do. I am sorry to say I know several families where the position of the governess is not half so good as that of the cook or the lady's maid. And you know that that is not as it ought to be, Miss Travers."

"No," said Maud timidly, almost painfully impressed by her sense of the good fortune which had brought her to Mrs. Arbuthnot's.

"Of course it isn't. What puzzles me is, how can people expect their children to be benefited by the instructions of a person whom they are taught by their parents to look down on as an inferior? And you know a governess may be quite as good as those in whose family she is teaching, Miss Travers, and sometimes (between ourselves) a great deal better."

Maud made no answer. She liked Mrs. Arbuthnot very much—very much indeed—and yet somehow she did not feel at all at ease with her.

"Now with me it has always been so very different. If there is one thing more than another that I have tried to impress upon my girls, it is that a governess is—or ought to be at least—a lady, and is entitled to be treated as such. And I flatter myself they were never guilty of such a thing as looking down on a governess in their lives —were you, my dears?"

"I hope not, mamma; it is only ill-bred people who do," said Laura sententiously.

"Quite right, my dear, I know who you are thinking of. That is just what I say, Miss Travers. —the whole thing is so ill-bred. And so unchristian too. Such a violation of the precept to do as you would be done by. Suppose my dear girls were to be forced to maintain themselves by teaching—thank Heaven, there is, I fondly trust, no chance of such a thing being necessary—but suppose it, how would they like to find themselves looked upon as belonging to an inferior order of society? Suppose" . . . . .

"Oh! mamma, don't suppose such dreadful things," said Frederica. "I think that if ever I was to come to that, I should fairly go out of my wits. For a person with the feelings of a lady to be at a stranger's beck and call must be something fearful—that is, at least, where people are so disagreeable and stingy as some that I could mention. You know who, mamma. Twenty pounds a year and no washing, for English, French, German, music and drawing, with the rudiments of Latin too, I think. What do you say to that, Miss Travers? And half-a-dozen rude children, and a lady—at least she calls herself one—who doesn't care what nasty unfeeling things she says to people beneath . . . . who are not quite so well off as herself. Isn't it dreadful?"

"You may imagine what sort of person she is, Miss Travers," said Mrs. Arbuthnot solemnly, "when I tell you that the last governess was turned away without even getting so much as her due

legal notice. Shameful to trample on an un-
offending girl in that manner only because she is
too poor and obscure to defend herself!"

"Yes, but it was not altogether Mrs. Higgins's
fault in that instance, mamma," put in Frederica.
"The girl had been receiving letters from the
writing-master, who was a married man, you
know—so that made it quite different."

"Of course in that case," said Mrs. Arbuthnot.
"But are you sure that was the way, my dear? I
thought it was because Mrs. Higgins objected to
her wearing flowers in her bonnet."

"Why, mamma, what ever can you be thinking
of?" remonstrated Laura. "That was Mrs.
Hopkins's nursemaid."

"Was it? Oh yes! now I recollect. What a
shame of Mrs. Hopkins to be sure! But some
people have no feeling for their servants, either.
The fact is, the employed of all classes are scanda-
lously treated. To come back to what I was saying, however—I hope and believe you will find
things very different here. It has always been my
great aim that everybody living under my roof
should be as happy as it is in my power to make
them."

Here in truth Mrs. Arbuthnot only did herself
justice, being a warm-hearted little woman, over-
flowing with good-nature. And Maud was sure

that it was so, felt that Mrs. Arbuthnot and the girls had done their very best to give her a hospitable reception and put her at her ease in her new home, and was grateful to all of them accordingly. But yet she had never expected to feel the degradation of her position so keenly as she felt it now.

Mrs. Arbuthnot sat looking at Maud for a few moments in silence, and then, as though irresistibly impelled to an expression of approbation by her study of the sweet face with its sad downcast eyes, exclaimed in her cheery good-humoured voice :

"I cannot tell you, Miss Travers, how fortunate I esteem myself in having been able to secure your services. Do you know there is something about you which tells me that we are sure to get on together capitally? and I am never mistaken in an instinctive feeling of that kind. At least perhaps, when I say never, I ought to make an exception in the case of our last cook, though that was hardly an exception either, for she was as pleasant a woman as you might wish to see, and would have suited us admirably, I am sure, only unfortunately, poor thing, she drank. A terrible failing, Miss Travers—quite the scourge of our lower orders. But, as I was saying, I feel so happy in having secured you, and so grateful to Lady

Rosamond. A very sweet woman, Lady Rosamond, is she not?"

"Lady Rosamond!" echoed Maud in some perplexity.

"To be sure, I suppose you can never have seen her, though. I remember she said she knew nothing about you personally; only the very high recommendations of her friend, Mr. Digby, or Diggory—which was it? I have such a shocking memory for names."

"Lady Rosamond!" repeated Maud in increased bewilderment. "I do not understand. You are not speaking—you cannot be—of—of Lady Rosamond Carleton, surely?"

"But of course I am, though. Why, Miss Travers, do you actually mean to say you never knew it was through her we first had the pleasure of hearing of you? How very strange! My dear girls, only think; Miss Travers did not know that it was Lady Rosamond who recommended her."

Maud understood all now—understood how Nathaniel's delicacy had prevented him from mentioning the name of the friend through whom her engagement with the Arbuthnots had been obtained, lest he might thus seem to be laying her under an obligation to a person she had been brought up to regard as an hereditary enemy. She understood, and, in spite of the awkwardness in which her ignorance had momentarily placed her, felt more grateful than ever to the poor pedant whose kindness was so tender and considerate.

"I knew that Mr. Digges had a friend of that name," she explained, "but he did not tell me it was through her" . . . . .

"I see, I see; Digges did you say? Ah yes! that was the name, of course. Well, your friend Mr. Digges ought to feel very proud, Miss Travers, I can assure you, for you have no idea how high an opinion Lady Rosamond has of him. She told me herself there was nobody whose recommendation she would take in preference to his—nobody in whose word she had more perfect confidence, I think she said. So of course nothing could be more satisfactory to me than that, for though it is not my general way to accept the recommendation of any one I don't know myself, a friend of Lady Rosamond's I would trust just as readily as my own."

Strange, as Maud could not help thinking even while Mrs. Arbuthnot spoke, how respect and friendship seemed to follow this Lady Rosamond everywhere—the respect and friendship of all save only Gilbert Fleming.

"Oh! I have an immense opinion of her judgment, and she has been so kind in this matter, you have no idea. It is some weeks now since I first

made up my mind it was time Cecilia should have
a governess, and most fortunately it occurred to me
that I would take the liberty of asking her ladyship
if she could recommend any one, for really in these
times there is such an enormous supply in proportion to the demand, and they are often so very
inferior, poor things, that it is necessary to exercise
a little circumspection. Well, Lady Rosamond
was so kind about it, and put herself to so much
trouble—just what I had expected from her. She
wrote off to this Mr. Digby at once, but he didn't
happen to know of any one at the time; and there
the matter dropped for a while, until a week or two
ago I heard from her that she had had another
letter from Mr. Digby recommending you. So very,
very fortunate, was it not? And how pleased she
will be to know that we have you with us, and that
we like you so much—it will quite interest her, I
am sure. We must take you with us to call on her
one day very soon."

"Does she live very near, then?" asked Maud,
in a little trepidation at the idea of finding herself
in the immediate neighbourhood of one with
whom, as she remembered, the Ormonds still kept
up a friendly intercourse. But she was relieved at
once by the answer:

"Not very near, I am sorry to say—about a
dozen miles. We often regret the distance, for

otherwise I am confident we should be quite intimate friends, we like both her and Lady Blanche—that's her sister who lives with her—so very much. But, as it is, we visit very little; these distances are such terrible barriers to friendship. You see, Miss Travers, we don't keep a carriage; the fact is, that where there are only ladies, coachmen and grooms and people of that sort are so very difficult to manage that we really prefer to do without one. It is very lazy of us, I suppose, but it is such a saving of worry."

" Oh! so infinitely pleasanter," said Laura.

" Quite a luxury," said Frederica.

" But at any inconvenience, my dears, we must positively take Miss Travers over to Ilscote some day very soon. I know Lady Rosamond will like to see her, and it will be a nice opportunity of showing her something of the country. There is a railway part of the distance, and we can either drive or walk the rest. What day should you say is likely to suit you best, Miss Travers ?"

"It is very kind of you," stammered Maud. " But really I could not think "   .   .   .   .   .

"Now positively I won't hear of any excuse," said Mrs. Arbuthnot, who, besides being naturally kind-hearted, and fond of giving pleasure to those she patronised, was perhaps not sorry on her own account to have such an opportunity of paying her respects to her titled neighbour. "You know what my principles are, and I need not tell you I shall never make any scruple of letting you mix with my friends as freely as I do myself. You must consider my circle quite as your own, Miss Travers, you must really. Will to-morrow suit you, do you think? The journey there and back occupies the best part of a day, so it will be better to take to-morrow, and then it won't be any interruption to the lessons. We shall all go together, and make a pleasant holiday of it."

"But—but—I don't want a holiday, I assure you. I would rather begin lessons at once, please. I would indeed."

"Very good and conscientious of you, Miss Travers, but upon my word I won't hear of it. A little trip will do you good and brace you up for your work; you are looking rather pale, I should say, and I know from Mr. Digby that family circumstances . . . . Don't be afraid that I am going to make any allusion, my dear, I am the last person in the world to do such a thing when I know that a subject is painful, and most sincerely do I sympathise with you in your loss. But I must insist on your rousing yourself a little, positively—it doesn't do any good to give way, you know. To-morrow then for Lady Rosamond's; it is quite settled."

Maud hardly dared to say more in deprecation of the proposal; and besides, she was not without a certain desire to see this Lady Rosamond of whom she had heard so much, and to whom, in spite of the vehement prejudices of her father, she could not help feeling a certain attraction, remembering what Philip Ormond had once said of her. Alas! had he not gone on to express a wish that Maud and this friend of his mother's could be brought together? There was a sort of pleasure in accomplishing a wish of his, even under circumstances so cruelly different from any he had dreamed of. So she made no further opposition, and it was understood that she should be taken to visit Lady Rosamond the next day.

This point once settled, her kind little hostess conducted her upstairs, and, with many injunctions to ring for anything she required and instantly to report the slightest want of due attention or respect on the part of the servants, left her comfortably installed in a snug bed-chamber— almost as cheerful and luxurious as those appropriated to the Misses Arbuthnot themselves. Surely Maud had been particularly fortunate to have lighted on such pleasant quarters as these, in the midst of a family so thoroughly estimable and kindly disposed. In truth she had been very fortunate—extraordinarily fortunate—

and she knew it; and yet no sooner had Mrs. Arbuthnot left her alone than she burst into a flood of bitter tears which, had that lady and her daughters been other than they were, she would probably have been able to restrain. Delicacy of feeling—that instinct which confers the inborn unteachable faculty of selecting topics of conversation so as to avoid all suggestion of what can possibly give pain to others—is a quality denied to a great many worthy persons, benevolent and warm-hearted, sincerely anxious to make all around them happy, and even possessing a certain degree of refinement. It may be but a minor virtue; yet how wofully its lack dims the lustre of other attributes far more solid and meritorious!

CHAPTER X.

A PARTING.

WHILE Maud, oppressed by a mingled sense of forlornness and humiliation, sat weeping alone in the chamber where Mrs. Arbuthnot had left her, a spirit of dreariness and desolation fitly corresponding with the gloom of her own heart reigned in the home of which but a few days since she had been the happy and honoured mistress. It was the eve of the day appointed for Mr. Fleming's final departure from Carleton Grange, where henceforth his ancient foe Sir Arthur Ormond was to bear sway; and the place was in the state of confusion and dismantlement necessarily involved in the impending change. The spacious rooms, lately echoing the sound of Maud's clear silvery laugh among their costly furniture and decorations, stood hushed and empty—the sombre light of the declining day reflected grimly from their bare floors and naked walls. Carpenters and upholsterers had been busied for days in undoing the result of weeks of previous labour, and in the stately reception rooms little remained to speak of their recent splendour, save here and there a roll of carpet or pile of chairs and tables waiting for removal to Linchester on the morrow—there either to share the fate of the bulk of the furniture in the auction-mart, or to help in the fitting up of that modest dwelling near the bank where Mr. Fleming had lived during Maud's school-days, and of which he was now about to resume possession.

But in all that dreary mansion the dreariest chamber, though not yet so completely dismantled as the rest, was that in which Mr. Fleming sat brooding alone—dreariest not in its own aspect, but in that of its solitary occupant. The fast-fading light cast from the western horizon showed him sitting before an untasted dessert, with his head resting on his hand and his eyes dreamily staring into vacancy. Thus, motionless and almost rigid, he had remained for upwards of an hour— ever since Mrs. Nicoll, having finished dinner, had left the seat which she had occupied opposite to him, and in all the pomp of crape and bombazine rustled past him to the door. He had come home from business somewhat earlier than usual that day, with the intention of turning his after-dinner leisure to account in arranging his books and papers for transmission to Linchester on the mor-

row; but his thoughts had found him other occupation for this his last evening at the Grange, and,
forgetful of all he had meant to do, he sat in
moody meditation, regardless of the flight of time
or of the darkness that gathered around him. His
face was paler than it had been a few weeks before,
and was marked by additional furrows which gave
it a yet more stern and gloomy expression than it
had been wont to wear. It was evident that either
by the final collapse of the scheme which had so
long enabled him to control the revenues of the
Carleton property, or perhaps by the tragic fate
believed to have befallen the innocent girl who had
been its unconscious instrument, a blow had been
dealt him as wasting in its effects as the passage of
ten years over his head.

And, in truth, to the mental suffering whose
ravages were now visible on his countenance both
causes had contributed; the latter to an extent
that might not have been anticipated by any one
acquainted with the coldness which he had ever
displayed towards the supposed heiress—to an
extent certainly not suspected by Maud herself.
He had grown accustomed to her presence in the
house, to the sound of her tripping step and pleasant voice, to the sight of her joyous smile and
graceful figure, to the thousand little marks of
filial duty and affection which, unencouraged, she

was constantly showing him—the bright look of greeting with which she would come down the avenue to welcome him home from business, the bouquet of choice flowers with which she was always careful to decorate his study, the caressing touch of the soft hand which she occasionally ventured to lay timidly on his shoulder when she besought him to give himself a day's holiday or pressed him to eat a more hearty breakfast before going out. So accustomed had he grown to these things that now he found himself for ever looking for them, and for ever disappointed when they came not. They had not given him conscious pleasure at the time; it had often been almost an effort to him to endure them; but he missed them now nevertheless. When the door opened and her form appeared not on the threshold, when voices sounded near him and hers was not among them, when he entered the house and left it and none came forward to bid him tender farewell or joyous welcome, when he rose from an unfinished meal and none softly chid him for self-neglect, he did not weep or sigh or otherwise lament, but he was aware of a strange uneasy sensation as of a man in whose existence has been torn a great void.

He thought much of the river in which, as he supposed, had disappeared for ever the sweetly smiling face and gently caressing hands he missed, and from his inmost soul he hated it—hated it none the less that he believed its agency to have delivered him from a danger he had dreaded more than death. For instinctively he felt that Maud would never have consented to keep his secret for him at the expense of Sir Arthur Ormond's rights; and he knew that if she had still been with him the story of his guilt would by this time have been in all men's mouths. He knew this, and knowing it felt that he could not bring himself to mourn . her fate as he would fain have persuaded himself that he did; and yet the very consciousness that that cruel fate had been to him not the affliction it had seemed, but a positive source of relief, magnified its horror for him twenty-fold. The knowledge that he benefited by her death, that he could not without hypocrisy tell himself that he mourned it, made him feel almost as her murderer. And then, ever and anon, a suspicion would shoot through his brain—a suspicion so horrible that he had to thrust it hastily away lest it should overturn his reason—that perhaps he had been her murderer indeed; that the harshness he had used towards her that fatal night, the vehemence with which he had enjoined a secresy revolting to her sense of right, might have wrought that gentle spirit to a mood of frenzy in which the idea of the river . . .

He tried hard to think it was not so—to accept the common theory, started by those who had no reason for harbouring any other, that the catastrophe had been the result of an accidental slip made in stooping to recover a trinket let fall close to the water's edge; but, strive as he would to cast it from him, the dread suspicion still came back, turning his blood cold as it crossed him. More torturing a thousand times than all his remorseful memories of the filial fondness he had so ill requited, than all his bitter pangs of mortified pride in giving up to the man he had held his foe that ancient home he had thought to make his own, a ghastly vision, now hazy, now distinct, was ever present to his imagination—the vision of a fair girl, bent on saving him from public shame, hurrying through the darkness of the night down to the river brink. Truly there was that in Gilbert Fleming's thoughts which well might make him look grim and gloomy—as grim and gloomy even as he looked sitting among the dusky shadows of the half-stripped room which after that evening he was to know no more.

He lifted his head from his hand at last, and turned his haggard face towards the entrance, roused by the sound of footsteps in the hall without. The door was immediately afterwards thrown open, and a servant appeared ushering in a gentleman whose features were hardly discernible through the twilight, but who in a moment more was announced as "Mr. Francis Godfrey."

Mr. Fleming started at the name, and, had the evening been a little less advanced, it might have been noticed that his eyes, as they rested on the new-comer, gleamed with a fierce and angry light. He hated the man as the author of all the evils that of late had come upon him; for even were his worst suspicions as unfounded as he prayed they might be, but for that man would not the hour of the catastrophe have found Maud sleeping peacefully in her bed? He hated him with a bitter concentrated hatred which, do what he would, he could not at all times conceal. But yet, while he hated, he feared too; and, so far as in him lay, he must control the manifestation of the anger which seized him always at sight of Francis Godfrey's face. He rose therefore with a bow, and, mindful of the presence of the servant, who stopped to light the lamp and close the shutters, even forced himself to extend his hand with some appearance of the cordiality due to an intimate friend.

"I had not expected to see you this evening," he said with a voice in which it required no very keen observation to detect a tone of disappointment. "I supposed you would be in London by this time."

"I thought it would be a surprise for you," said the young man, dropping down on a chair near that of Mr. Fleming, with an air of easy unconcern so marked as to suggest the idea that it was partly assumed for the occasion. "But I made up my mind this morning I would stop in the village over another day on purpose to have the pleasure of seeing you once more, so here I am; as you perceive. It may be some little time before I have an opportunity of coming to this part of the country again, and though our after-dinner tête-à-tête yesterday evening was very pleasant, as usual, I could not make up my mind to be satisfied with it for a final parting."

Mr. Fleming glanced towards the servant and laughed constrainedly.

"Could you not? That was very kind of you."

"Upon my word I couldn't, and the more I thought of it the more determined I became that there must be another. I suppose anything in the way of a good-bye would content you, but my disposition is peculiarly affectionate—clinging, I may almost say—and I have been waiting all day for this opportunity of repeating my adieux. I am glad to see I am in time to help you with your wine—it has always been specially to my liking."

He poured out a glass as he spoke and emptied it at a draught; though his flushed face and glistening eyes, as seen by the light of the lamp which was just then placed between the two gentlemen, seemed to betoken that he had already been indulging in the pleasures of the table pretty freely. But men can generally bully to better advantage when they have been drinking, and perhaps Mr. Francis Godfrey did well in thus priming himself.

The servant remained in the room a few moments longer to adjust the lamp, and there was a short interval of silence. Presently, having waited till the man had retired, Mr. Godfrey began, in a voice which seemed to be designedly sullen and defiant:

"Well, Fleming, I suppose you guess pretty well what I have come for. I have been thinking over the terms again, and I was an ass to agree to them. It won't do, my friend, it won't do, and that's all about it."

Mr. Fleming's lip curled with anger and contempt, but he maintained his usual staidness of manner, and answered, in tones argumentative rather than passionate:

"I thought I had sufficiently explained to you why it must do. I have told you exactly what my circumstances are, and from your knowledge of them you must understand that I simply cannot afford to give more than I have already

offered. I have disscused the question with you
a great many times already, and am prepared to
discuss it if you please as often again, but you
will find that the conclusion must always be the
same."

"I am not so sure of that," growled the other.
"Two hundred a year for a secret you had better
pistol yourself than let out! It was worth seven
hundred a year to my father—you haven't forgotten that, I suppose—and I don't see why it
should be worth-less to me."

"Some people have a wonderful gift of turning
treasure into dross," said Mr. Fleming bitterly.
"Your father took care not to maim his milch
cow, Mr. Godfrey, but you have managed matters
so as to reduce me from a rich man to a poor one.
Carleton Grange is gone from me now, and, as I
have told you before, you as my pensioner must
take the consequences."

The young man tossed off another glass of wine.

"I know what you have told me well enough,"
he retorted savagely, "and I don't want to be
told it again. But you needn't talk to me about
being a poor man because you have lost the
management of Carleton Grange. A partner in
Walford's bank is not a poor man, though he may
have let all the landed property in England slip
through his fingers. You have made a fool of me

long enough, and damme, I am not going to stand it any more. What do you say to that?"

"Only what I have said before. My share in the business is not large, and my income from it is barely sufficient for the annual payment which I have bound myself to make in discharge of debts contracted when I was a young man. Two hundred a year is the utmost limit of the sum I can afford you without breaking faith with creditors whom I have undertaken to satisfy."

"Creditors, forsooth! And what are the claims of all the creditors in the world—what is their hold upon you—in comparison with mine? You'll find you can better afford to break faith with them, as you call it, than to provoke me into cutting up rough. Don't you know you are absolutely at my mercy?"

The crimson rushed into the banker's face, and the veins of his temples swelled to the size of small cords.

"Idiot!" he exclaimed in a tone which made Francis Godfrey, insolent swaggerer though he was, positively quail before him. "Take care what you say, or you will discover how presumptuously you over-rate the power which circumstances have given you over me. You think I am a slave to the world and its opinion; ay, and so I am, so much that if I cannot keep intact the reputation I have made for myself for my dead wife's sake, if I cannot honourably acquit myself towards all who ever trusted me with the value of a shilling, I shall not care how low I fall— content if by sounding the depths of public obloquy I may escape the degrading consciousness of owing anything to such as you. Understand, either I remain the trusted and respected man of business who has repaired all early faults, discharged all early obligations, by years of un-flinching toil and perseverance, or I will stand before the world as infamous as you choose to make me out. Do your worst; betray me if you please; but never flatter yourself that I will defraud others to swell your unlawful gains. You know what price I am ready to pay for your silence; you know why I can give no more; and you can accept or refuse at your pleasure. But beware how you menace me, or I withdraw my offer altogether."

It was manifest that the young man was shaken. This sudden burst of wrath had gone far to dissi-pate the fumes of the wine he had been drinking, and he had become sober enough to appreciate the consequences involved in the execution of the threat just employed. He was visibly cowed, as the inferior nature ever must be in the presence of a superior nature which chooses to assert itself;

and, probably reflecting that this was a case in which persuasion might be more politic than intimidation, made an attempt to conceal the angry feelings burning within him, and muttered, with an air of sulky deprecation :

" Come, come, Fleming, there is no need to fly out upon me in that style—you know well enough I didn't mean to offend you. Of course I don't ask you to give what you haven't got—I'm not such a fool as that; only I do say two hundred is deuced shabby, and I'm sure you must feel it yourself. For your own credit as well as mine you ought to try to come down a trifle more handsomely, for I haven't been brought up to live on two hundred a year, and considering that by this time I should have been the husband of your daughter if she had lived " . . . . .

" Never!" cried Mr. Fleming with startling emphasis. " Now that I know what you are, I would have interposed at the altar itself rather than abandon her to such a fate. You her husband—you!"

There was undisguised contempt, almost disgust, in his tones; hatred had over-mastered fear, and for a while the power of dissembling was gone from him. And apparently he had thus unwittingly hit on the best mode of dealing with such a man as the one before him, for the visitor gave

way to no fierce blaze of passion on hearing himself so addressed, but only scowled a dark vindictive scowl, and answered through his set teeth :

"It isn't for me to contradict—you know best
what you would have done, no doubt. You were
so fond of the girl when she was alive, were you
not ?"

Mr. Fleming felt the taunt, and again a rush
of blood suffused his face. For a moment he was
dumb, as though with shame that the unfatherly
coldness of which he had been conscious towards
the innocent girl who had so loved him should
have been detected by this man.

"You are an insolent villain," he burst out at
length. "Whatever I may have been, it is nothing
to you; enough that she was a being as infinitely
superior to you as light to darkness, and that
I will not suffer you to profane her name by
coupling it with yours. She was an angel, and
I thank God for her that she has escaped you."

He paused an instant, then resumed in a calmer
voice, recalled to himself perhaps by the look of
anger, deadly though suppressed, that gleamed
menacingly from under the knitted brows opposite
to him.

"But all that belongs to the past now; and
there is no need to dispute it further. As to
what concerns the future, I have only to say that

if the pension I have agreed to pay does not content you, so much the worse for both of us, since it is flatly impossible that I can give more. Make up your mind quickly and once for all, for I do not choose to be the sport of your caprices. Will two hundred a year buy you, or will it not?"

"I suppose it must, if that's to be the way of it," said the young man in sullen accents, keeping his eyes fixed morosely on the ground. "Though how I am to live on a beggarly pittance like that" . . . .

"You need not live on it unless you please. You have been brought up to a profession, and with very moderate labour you may find it easy to double or treble your income. It is a paying profession for those who can suit their ideas of art to the public taste," Mr. Fleming added with a touch of bitterness in his voice.

"Humph. Well, if I must be a slave I must, for live on two hundred a year I can't. But it will go confoundedly against the grain to find myself plodding at the easel again. Nature never intended me for it, you know."

"Perhaps not," said Mr. Fleming drily. "But it is too late now to think of changing your profession; you must take things as they are and make the best of them."

"Oh! as for changing, I don't want to change

—one kind of drudgery is as good as another. What I mean is that Nature intended me to be a gentleman."

"Indeed!"

"Yes, and it's that which makes it so cursedly hard on me to have to go back to a life of slavery."

"Slavery! surely not quite so bad as that, with two hundred a year to sweeten it."

"Hang your two hundred a·year. What is two hundred a year in London, I should like to know?"

"You still propose to settle in London then? You prefer it to Rome or any other Continental city?"

He felt that his bribe was not large enough to bear clogging with any conditions as to residence, but he would have been thankful to hear of thousands of miles being put between himself and that man.

"Prefer London? Why yes, decidedly. No place like London to fix one's head-quarters in. And I shall be comparatively near you, Fleming, too—that's another advantage."

Mr. Fleming started.

"Near me! You can have no possible motive for wishing to be near me. I shall take means to send you your remittances regularly, but with that exception all communication must from this date be at an end between us. Remember that, if you please."

"What! you want to wash your hands of me altogether, do you? Be easy—you may rest assured that, after what I have seen of your disposition towards me, I shall never trouble you if I can help it. But it is pleasant all the same to think one has a friend at hand to fall back upon in case of need."

"Pray do not think anything of the kind—with regard to me at least. What I have promised to give, and you have consented to take, is the utmost I can do for you, and we part to-day on the understanding that we are never to meet again."

"Charmingly plain-spoken, upon my word. Well, I see you are longing to be rid of me, so I'll take the hint and be off at once. Good-bye, and be punctual with the remittances."

He stood up and paused, almost as if he expected that his host would offer to shake hands at parting. But Mr. Fleming was not enough of a hypocrite to be able in his present mood to go through any formalities of friendship with such a visitor, and merely said coldly:

"Good-bye, I wish you all prosperity in your new career. You understand what I have said, I hope. We part for the last time to-day."

"Oh yes! I quite understand your amiable
sentiments towards me, and appreciate them very
highly, you may be sure. Good-bye."

In another moment the sinister face had passed
from the range of Mr. Fleming's vision, and presently the closing of the front door announced that
Francis Godfrey had quitted the house in which
his presence had been of such ill omen. But Mr.
Fleming never stirred a muscle, and still sat stern
and gloomy as before, seeming to have found no
relief even in the departure of his detested companion. Neither had he, for, hope as fervently as
he might to have done with him for ever, he could
not help being haunted by a vague uneasy fear
that he might see that sinister face again.

CHAPTER XI.

ILSCOTE was a snug little village some dozen miles from Grantwick, picturesquely situated at the foot of a gently sloping stretch of rich woodland. A little way out of Ilscote was Ilscote Lodge, whither Maud was to be now taken under Mrs. Arbuthnot's guidance; a pretty house built in the style of nineteenth-century Gothic, and overlooking the village from the hill-side, where its tall white gables and glittering oriels made it a conspicuous object in spite of the trees among which it was half buried. Though the house was small in proportion to the extent of its grounds— the better thereby befitting the requirements of the two quiet ladies who were its tenants, and who laid themselves little out to receive company— it and its surroundings were in such perfect keeping that it looked more stately and manorial than many a mansion containing half-a-dozen times its number of cubic feet. Modern as it was, there was nothing about it of the *parvenu*—nothing compatible with the theory that it could possibly be the retreat of a retired West-End fishmonger.

And what it was to an external observer, that also it was within. The rooms, though not large, were furnished with a taste and choiceness which made them little gems in their way; while the pleasing view obtainable from the windows of most of them into the richly stocked flower-garden and shrubbery rendered them as cheerful as they were luxurious and elegant. Perhaps, however, the most thoroughly inviting and comfortable apartment in the whole house was not any of the suite of state rooms on the ground-floor, but a smaller one upstairs, which, though only on the first floor, was placed high enough to overlook the windings of the long avenue by which the house was approached from the village, and to command a view of the smiling sylvan landscape beyond. Besides its natural advantages of a fine prospect and warm southern aspect, this room was furnished and fitted up, if not in quite such costly style as the others, more tastefully and attractively. The draperies were lighter in colour and texture; the flower vases were turned to their legitimate purpose of holding flowers; the books were scattered here and there — on the piano or on the small-work table under the bird-cage in the bay window — with that graceful disregard of symmetrical arrangement which bespeaks constant use ; and a piece of woman's work was generally to be seen in some part or other of the room, giving it a more cheerful and inhabited air than was possessed by the others. This was Lady Rosamond's boudoir, arranged and decorated after Lady Rosamond's own fancy; though Lady Blanche used her right of entry so freely that long prescription had made the room almost common property between the two sisters. For Lady Blanche knew as well as any one what comfort was when she found it, though the constitution of her mind with regard to it, like that of a great many other people, was rather appreciative than reative.

Into this pleasant chamber, looking particularly pleasant in the warm sunshine of a cloudless morning, Mrs. Arbuthnot and her party were shown on the day following Maud's arrival at Grantwick— Lady Blanche, the nominal mistress of the establishment, being engaged downstairs, consulting with her sister and an upholsterer on the important subject of some new hangings which she had decided to be necessary in the ordinary reception rooms. This was the first time that any of the Arbuthnots had been admitted to the cheerful retreat upstairs, and while they waited they made the very best use of their powers of observation—

as far at least as was consistent with a rigid adher-
ence to the chairs on which they had originally
deposited themselves, and with a preternaturally
stiff motion of their necks when they turned round
to look.

"It is a very nice room," said Mrs. Arbuthnot,
in a solemn awe-struck whisper, as though she
were speaking in church. "I like these curtains
better than the ones in the drawing-room, don't
you, Laura?"

"I think I do," answered Laura in the same
tones. "The gold scroll on the border is so handsome, isn't it? They must have sent to London
for them, shouldn't you say so?"

"I'm sure they must," whispered Mrs. Arbuthnot. "And I don't believe they could have got
them for a penny less than five-and-twenty shillings
a yard — I know by the look from this distance.
As Laura says, the scroll is very handsome, isn't it,
Miss Travers?"

"Oh! very," said Maud absently.

"Altogether the whole room is furnished with
great taste. Cecilia, don't do that."

"Just one inch more, mamma," said Cecilia,
who was cautiously lifting the cover of a piece
of unfinished Berlin wool-work that was lying
folded on the table. "I only want to see the
pattern."

" Put it down at once, Cecilia. How often am I to tell you how unladylike it is to pry so? Well, did you see what it was?"

"A wreath, I think — I saw flowers quite plain, and I'm almost sure it wasn't a bunch."

"Not so loud, Cecilia. It is for a cushion, I dare say, or perhaps a piano-stool. That's a very pretty table·cover, isn't it? The border is the same as the scroll on the curtains, you see. And finished off at the corners with a coronet in silk braid — an earl's coronet, I suppose. Lady Rosamond's papa was an earl, Miss Travers. I don't know whether you are aware of it."

"A coronet, mamma! it isn't anything of the kind," said Frederica, with as much scorn as a barely audible whisper is capable of conveying. "It's only a basket of flowers and fruit—grapes, I think, and very nicely worked too."

"Oh! is it? Well, I thought the coronet was rather odd. But I am so dreadfully short-sighted."

Meanwhile Maud had not been altogether unobservant of what was around her. Immediately on entering the room her eyes had fallen on two oil portraits which hung side by side over a little writing-table in a recess, and they had occupied the chief share of her attention ever since. One represented a young man — of a countenance handsome and singularly pleasant to look at, and a form comely and vigorous — habited in a costume which showed the work to have been executed some fifteen or twenty years before. The other portrait, which was similarly indicated as belonging to about the same period, was that of a child — a blooming fair-haired little girl of some two or three years old, whose tiny softly-moulded face smiled innocently down from the canvass, bright and cherub-like. On both those pictures Maud looked with an interest stronger than she had been able to feel for some time back in any subject foreign to her personal cares—perhaps attracted to them by a fancy which struck her that, in some way or other, the features of the child were not altogether unfamiliar to her. But where and when she had seen any resembling them she could not with her utmost endeavours recollect; and she was striving to shake off the uncomfortable impression always produced by a baffled effort of memory when her attention was attracted by a new remark from Laura Arbuthnot, by whose inquisitive eyes the pictures had just been discovered.

"I wonder whose portraits those are," she whispered. "Look, mamma—make haste before any one comes."

Mrs. Arbuthnot turned her eye-glass promptly in the direction indicated.

"Dear, dear! how very interesting!" she murmured, in tones even lower if possible than any she had yet employed. "I am quite glad to have seen them. I'll tell you what they are, my dear— at least I feel quite sure of it—the portraits of Mr. Carleton, Lady Rosamond's husband, you know, and her poor little girl. Now that I think of it, I have been told she had their pictures hanging in her room upstairs, so these must be the ones."

"Of course they must," said Laura, and she scanned them more curiously than ever.

"A dear little thing she must have been," said Mrs. Arbuthnot, examining the child's portrait through her glass. "No wonder poor Lady Rosamond was in a terrible state at losing her—and in such a way too. A most dreadful affair, Miss Travers; perhaps you have never heard of it, for it happened a great many years ago now, but they say Lady Rosamond has never got over it. I think she was in France visiting" . . .

"Mamma, there's some one coming," interposed Laura quickly.

Mrs. Arbuthnot closed her eye-glass in a great hurry.

"I'll tell you afterwards," she added hastily, finishing off the conversation with a look of intelligence at Maud, and then turning towards the door a face wreathed with smiles to greet the person who was about to enter, and whom a moment more proved to be Lady Rosamond herself.

She was a graceful and even now very pretty woman, in spite of her deep mourning and the widow's cap which she yet persisted in wearing. Her figure was still as slender and flexible as it had ever been, thus combining with a more than usually clear complexion to make her look, at least on a first glance, considerably younger than she really was—she was barely forty even reckoning by years. Yet a close observer could hardly have failed to discover in her face, pure and fresh as it still was, traces of sorrow and suffering such as can be looked back upon by few who have lived in the world twice as long. The soft lustrous brown eyes had an expression of sadness in them which it must have taken years of deep abiding grief to render permanent. The same look of depression, too, hovered about the corners of the sweet delicate mouth, varying in intensity according as the face was in motion or repose, but never quite dispelled by the brightest smile which ever now mantled on those still rosy lips; while here and there a thread of silver was to be detected in the smooth braids of her shining brown hair—hair of that fine silken texture which in the course of nature seldom becomes grey till at a late period of life. And yet the melancholy stamped on her every lineament, communicating itself even to her gait and bearing, seemed to enhance the attractiveness of her appearance rather than to detract from it—so well that subdued air of patient resignation agreed with the naturally gentle character of a beauty which had always been simple and unassuming. A fair and winning woman Lady Rosamond was still ; all the more winning, perhaps, in the appeal which the mute traces of her sorrow made to the sympathy of those who came across her path.

This mild beautiful apparition was utterly incongruous with all Maud's preconceived impressions of the Lady Rosamond of whom she had so often heard ; and the surprise of beholding it imparted a singular flutter to her nerves—so sorely taxed of late as to be more than usually apt to be thrown into commotion by anything unwonted or unexpected. Not that it was the strangeness and unfamiliarity of the face that thus affected her ; it was so sweet and kind in its expression, and the look of resigned grief which it wore harmonised so well with the present mood of Maud's own spirit, that she could have taken it rather for that of a friend long known and loved than for one seen first to-day. But she had so little expected to meet with such a face here—to find it belonging to the woman her father hated—that she absolutely started as her eyes fell on it, and she felt her heart and all her pulses vibrate.

"This is very kind of you, Mrs. Arbuthnot; I hope you are quite well," said a gentle voice—a voice in such exact accordance with the character suggested by the aspect of the benign melancholy features, that it seemed to Maud as though she had expected to hear it, and again her pulses thrilled.

Lady Rosamond shook hands cordially with Mrs. Arbuthnot, and then, turning for the first time towards the corner where Maud sat, advanced with extended hand, under the momentary impression that the slight figure of which she had caught a glimpse in entering was that of Laura or Frederica Arbuthnot. But ere she had made more than a pace or two forward, her eyes met those of Maud, which, in obedience to the feeling of interest excited by her appearance, had for the last few moments been intently fastened on her movements—so intently that they could not now be withdrawn at an instant's notice—and Lady Rosamond found out her mistake.

It is always startling to find one's self confronted by a face other than that for which one has been prepared, and to Lady Rosamond at this moment the discovery of her error seemed more than ordinarily embarrassing. She paused abruptly, and stood still for an instant in evident agitation, her eyes fixed on Maud with a surprise which her usual kindly readiness to welcome a visitor, and especially a stranger, did not enable her to con ceal. Mrs. Arbuthnot observed the awkwardness thus occasioned by her default, and hastened to explain :

" I must beg you to excuse me, Lady Rosamond. I had almost forgotten to introduce Miss Travers the lady whose services you have so kindly as sisted me to procure for Cecilia. I thought you would not object to my bringing her to call on you, being a person in whom your friend Mr. Digby takes so much interest, and " . . . .

" It was very good of you," said Lady Rosamond, recovering with a little effort from her embarrassment, and taking Maud's hand with a frankness which sufficiently proved how involuntary had been her momentary delay. " I am very glad to have the pleasure of making the acquaintance of Miss Travers—very glad indeed," she added with increased emphasis, favourably impressed apparently by the expression of the eyes which were now timidly raised, and on which hers fastened with a look of manifest interest. Another moment she paused before Maud, and then, almost reluctantly as it seemed, turned away to bestow a welcome on Laura and Frederica.

Meanwhile the unexpected kindness which she had thus met from one of whom, as she remembered but too well, she had been accustomed to think hardly, had produced in Maud a singular revulsion of feeling. She remembered how cruelly she had formerly misjudged this patient sorrow-stricken lady; and though she might have reasonably argued that no blame was due to her for a partial adoption of her father's prejudices—partial, for in the bitterness of those prejudices she had not shared—it seemed to her as if she could never sufficiently atone for the injustice. An aching sense of self-reproach filled her heart, and, over-flowing with penitent tenderness, it yearned towards the gentle mourner the warm impression of whose touch she still felt lingering on her hand—yearned as if longing to ask pardon for past wrongs, though committed only in thought, as if longing to make reparation for them by deeds of sympathy and love. She felt how vain the longing was, and sighed—turning a look half of interest, half of unconscious apology, towards the sofa at the other end of the room, on which by this time Lady Rosamond had placed herself by Mrs. Arbuthnot's side. But again they encountered those of her friendly entertainer, and she lowered them hastily and in confusion.

"I hope Mr. Digges was quite well when you

saw him or heard from him last," said Lady Rosamond, seizing the first opportunity of addressing her that Mrs. Arbuthnot's loquacity allowed.

"Quite well, thank you."

She was too much flurried at the moment to say more, and there was a pause, which Mrs. Arbuthnot was the first to break.

"I am sure Mr. Digges is a person to whom I ought to feel very much obliged—next to yourself, Lady Rosamond. I am so pleased at having secured Miss Travers, you can't think. I have quite taken a fancy to her already, and so have the girls. Cecilia was only telling me this morning she never had a governess she liked so much. And you know that is such a point gained, Lady Rosamond. Unless a pupil can be brought to regard a teacher in some other light than that of a stranger hired to instruct her" . . . . .

"Oh yes! I quite agree with you," hastily interrupted Lady Rosamond. "You come from London, I believe, Miss Travers? I hope you had a pleasant journey."

"Yes, thank you," said Maud. "The country is looking very beautiful just now."

"So it is," assented Mrs. Arbuthnot. "This is what I call the season of all others for appreciating the advantages of a rural life. Well, as I often tell my girls, there may be drawbacks on living in the country, but at this time of year at all events they are far more than made up to us. Who would envy the artificial pleasures of fashionable life in London while Nature is doing so much to attract us?" continued the worthy lady fervently, forgetting with excusable poetical license the ana-chronism involved in talking of fashionable life in London in the month of August. She paused a moment, and then added, as though the question were suggested by a natural association of ideas : " Have you heard anything lately of your friend the Honourable Mrs. Merton? Her daughter is as much admired as ever, I suppose ? "

Mrs. Arbuthnot was an indefatigable talker, and the answer to this question she so energetically followed up by comment and new inquiry that it was some minutes before Lady Rosamond found another opportunity of addressing Miss Travers. But not the less did Maud appreciate the kindness with which the mild lady had spoken to her, the evident anxiety with which she had interposed to shield her from the heedless shots of well-meaning Mrs. Arbuthnot's tongue ; and she felt penetrated with a sense of grateful obligation which, magnified by her remorse for the past injustice she had un-wittingly done to a woman so tender of others and yet herself so sorely tried, almost brought the tears into her eyes. After her experience of the cold indifference of the strangers among whom her lot had been cast in London, and the yet more oppressive ordeal of Mrs. Arbuthnot's patronising good-nature, no wonder that the welcome of one who to frank and cordial kindness joined evident refinement and delicacy of sentiment produced an unwonted effect on her. It was so long since her feelings had been treated with anything like tenderness or consideration. Her heart swelled even to bursting, and a strange sensation thrilled through her nerves as though of unexpectedly finding something that had long been lost and vainly looked for.

Presently the door again opened, and another lady entered whom Maud at once rightly conjectured to be Lady Blanche Arden. She was some ten or twelve years older than her sister, with features fine and aristocratic though somewhat pinched, and a tall commanding figure, a little meagre and gaunt perhaps, but distinguished by a certain elegance of motion as of one who was, or had been, accustomed to mix much in good society. She was handsomely attired in a rich silk dress made in the newest fashion ; and a modish little French cap, with long ribbon streamers attached, was perched on her head with an air which might have been almost called coquettish in a less decorous and stately person. Her manners presented a curious combination of the mincing and the dignified—mincing as those of elderly young ladies generally are, but dignified as became one who had not forgotten that, though left nowhere in the great matrimonial race, birth had made her an earl's daughter and given her precedence over the proudest untitled matron breathing. The air of patrician languor which she could assume in the company of those whom she conceived to be her social inferiors, especially if she thought that they did not sufficiently recognise the distinction, had driven many an aspiring dame to the verge of distraction, and rendered her far less popular in the society in which she moved than the gentle unassuming Lady Rosamond, in whose whole composition there was no grain of haughtiness to be found. Altogether, two sisters are not often seen between whom it would be less easy to trace a likeness either in manner or feature than between the two daughters of the Earl of Lexington. It is true that, as the elder lady entered, there was something about her type of countenance which struck Maud as being familiar to her, and she naturally inferred the existence of a latent family resemblance; but in what that resemblance consisted she would have found it impossible to specify.

Mrs. Arbuthnot, who had always shown herself

duly impressed with a sense of Lady Blanche's social importance, happened to be a special favourite with her ladyship, who extended her hand with much graceful condescension.

"Excuse me for detaining you so long, but Lady Rosamond and I have been selecting patterns for a new suite of furniture. We are much obliged to you for this visit, I am sure."

"It is very kind of you to say so," responded Mrs. Arbuthnot reverentially. "Will you forgive me, Lady Blanche? you see I have taken the liberty of bringing a friend with me, Miss Travers—Cecilia's new governess in fact. Lady Rosamond was kind enough to interest herself in obtaining the situation for her, so I knew I might venture."

Lady Blanche looked at Maud, and inclined her head graciously; to admitted inferiors she was almost always bland and patronising.

"I hope the engagement will prove mutually satisfactory," she said, with a magnificent air *de grande dame* which must have cost her some practice.

Maud blushed, and timidly murmured forth a half audible acknowledgment of her ladyship's good wishes. She was afraid of Lady Blanche, and yet she thought she rather liked her too. But indeed the strange effect of Lady Rosamond's placid aspect and sweet voice was still far too present with her to allow her to pay much attention to any one else.

Lady Blanche took a chair near Mrs. Arbuthnot's sofa, and began affably to question that lady on the state of her health and that of her daughters. And then it was that Lady Rosamond, judging that Mrs. Arbuthnot was sufficiently entertained, suddenly quitted her place on the sofa, and, as though yielding to impulse, promptly crossed the room and took a seat by Maud, who almost trembled with nervous yet pleasurable excitement as she found herself so near the kind face she had previously been watching with such interest.

"Have you known Mr. Digges long. Miss Travers?" Lady Rosamond said in her mild pleasant voice, rather by way of beginning a conversation than with any desire for information, for, as though anxious to avoid all appearance of prying, she added, before Maud had time to answer: "I am sure you must agree with me in liking him very much—everybody who knows him, I think, does."

And this kind saint-like lady, who thus strove to set the poor governess at ease by inviting her to join in a eulogium on the friend they had in common—this was the woman whom Maud had once made it a point of conscience to dislike and think meanly of. Her very heart ached with the remembrance of the wrong, and with impotent longing to expiate it. She almost felt as though she could kneel down and kiss the hem of Lady Rosamond's garment.

"Yes, I like him very much indeed," she said with an effort. "I can never sufficiently thank him for all his kindness to me."

"He is one of my best and most valued friends," said Lady Rosamond, taking no notice of the last part of Maud's reply. "I have known him for a great many years"—she sighed, perhaps remembering how far happier than now she had been when the acquaintance had first been formed—"and there is nobody living for whom I have more respect. He is so thoroughly unselfish and single-minded."

Maud's shyness and timidity were fast melting away under the charm of Lady Rosamond's manner, and she was about to echo her new friend's praises of the schoolmaster with more frankness than she had yet shown, when she was interrupted by Mrs. Arbuthnot, who, having duly exchanged civilities with Lady Blanche, turned round to Lady Rosamond to exclaim:

"Oh! by the by—I have been wanting to ask you about it ever since I have been here, but something has always come in the way—have you heard any more particulars of that dreadful acci-

dent at—at—what is the name of the place?
Hernebridge, isn't it? The poor young lady who
was lost in that shocking way, I mean—I suppose
there is nothing further known about how it
happened?"

"I—I believe not," said Lady Rosamond, and
through all the tumultuous beating of her own
pulses Maud fancied that she heard the silvery
voice tremble.

"A terribly sad thing, to be sure! And excuse
me for asking the question, but I believe it is
quite true what I hear some people say, that this
Carleton Grange, where the poor young lady seems
to have lived, is the same place you were connected
with for so many years; is it not?"

"Yes," said Lady Rosamond, rather faintly.

"Dear me! dear me! only think. And can
you inform me, then, if it is a mistake, or if Mrs.
Hopkins was right the other day in telling me
that the property goes now to your friend Sir
Arthur Ormond, whom I think I once had the
pleasure of meeting at dinner when he was
staying here? Is that really true?"

"Quite true," murmured Lady Rosamond.

"Well! only fancy how lucky some people are!
And he was such a rich man already, I believe!
Why, then, I suppose it is likely you will be
visiting him at the Grange some of these days."

"Perhaps"—came the almost inaudible response.

"Oh! of course you will. I have heard you never cared to go near the place while there were strangers living in it; out t will be quite different now, you know. With such an old friend established there, you will feel almost as if it was your own again, I should think."

Maud saw that the little white hands which lay folded together on Lady Rosamond's lap tightened their clasp almost convulsively, and could not refrain from lifting her eyes, not in curiosity but deep compassionate interest, to the face that a few moments ago had looked at her so kindly. Yes, it was evident that Mrs. Arbuthnot, with her thoughtless chatter, was inflicting absolute torture on that patient suffering lady, whose wounds were not yet sufficiently healed to bear such rough handling. The soft eyes were veiled by a pair of downcast lids that quivered as though with pain, and there was a nervous trembling about the corners of the gracious mouth which so thrilled Maud with tender pity that she would have been ready to give anything for the right of ministering comfort to a sorrow so meekly borne, and imposing silence on the inconsiderate tongue which thus persisted in stirring its source anew. But vain and unavailing was her sympathy, and she could only sit compassionately watching the effect of the

cruel random shafts which she would so gladly
have averted.

"How pleased you will be to see the old place
again after so many years! There is nothing so
delightful, I think, as these renewals of early
associations. Do you expect to find it much
changed?"

Much changed! The house where she had lived
with her husband and her child, and where their
voices were now hushed! Lady Rosamond could
bear the torture no longer, and, stammering out
something about seeing after some refreshment for
her visitors, rose to leave the room. As she did so,
her eyes, now swimming in tears, met those of
Maud, still fixed on hers as though under the
influence of a spell. Apparently she interpreted
the sympathising expression of the look too truly
to be offended by its steadfastness, for she smiled
encouragingly through her tears, and as she left
the room Maud knew that the last glance of those
friendly eyes was turned on her.

Even Mrs. Arbuthnot was not so obtuse but that
she began to suspect that something had been said
which would have been better left unsaid; and,
turning to Lady Blanche, who had sat frowning at
her in grim but unobserved displeasure, depre-
catingly inquired:

"Dear me, I hope I have not done anything

I ought not? I am afraid Lady Rosamond looked rather agitated. I trust you don't think it can have been in consequence of anything I said just now?"

"My sister is not strong," answered Lady Blanche with frigid stateliness, " and after what she has gone through it is natural that she should be easily affected by references such as you have now thought fit to make. I should have hoped you would have understood that the subject was a painful one."

" I am so sorry," said Mrs. Arbuthnot penitently, "so very, very sorry. I'm sure I would wish to cut my tongue out, almost, rather than give pain to any one, to say nothing of Lady Rosamond, or you either, Lady Blanche, for I don't think it would be possible for me to feel more respect and admiration for anybody in the world than I do for you two, and " . . . . . .

"That will do," interposed Lady Blanche with magnanimous condescension, for she was not an ill-natured woman, and Mrs. Arbuthnot had made the *amende honorable*. " That will do—I am sure you did not mean it. Only my sister has suffered a great deal, and you must remember in future that though she tries to bear up under her sorrow as well as she can, she is always brooding on it in secret. I know she is—poor Rosamond, I know she is—though she makes-believe to be so cheerful."

There was a little break in Lady Blanche's voice ; evidently sisterly affection was getting the better of stateliness.

"Poor Lady Rosamond—poor dear Lady Rosamond!" sighed Mrs. Arbuthnot, while tears of unaffected compassion sprang to her eyes ; for if her perceptions were blunt, she had a kind heart, readily moved by the sorrows of others when once she was made cognizant of them. "And she so good and deserving of happiness! It is piteous to think of her suffering so much—piteous indeed."

Mrs. Arbuthnot's expressions of sympathy were too much for even the noble spinster's sense of dignity, and patrician hauteur melted away in a flood of tears.

"Yes, she deserves happiness if anybody does," Lady Blanche answered, almost sobbing, while the ribbons and lappets of the little French cap became so violently agitated as quite to spoil their effect. "So much as she has gone through—and goes through still every day she lives, I feel only too sure of that—and yet never a word of complaint or reproach, not a look even. Of course I know very well I was not responsible for anything that happened—thank goodness, I have that satisfaction.

But—but I've often thought that some people in her position might have tried to make out that it was my fault somehow, and she has been so sweet-tempered and forbearing . . . . Though it wasn't anything of the sort, of course."

" Dear Lady Blanche, we are all quite aware of that."

" No, that I am sure it wasn't," went on Lady Blanche, while the ribbons trembled more than ever. " I don't believe anybody could have loved a child more than I loved that dear little girl of Rosamond's, really I don't. Children in general I can't say I care for much, they try my head so terribly, but for that one I would have made any sacrifice almost, for Rosamond's sake, you know. Not that she was so much like what Rosamond had been, for she took more after the Carletons, still that made no difference to my feelings. But of course my first duty was to poor papa, and supposing he had been taken ill while I was travelling about with other people's children, how could I ever have forgiven myself? And you know I did come to England after it was all over, and had the roughest passage that had ever been experienced for a fortnight, the sailors said. So you see I have nothing to reproach myself with— nothing."

" Lady Blanche—dearest Lady Blanche!"

"And I went to the steamer myself to see her on board, and was so particular in telling the servant to be careful to wrap her up warm and all that sort of thing. I'm sure her own mother couldn't have taken more pains with her than I did. I remember even noticing that the ribbons of her hat had come unfastened—a sweet little mourning hat I had got my own maid to make up for her the evening before—and actually I tied them again with my own hands; I know I did, for I recollect getting the strings in a knot and having to set the servant to undo them. Nobody could have done more than that, you know."

"Impossible, Lady Blanche, I am sure. Pray, pray don't agitate yourself by thinking of it."

"It comforts me so much to remember all these little things now," said Lady Blanche, drying her eyes, "for of course it is pleasant to feel one has done one's duty. And if ever any one did their duty, I did mine by that sweet little child—indeed I was so fond of her that I quite spoilt her. You may imagine when I tell you that just before we left the house she put out her dear little hand to lay hold of a locket I wore on my watch-chain— a very nice locket it was, set with pearls, and with my great-aunt's initials worked in her own hair inside—and that very minute I had it off and tied it round her neck with a bit of ribbon for a keepsake.

My great-aunt had used us very ill with reference to some property, and I was so sorry to let the little darling go over the sea by herself that I could refuse her nothing. So if I had known I was never going to see her again I couldn't have been kinder—though I'm sure I had no more idea when I stooped down to pass it round her sweet warm little neck . . . . . Oh! dear, dear! it is dreadful to remember it all so plainly."

There was a new burst of tears, and for a few minutes Lady Blanche buried her face in her delicate lace-bordered handkerchief and sobbed almost hysterically, regardless alike of dignity and of the concern expressed by compassionate Mrs. Arbuthnot. Nor was Mrs. Arbuthnot the only sympathiser present. Though unable to make any attempt at consolation, Maud was not the less deeply affected by the spectacle of the grief which this lofty lady had been surprised into manifesting. She had, indeed, entered into her feelings with so keen a participation that, as she listened, it seemed to her as though the scene which was evidently so vividly present to the mind's eye of the narrator rose before her own; and she could almost imagine that she saw the action with which Lady Blanche had hung her gift round her niece's neck. But let her feel as much for and with the poor lady as she would, she knew that it was not for her

to give expression to her sympathy; and with an
effort of self-control she remained mute and dry-
eyed, her heart inwardly aching for Lady Blanche,
and for Lady Blanche's sister a thousand times
more.

Presently a servant entered with cake and wine
for the visitors, and Lady Blanche, her pride
coming at last to her aid, suddenly ceased weeping
and drew herself up with a stately stiffness of
demeanour which did not again desert her.   A
few minutes afterwards, Lady Rosamond returned
to the room to assist in doing the honours—a little
paler than when she had entered it last, and with
her eye-lids slightly swollen, but so patient and
gentle of aspect, and so cordially hospitable towards
her guests, that Maud felt more tenderly reverent
than ever, and almost envied Lady Blanche the
privilege of sharing and solacing the sorrows of
so meek a sufferer.   For a few moments she hoped
that Lady Rosamond was coming back to her side
to renew the conversation interrupted by Mrs.
Arbuthnot's idle loquacity; but in this she was
disappointed, for Mrs. Arbuthnot again intervened,
and Lady Rosamond, casting what seemed almost
a wistful glance at the vacant chair near Maud,
seated herself on the sofa to reply to some frivolous
question addressed to her by her matronly visitor.
Before an opportunity of getting away from that

lady presented itself, it was discovered by the Arbuthnots that their stay had already extended to such a length that if they did not at once take their departure they would be too late to catch a certain train back to Grantwick. They had to perform their adieux, therefore, rather hastily, and hardly had Maud had the pleasure of once more feeling the soft pressure of Lady Rosamond's fingers on her own when she had to make way for Frederica and Cecilia Arbuthnot, who came next to her in the order of leave-taking. But just as she had quitted the room, and, with a vague sense of incompleteness and disappointment, was preparing to follow Mrs. Arbuthnot downstairs, she felt a light hand laid gently on her shoulder, and turned round with a thrill of pleasurable surprise. Lady Rosamond stood beside her, looking at her with her kind mournful eyes.

"Will you please give my best remembrances to Mr. Digges if you should be writing to him? I had almost forgotten to ask you."

Maud promised that she would, and Lady Rosamond took her hand to bid farewell once more.

"Good-bye, Miss Travers. I am so glad to have seen you."

"You have been exceedingly kind to me," said Maud. "I have to thank you very, very much."

"No, no, indeed you have not. Good-bye."

But even yet Lady Rosamond did not relinquish Maud's hand, and, holding it still, she said :

"I may look forward to seeing you often, I hope? It will be a great pleasure to me."

Mrs. Arbuthnot's voice was heard from below asking for Miss Travers ; there was a hasty word of farewell on each side, and Lady Rosamond let go Maud's hand and turned slowly away from the staircase, as regretful apparently as Maud herself at the necessity of parting so soon.

And very regretful indeed was Maud at having to quit so gracious a presence, and go back to the every-day life which, even in the midst of excellent and well-meaning people, threatened to be so comfortless and uncongenial.   In finding herself called upon to leave the roof of Lady Rosamond for that of Mrs. Arbuthnot, she felt as one who wakes to a reality, dreary, hard, and cold, after a dream of Paradise.

CHAPTER XII.

AT HERNEBRIDGE.

THE months flew by, summer had mellowed gradually into autumn, and autumn decayed into winter, and Hernebridge and its neighbourhood had nearly recovered from the excitement occasioned by the loss of the heiress and the consequent change of ownership at the Grange. Nearly, but not quite, for a few households there were which were still saddened by the recollection of her whose voice was believed to be hushed for ever, and where her absence still continued to be felt by some or all of the inmates as a blank. Long after it had become possible to gossip with the Hernebridge grocer or haberdasher, or even to hold confabulation with the landlord of the ' Hen and Chickens,' without hearing a word said of Miss Fleming and her fate, her memory was still cherished and her loss mourned in those poorer homes to which her residence at the Grange, short as it was, had brought comfort and solace, and which now, in the biting days of winter, suffered for want of their benefactress. Then of course there was the Grange itself, where Mrs. Jenkins, as Sir Arthur Ormond's deputy, held forlorn rule over dismantled rooms and untrimmed grounds— spending her days in bewailing to the reduced staff of servants who shared her solitude the fallen glories of the household. The most faithful of all Maud's retainers, Josephine, had indeed long since ceased to be a member of the establishment, having followed Mrs. Nicoll to Linchester, and then—tired of so exacting a mistress—taken service as lady's maid in the family of Mrs. Walford, a post obtained for her at the special instance of Mr. Fleming. But though after her departure no sound of weeping and wailing had been heard within the old walls, it would have been difficult to imagine any place more drearily unlike itself than Carleton Grange this winter.

And in yet another quarter, the quarter in which of all others such a result might least have been expected, there prevailed a spirit of gloom and depression due to the same cause which had brought desolation to the Grange— due to it none the less that only one person understood how cause and effect were connected. Since the year that had witnessed the death of the baronet's eldest son, Ormond Hall had never been so dull and cheerless as during the last few months. For Philip, still suffering from his hidden and unsuspected wound, could not with his utmost efforts force himself to be other than silent, sombre, and reserved; and Sir Arthur, always accustomed to a good deal of humouring from those about him, insensibly caught the infection of his son's low spirits. He felt that there was something wrong, though he knew not what, and grew hipped and querulous, finding fault with everything and everybody— the weather, Mr. Hickey, the parish authorities, and Philip most of all. In short, nothing went well with the old man this winter, and Philip, the involuntary cause of his state of peevishness and discontent, had to go through not a few very trying ordeals in consequence.

"I don't know what's come to the house this year," Sir Arthur would grumble forth as he sat at home on a wet morning watching the rain beat on his study windows. "A man might as well be buried alive at once as penned up in a dismal hole like this without a soul to speak to from week's end to week's end. If only your poor brother had lived . . . . . It's all your fault, Philip."

"My dear father!" Philip would expostulate.

"But I say it is—confound it. If you had been

a young man like other young men, there would have been a wife brought home to cheer us up long ago.   Things will never go right with me till there is, but of course that is nothing to you Though one might have thought that even if you didn't mind about letting me fret my heart out with dulness and loneliness, you might have cared something about your duty to the future.   An old family name and property like ours, and now the Carleton estates just come in—and only you and me left to represent them!   I wonder you can reconcile it to your conscience.   But you intend never to marry, I suppose," the old man would conclude sneeringly, little guessing how truly he spoke.

But Philip could not find it in his heart to grieve Sir Arthur by declaring his views with unnecessary distinctness, and to such reproaches would answer evasively, with an attempt to conceal the inward pain they caused him:

"Perhaps not, father—certainly not unless I can find a woman whom I can love with my whole heart and soul, well enough to feel satisfied in making her my wife.   I am afraid there is not much chance of that—not at present, at least —but who knows what may happen some day? There is no positive reason against it, at all events."

No indeed, no positive reason, as Philip often told himself. Had not the woman whom he had loved with his whole heart and soul once—so deeply that, could he but have been assured she had been altogether his, as he had been altogether hers, he would have felt it treason to give her a successor in his affections even if he could—had not she been another's at the very time he had presumptuously flattered himself that she was all his own? For as another's he had at last taught himself undoubtingly to regard her. He had pondered so much and so long on the words he had heard uttered by Francis Godfrey in presence of Maud's father that he had grown accustomed to the idea which they embodied; while, on the other hand, the months that had passed since her disappearance, and the effect of the fierce conflicting emotions which had so rapidly succeeded each other in his bosom, had dimmed his recollection of the blushing downcast looks which had seemed to him at the time an unspoken avowal of love— so dimmed it that he was ready to admit it might have been his heated imagination only which had invested them with their eloquence. Thus he deemed himself free, though he cared not to use his freedom, though he believed that, having loved once, he could never love again. And, believing this, he would feel at times something like a shade of resentful bitterness—not against Maud, that could not be—but against the fate that had thrown him in Maud's way, that had let her awaken in him a sentiment which, inspired by a woman free to return it, might have been to him the source of happiness ineffable. The pure and holy love he had felt for Maud—that love which, but for Francis Godfrey's slander, her death would never have hindered him from counting as the greatest blessing ever vouchsafed to him—had come now to be looked on as the one great misfortune of his life; so much the greater that even yet he could not altogether shake it off, but it clung to him still, a legacy from the past by which his whole future must be coloured.

"Positive reason!" would Sir Arthur pettishly rejoin—"who talks about positive reasons? I declare I believe sometimes that you have so turned your head with metaphysics and stuff that you don't know what you are speaking about. There's one very good reason why you don't find a woman to suit you, and that is that you don't give yourself the trouble to look for her. If you cared a brass farthing for me or my wishes, you would go into society like other young men, and we should soon find out then whether you could fall in love or not. I think if you had any regard for me you might oblige me so far, I really do. Your poor dear brother . . . . . But you don't consider my feelings as he would have done."

"My dear father, I would not willingly grieve you for the world. If that is all you want me to do . . . . . I don't like company, as you know; but I will see about it—some day—indeed I will."

The weeks rolled on, however, but Philip could not make up his mind to see about it; and all that winter through he remained solitary and isolated, brooding silently over the great trial of his life, and driving the old baronet to the verge of despair by continued disregard of his wishes.

The schoolmaster's was another household where the calamity of the past summer had been not only deplored but felt as a personal loss; nor had it yet recovered from the blow. Not a member of the family whose sum of happiness was not more or less impaired by the withdrawal of the bright young face the sight of which had ever been so welcome. But while all missed the kind friend and patroness who had always been ready to chat pleasantly with the younger girls, to interest herself with the keenest apparent zest in Tommy's amusements, and to let Moses put his paws on her dress in the muddiest of weather, Jemima and her uncle mourned with a poignant sorrow of which the younger members of the household were not yet capable—all the more poignant perhaps that each of the two looked at the sad event from so widely different a standing-point that neither was able to say a word which could be of the slightest comfort to the other. Nor was Nathaniel to be less compassionated than his niece, even knowing as he did that death had spared her whom the sorrowing Jemima believed to have miserably perished. Besides his compunction at witnessing that grief of poor Jemima's which a word of his might go so far towards alleviating, his sympathy and solicitude for Maud in her poverty and exile cost him almost as much pain as belief in her death might have done. When he thought of her toiling for her bread alone and among strangers, cut off from all the friendship and love that had formerly been hers, he would be overcome by an agony of self-reproach for the assistance he had rendered her in her flight—assistance rendered because he was weak and could not see her plead in vain, not, Heaven knew, because he was willing to let her go. Willing to let her go! no truly, that he had never been. He had felt from the first that with her departure from Hernebridge the sunshine of his life would be quenched. Well, if he had been weak, the punishment was heavy, for without her all was as bare and bleak and cheerless as ever he had imagined it, and he was left sorrowing in outer darkness with no solace save what he could find in conning and re-conning the brief missives which he would from time to time find waiting for him at the Linchester post-office. Even his violin and his books had lost their old power of fixing his attention, and often, when seeming most absorbed in one of his two favourite occupations, his mind was given to mournful meditation, while that of the more fortunate Jemima was engrossed in cooking or stocking-mending, to the temporary exclusion of all other cares. No wonder that, with its head thus oppressed with secret sorrow and anxiety, the schoolmaster's household should be a dull and gloomy one that winter.

Not that those days, dreary as they were, passed without bringing some elements of satisfaction and even of rejoicing. Notwithstanding the depression of Nathaniel's spirits, his family affairs had never been so flourishing as they became about this time. The school was prospering bravely; and, by dint of hearty good-will and a capacity for steady plodding, Bob was rapidly advancing in the esteem and confidence of his employers at the bank. Nor was a substantial mark of their favourable consideration of his services destined to be long wanting. One evening towards the end of winter he came over from Linchester to take tea at the school-house, looking quite red and flustered with excitement, though withal very sheepish, as was generally the case when he had anything to say concerning himself.

"I've got some news for you to-night," he began shyly when the first greetings were over, and he had blundered somehow or other into a chair, where he sat pulling about the shaggy head and ears which Moses hospitably rubbed against his legs in sign of welcome.

"Indeed!" said Nathaniel, compelling himself to be interested. "Good news, I hope, my boy?"

"Why yes, I think you'll say so," answered Bob, nervously rumpling Moses's head till it looked quite disreputable in its state of dishevelment. "I'm promoted to be second clerk at Walford and Co.'s, that's all. With a hundred and twenty pounds salary to start with, and to be raised to a hundred and fifty next year. I thought you might like to hear of it, and asked for early leave on purpose to catch you at tea."

There was a short pause, necessary for the due comprehension and digestion of so astounding an announcement.

"My dear boy!" said Nathaniel, and he would

have grasped his nephew's hand but that Bob was hanging his head too bashfully to take any note of unspoken congratulations. "My dear, dear boy!"

"A hundred and twenty pounds!" gasped Jemima, and then for some time she sat still in silent, almost gaping, astonishment—her house-wifely mind lost in contemplation of the vastness of a sum so infinitely larger than any which she had ever had to do with.

"I say, Bob, I shall have a box of carpenter's tools now, shan't I?" put in Tommy, who had a vague idea that Bob had just come into illimitable wealth. "Jem says she knows I should saw the legs off the tables and chairs, but I'll promise faithful I won't, and if I did it would be no such great harm, for of course there will be plenty of things in the box to mend 'em again. Billy Muggins has got such a beauty, with a set of such lovely long nails, long enough to go right through the board his mother makes the pies on and come out with their points the other side of the parlour table—it was only this morning he told me how his father had been walloping him for it. And Bob, when you come to see us you'll always be sure to bring me some of that jolly brown stuff stuck all over with almonds—I forget the name but you know what I mean, and so does Jem. The

same you brought me such a famous piece of last
time you came—the day before I had the stomach-
ache so bad. I may have as much of it as I like
now, mayn't I ?"

"Be quiet, you greedy child," said Anne.
" Bob's got something else to do than think about
you, I can tell you. Bob, you never saw such a
lovely hat and feathers trimmed with blue as there
is in the draper's window just now, and mine is so
shabby, for you know I didn't have one when
Amelia had hers, and " . . . .

"Just like Anne !" interrupted Amelia scorn-
fully, " she never thinks of anybody but herself.
As if I didn't need a frock fifty times worse than
she does a hat ! There's a new stuff, Bob, just
come in very reasonable " . . . .

" I can tell you you shan't have anything either
of you till we get uncle's chair stuffed and covered,
and a new roasting-jack for the kitchen," severely
interposed Jemima, the indignation with which
she listened to this conflict of claims effectually
rousing her from her first bewilderment. " Never
mind them, Bob, they are only children all of
them. But you've never told us how it all
happened. When did you know of it first ?"

"Only this afternoon," said Bob, blushing
almost as violently as a girl called to dilate
upon her love affairs. "I don't mind telling you

all about it if you care to hear, for of course you and uncle ain't like strangers."

"Of course we ain't," said Jemima impatiently. "Well?"

"Well, I had been out to eat my bit of dinner as usual, and was just in the act of hanging my hat up on the peg before settling down to my work again, when Grimble—that's the porter, you know, and a precious old Turk it is—comes up very smooth-spoken and civil, and asks me would I please to step into Mr. Fleming's room? I was terribly put out to be sure, for I could think of nothing there could be to speak to me about unless it was some mistake in the books; but there was no time to consider, for Grimble he was waiting to show me in, and of course I had to go with him as quick as I could, though I don't deny I wondered what made the old chap so precious polite, it not being his usual way, but quite the reverse. And I had to stare more than ever the next minute, for when we got outside Mr. Fleming's door Grim turns sharp round on me and pulls his hair and says something about best congratulations. I dare say he thought me very stupid, for I couldn't think of anything to answer at first, and just as I was going to ask him what he meant he opened the door and shoved me in, and there I was alone with Mr. Fleming."

Bob paused, apparently oppressed with the mere recollection of that awful moment, and Jemima had to encourage him.

"Well, and what did Mr. Fleming say?" she asked. "Mind the kettle doesn't boil over, Amelia."

"He said—I don't know what he didn't say," answered Bob, holding down his head shyly. "He said that I had given great satisfaction, and that he hoped I should continue as I had begun, and all that sort of thing; and before I had so much as time to thank him for his kind expressions, he asked me if I should mind having a little more to do for the sake of extra pay. Of course I told him No; never thinking, though, what he was driving at; and then he said that owing to private circumstances—I thought just there he seemed to give a kind of sigh—he would have more time to devote to business than formerly, and that one of the clerks was to be got rid of in consequence. I regular quaked at that, for I knew I was the junior, but he smiled and said that he had been talking it over with Mr. Walford, and that they had decided to turn off the second, whom they hadn't been very well pleased with lately, and to try me at his desk instead of getting a new one. And then he went on talking very kindly, and saying he hoped I should do, for he took a great interest in me". . .

"Ah! I know who you've got to thank for that," interrupted Jemima a little tremulously. "The dear beautiful young lady that's gone to be an angel in Heaven—it's all for her sake he makes such a deal of you. I hope you don't forget that, Bob."

"Of course I don't," said Bob promptly, for vanity was not one of his faults. "Why, I could see quite plain he was thinking of her to-day all the time he was talking to me—he was looking so grave and sad like. He has taken it very quietly, has Mr. Fleming—it's his way—but he has felt it all the same, you may be sure. And no wonder, for such a young lady as her you don't see the likes of every day."

Bob sighed, and something like a tear stood in his eye—he was not ungrateful to the memory of his benefactress.

"You may well say that," said Jemima, drawing the back of her hand across her eyes. "She was an angel even when she was alive, and that's why she was taken away so soon to be one in reality, I suppose. Wasn't she, uncle?"

"There is no one I respect—respected—more than Miss Fleming," stammered Nathaniel, feeling very guilty. "You know that, my dear."

"So you ought to, uncle," said Jemima through her tears, "for she was very fond of you."

Nathaniel's face grew scarlet.

" And of Bob, and me, and all of us," continued Jemima, giving unrestrained way to her emotions. " It was so nice to feel we had got somebody to care about us. Oh dear, dear! what a happy time it was when that sweet young lady" . . . Jemima wept violently, and Nathaniel, hardly less affected than herself, endeavoured to give a new turn to the conversation.

" But Bob, you have never told us yet what you said to Mr. Fleming for all this. I hope you let him see sufficiently that you appreciated his kindness."

Bob shuffled about nervously on his chair.

" I was always a bad hand at speechifying, and always shall be, I'm afraid. But I felt very thankful, you may depend, and I tried the best I could to let him see it. And uncle, I hope you won't be angry with me, but it's better you should know of it" . . . .

" Well, my boy?" said Nathaniel encouragingly, seeing that Bob paused, a little embarrassed.

" I took the liberty of bringing in your name too, uncle. Perhaps I oughtn't to have done it, knowing that you and he weren't friends, but I was taken all aback as I may say, and it didn't seem natural to me to leave you out. So I just said how grateful and obliged I felt for his kindness, and that I was sure my uncle Nat would be equally so when he heard it. That was no harm, was it?"

A few months before, nothing would have been more distasteful to Nathaniel than the idea of having been represented as lying under any direct obligation to the enemy and slanderer of Lady Rosamond. But of late his feelings towards Mr. Fleming had undergone a curious change—a change very perceptible and decided, yet hard to analyse. He did not like him any more than heretofore—less, indeed, for he knew him to have been guilty of crimes of which formerly he could not have suspected him. But with all this he felt that where Mr. Fleming — Maud's father — was concerned he could no longer be jealous of his own personal dignity. Maud would have borne any-thing from that man, and how should he, Nathaniel Digges, stand on punctilio, and grudge to turn the other cheek? So he clapped his nephew approv-ingly on the shoulder, and replied:

"Certainly not, my dear boy. I am very glad to hear that you put it so nicely. I trust to your good sense always to make what use of my name you please."

Bob looked relieved.

"Thank you, uncle, you are very good. But there's no chance of my doing anything of the sort again. I am sorry to say, Mr. Fleming didn't take it well at all—I couldn't help feeling quite a turn against him for all he had been so kind."

"Never mind, Bob, never mind—it won't do me any harm. What did he say then?"

"I can't remember his words exactly, but he drew himself up very stiff, and said something about my pleasing to remember that the interest he took in me was quite irrespective of any other member of my family, and that he had no more claim on Mr. Digges's gratitude than Mr. Digges on his—that was it, I think. It was all I could do to keep a civil tongue in my head when I heard him."

"I see he has not forgiven me yet for the way I put him down once about Lady Rosamond," commented Nathaniel, with a faint smile. "But I don't regret a word of what I said for all that. Only you must learn not to mind these things, my dear boy, you must indeed."

"How can he help minding?" indignantly exclaimed Jemima. "It would be enough to make a cat mind, I think, to hear his own uncle spoke against like that. I wish I'd been by, that's all— I'd have let him know what I thought of him for turning up his nose at his betters, and would if he had been fifty Mr. Flemings. A nasty, impudent, unfeeling" . . . .

"Jemima, Jemima, don't, pray don't," expostulated Nathaniel. "He is her father, my dear, remember that, and think what she would feel if she could hear you speak of him in that manner."

Jemima was silent, and Nathaniel went on:

"I don't like to hear you say such things, my dear. Whatever his faults may have been, he has been sorely punished for them, and we must try to forgive him, as she does—would have done, that is. Fancy how he must miss her, Jemima."

"That is very true," said Jemima, relenting. "I've often thought to myself how dull and lonely he must be."

"Ah! you would say so, if you knew as much of him as I do," put in Bob. "It's enough to give one the dismals to see him at work from morning to night in that dark back parlour of his at the bank, and yet he seems always better pleased to come than to go, so you may judge from that what his home must be. Dull with a vengeance, you may depend. I say, Jem, I wish you'd let us have our tea."

Jemima was melted, and set about the task of pouring out the tea without saying more in disparagement of Mr. Fleming. After all, even if he failed to appreciate her uncle, he was her brother's benefactor, and Maud's father, and then he must feel so very lonely.

CHAPTER XIII.

DESERTED.

YES, very lonely indeed did Gilbert Fleming feel—very lonely in that dark back parlour at the bank where he sat day after day over his books, with no prospect beyond save the dull cheerless home that awaited him in the next street—more lonely still in that home itself, wearily counting the hours till it was time for him to return to those labours which stood him in the stead of rest and recreation. True, his life was no more monotonous, no more solitary, now than it had been all those long years he had spent at Linchester during Maud's school-days, oscillating between that same dark back parlour at the bank and that same dingy home in the adjoining street. And yet whereas he had been contented then, or comparatively so, existence was a daily burden to him now. For in the interval he had known something better, had known what it was to have a home lighted up with the presence of youth and beauty

and innocent gaiety, had known what it was to be
waited for and welcomed by one who missed him
when he was away and rejoiced at his return; and
though it had not seemed to him that he cared for
any of these things at the time, he felt their want
now, and could not grow accustomed to it—rather
became more sensible of it every day. All the
domestic instincts of the man—and they were
naturally strong and deep, notwithstanding that
for years they had been dormant and he had
deemed them dead—had been, unknown to himself, awakened by the experiences of the few short
months during which Maud had been the presiding
genius of his home; and, do what he would, he
could not get them to sleep again.

It was strange, for other incidents of his
changed position he had gradually grown used to,
and much that at first had been irksome and gall-
ing he had now come to look on as a matter of
course. He never saw the difference now between
the stately country-house where for a few months
he had lived as master, and the sombre narrow-
fronted town dwelling to which he had returned
in one of the dullest streets of Linchester —
no longer was conscious of the diminution of
elegance and luxury which had taken place in
his surroundings, of the substitution of a single
cross cook for a staff of well-trained servants.

He had grown accustomed — though this had been an affair of more time — to a certain slight yet perceptible curtailment of deference on the part of Mr. Walford and the bank customers since he had ceased to combine with the character of a man of business that of a wealthy county magnate; and he had habituated himself to look with equanimity on the increased social importance of Sir Arthur Ormond. And, harder still, he had even learned to familiarise himself in some degree with the consciousness of being in the power of such a man as Francis Godfrey. Indeed, as time advanced and he heard nothing of this dreaded object of fear and dislike save that he had taken a studio in London and was supposed to be doing well, he almost succeeded in shutting the hateful fact altogether out of contemplation.

But much as time and use did for Mr. Fleming in his altered circumstances, they could not do everything—could not make him forget that last year, living at the Grange, he had had a home, however little he might have valued it, and that now, living in his dull house at Linchester, he had none. None, for after having known what it was to live under the same roof with one who cared for him and showed her care as Maud had done,

he could not bring himself to dignify with
that name the four walls of the dismal abode
where he dwelt now, with no companion to
share his solitude save Mrs. Nicoll—Mrs. Nicoll
who passed the morning in visiting, yet fretted
in the evening at finding herself alone with
him, every day growing more peevish and dis-
contented as it became evident how settled
were his sadness and depression.

Yet even Mrs. Nicoll, differing as she did at all
points from her who lately had been mistress
of his household, was better than nobody at
all, and this he had occasion ere long to find
out. One stormy winter evening, when he had
come home from his work fagged and harassed
as work always fagged and harassed him now,
and was sitting before the fire with a cup of
tea in his hand, dreamily gazing into the blaze
and thinking how much less dull than this the
longest evenings had been which he had spent
at the Grange the previous winter — he was
rudely startled from his reverie of the past
by the voice of his sister saying from the tea-
table :

"In a brown study as usual, I see ! Do you
think, Gilbert, you can manage for once to throw
it off while you listen to me for a few minutes ? I
have something to say to you."

"Something to say to me!" he repeated languidly, while he roused himself with some difficulty from his meditations. "Well, what is it?"

"What a shocking habit you have got, to be sure, of repeating people's words after them! That's one thing that comes of being so absent—you never know whether you are being rude or polite. These brown studies have always been your bane, Gilbert."

"I'm very sorry, Sophia, but really I can't help it."

"Well, I suppose you can't now, but it is a great pity none the less. You can't think how odd and unsociable such manners make you appear, besides being very disagreeable for those who have to do with you. I'm sure the house is quite dull enough without you coming home and staring at the fire all the evening, just as if you didn't care for having me to speak to. I've felt it very much, Gilbert, I have indeed."

"You must make allowances, Sophia, and I will try if I cannot do better for the future. Come, I am thoroughly roused now, you see. What were you wishing to say to me?"

"No, no, Gilbert, I know better than that," said Mrs. Nicoll, passing by this last question.

" Your habits are far too confirmed to be changed now, and it would only make you miserable to try. But you may fancy how dull it must be for me — so differently disposed as I am myself — to see any one go on so. And such low spirits too as I have been in since the loss of that dear girl " . . . .

Mr. Fleming winced.

" Come, come, Sophia, I promise " . . . .

" It isn't a bit of use for you to promise. But it is dreadfully dull—nobody knows how dull it is. And of course it's quite impossible to flatter myself that you can find the least pleasure in my society—it isn't likely, when you sit for hours without opening your mouth. I might be living miles off for all the difference it could possibly make to you, I am sure."

" Don't say that, Sophia. People may care for each other a great deal without there being much to say between them. And it would be strange if we did not feel happier together than apart, seeing that neither of us has a relation in the world besides the other."

" I can't let you say that, Gilbert, so far as I am concerned—about having no relations, I mean. You know I have always looked on poor dear Nicoll's relatives entirely as my own, and the feeling has been mutual, I am certain. Mrs.

O'Flaherty quite cried when she heard I was going over to keep house for you—so much so that I really felt it was almost wrong to come away, but of course, that poor dear girl being so young and inexperienced, I considered it a duty to do my best for her. Still I know nothing would please Mrs. O'Flaherty, or the Grogans either, so much as to think there was any chance of my going back again, and Kilderry always agreed so well with my constitution, and the garrison made it so very cheerful . . . . I loved it quite as a home, I can assure you."

Mr. Fleming turned a penetrating look on his sister. He had fully thrown off his reverie now, and his powers of observation were thoroughly awake.

"What is all this, Sophia? Am I to understand that you are really desirous of leaving me?"

His voice shook a little as he put the question.

"As you positively ask me, Gilbert," said Mrs. Nicoll, looking, to do her justice, rather shame-faced, "I think it might be the best arrangement for both of us. Don't you?"

"For both of us? Well, you seem to know best. As you say, life is very dull here."

"Of course I needn't tell you, Gilbert," said Mrs. Nicoll apologetically, "how much I feel for you and sympathise with you and all that, but then

I can't do you any possible good by stopping ; and indeed I believe you will be much more comfortable without me."

"You pay yourself a very poor compliment, Sophia."

"But you are such a strange person, you know, Gilbert, and upon my word I believe you will. The fact is, you and I are quite differently consti- tuted. I am formed for society and pine if I am deprived of it, while you are actually happier living by yourself. You were always cut out for a lonely life—you know that very well."

"Was I ?" said Mr. Fleming bitterly, and he wondered what manner of people those must be whom Mrs. Nicoll would deem cut out to live hap- pily with a wife and children.

But Mrs. Nicoll had settled the point of her brother's natural destiny quite to her own satis- faction, and, without thinking it necessary to adduce argument or illustration in favour of her theory, went on :

"Of course you are, and even suppose you were to find yourself a little dull (though I know you won't), you could come over and visit me sometimes, that is, if you are not too wedded to business to give yourself a holiday. We should all be de- lighted to see you, and you would be charmed with Mrs. O'Flaherty and the Grogans. Oh !

you may depend upon it, it is by far the best arrangement."

"I suppose it is," he said after a pause. "Though I don't expect Mrs. O'Flaherty and the Grogans will see much of me."

"Now don't speak like that, Gilbert, or I shall think you are cross with me, which would be very unkind and very unreasonable too, I must say."

"I think it would, and I am not cross at all, I can assure you. If you wish to go, it is far better that you should."

"And you won't find any fault with me?" asked Mrs. Nicoll doubtfully. "I should be sorry to part anything but friends, you know, Gilbert."

"There is no danger. You are as free as air, and I shall never think of finding fault. Is not the arrangement you propose the best for both of us?"

"There's a dear good sensible fellow!" said Mrs. Nicoll enthusiastically, for in spite of her views as to her brother's vocation for solitude, her conscience was relieved by finding that he took her project so easily. "I am so glad you see it in that light. Do have some more tea, Gilbert. And won't you let me cut you some bread and butter? just the least bit?"

It was long since Mr. Fleming had found himself the object of such blandishments, but he resisted them nevertheless.

" Won't you really? Well then, as you have quite done, will you excuse me if I leave you alone while I add a postcript to a letter I have been writing this morning to Mrs. O'Flaherty, just that I may let her know it is all settled. You see when once one has made up one's mind to a thing, there is no good in delaying."

" Certainly not."

" You will excuse me then, Gilbert. And you won't be much surprised if you don't see me again this evening, for it would be very desirable if I could manage to look over my things and see what I ought to get before I set off. So I may as well say good-night at once perhaps."

What a hurry she was in to go, to be sure! But after all, where was the wonder? he would not stay himself if he knew of any place where life would look less desolate.

" Good night, Sophia. Perhaps I ought to thank you for remaining with me so long as you have done."

Mrs. Nicoll graciously assured him he was quite welcome, and then, in high good spirits and good humour, sailed from the room; and Mr. Fleming was left alone.

Alone! yes, quite alone now. Mrs. Nicoll had

never been much to him, but she had been something, and henceforth he was to live in absolute solitude—none near him with whom he could exchange a word, save strangers on whose sympathy and affection he had no claim—none but hired attendants to wait on him in sickness, to close his eyes in death. Isolation—utter isolation—living or dying, such was henceforth his only prospect. He was not cut out to live alone, whatever Mrs. Nicoll might think, and, feeling that he was not, he buried his face in his hands with something like a groan.

He recalled the image of the fair girl he had known a while ago, of her who would never have been scared away by the dulness of a house in which he was content to make his home, and thought how immeasurably brighter life would seem if he could open his eyes and see her sunny face looking into his. Ah! if only that could be —if only . . . . He stopped himself, with a sudden pang at his heart. Could he honestly tell himself that he wished that sweet face by his side again, when he remembered the tongues which out of doors would have been busy with his name while that face smiled on him within? He shuddered and left the question unanswered—he was not sure what the true answer was. Yet even this uncertainty implied a mighty change wrought in his proud spirit by the gloom of these latter days. For he would have been sure a short time since—sure that no love, no tenderness, of Maud's could ever have brought him compensation for the loss of the social estimation he had striven so hard to make for himself. He was not sure now, and the doubt marked the difference between the Gilbert Fleming of the past and the Gilbert Fleming of the present.

CHAPTER XIV.

HARDLY less drearily than for the lonely man of business at Linchester, the slow months dragged on for Maud in her banishment. She was in a comfortable and cheerful home, surrounded by people for whom she felt a genuine liking, and who honestly did their best to show her kindness and consideration; but even apart from the circumstance that what they intended for kindness as often as not inflicted cruel humiliation, her thoughts and memories furnished her with far too painful subjects of contemplation to permit her to receive much comfort from any merely external influences.

Occasionally a ray of light would make its way through the darkness, and she would for a while be conscious of a sensation more or less pleasurable, but these intervals of relief never lasted long. Thus from time to time she received a letter from Nathaniel, which, besides assuring her of her father's health, was always welcome as a reminder that in one quarter at least sympathy and friendship still existed for her. Then once, with the help of Nathaniel, she had managed to transmit anonymously to Josephine a small present of money earned by herself—a gift which she looked forward to repeating—and the idea of being thus able to help a faithful friend to whom she had unwillingly caused so much sorrow was very grateful to her. But never since the wreck of her home happiness had the aching sense of shame and sorrow been so effectually lulled as on the rare occasions on which she was privileged to find herself in that benignant presence which had charmed her on the day of her first visit to Ilscote Lodge. In Lady Rosamond's sweet mournful face, in her kind eyes, in the soothing tones of her voice, there was something which for Maud, in her present state of forlorn friendlessness, was irresistibly attractive; and when submitted to its influence, she seemed to be lifted out of herself, to forget all her cares and troubles, almost her own identity—the whole interests of her life appearing for the time to be bound up with those of the gentle lady whom so shortly before she had held as a stranger.

And to her infinite gratification it seemed to her that Lady Rosamond, either divining her feelings or naturally predisposed to like a friend of Nathaniel's, was inclined to regard her with peculiar favour. Very soon after Mrs. Arbuthnot's call on her illustrious friends at Ilscote, Lady Rosamond had driven over to return it, when she had again shown a desire to cultivate the governess's acquaintance by engaging her as much as possible in conversation, and again expressed a hope that Miss Travers would come to see her often. Once or twice after this, Maud had accompanied the Arbuthnots when they went to pay a visit at the Lodge, and on each occasion had found herself treated with a friendliness and cordiality which would have made her desirous of returning thither even had she been conscious of no such special charm as she found in Lady Rosamond's society. But just as she was beginning to look on these occasional calls at Ilscote Lodge as the chief pleasure vouchsafed to her in her new life, and to count the days till the time for making them came round again, Mrs. Arbuthnot—who perhaps, good-natured as she was, was a little put out at finding the governess manifestly preferred to Laura and Frederica—suddenly discovered that it was not right to invade her ladyship's drawing-room with so large a party, and that Cecilia had better be left behind, of course under the charge of Miss Travers. Thus of late Maud seldom or never saw Lady Rosamond, and all through the dull winter, and almost to the end of the scarcely less dull spring, the monotony of her life was nearly complete. Then indeed something occurred which had at least the effect of fluttering her pulses and quickening the flow of blood through her veins.

It was a fine day in May, and the Arbuthnot family circle, including the governess, had just sat down to dinner, when Mrs. Arbuthnot—who had returned a few minutes before from a call which, as Maud knew, she and her two eldest daughters had been paying that day at Ilscote Lodge — said pensively:

" Yes, I really think the blue tarlatanes will do. They have been worn a good deal, I know, especially Laura's, but nicely ironed out and with an extra row of trimming round the bodies, they may be made to look very well, and I don't think any of the Ilscote people have seen them. The girls and I have been asked to dine at the Lodge next Wednesday week," explained the lady, turning to Maud, "it will be rather a grand affair, I fancy."

" Indeed!" said Maud. " I hope you will enjoy yourselves."

" Oh! there is no doubt of that, I am sure. By the way, Miss Travers," and here Mrs. Arbuthnot slightly blushed, "I must not forget to mention that Lady Rosamond was kind enough to say she would be glad to see you too, but I told her I

didn't think you cared for going out in the evening. That was quite right, I hope?"

"Quite, thank you," said Maud, who, in spite
of the pleasure it always gave her to be near
Lady Rosamond, was only too glad to be spared
the necessity of mixing in general society. "I
shall really much prefer to remain at home."

"Just what I told Lady Rosamond," said Mrs.
Arbuthnot triumphantly. "It is no kindness to
force people to go into company whether they like
it or not, and for my part I am not quite sure
whether it isn't worse tyranny for employers
always to be pressing their governesses to go here,
there, and everywhere with them than to restrict
them altogether to the school-room. The poor
things don't like to refuse, you know, but ten to
one they would sooner stop behind, and after all
it's very hard that when they have been doing
their duty conscientiously all day, they should not
at least have the evenings to call their own. I
can't imagine how people can be so inconsiderate.
But that is not my way, Miss Travers, as you know,
so I told Lady Rosamond that you would be very
much obliged to her, but that I was sure you would
wish to be excused from all evening visiting. Just
the answer you would desire to be made, isn't it?"

"Oh yes! indeed it is. I am very much
obliged to you for having refused for me."

"I was certain you would be. I should not have done it if I had thought there would be any chance of your enjoying yourself, but I knew so well how you would feel about it. Only fancy a stiff dinner party of eighteen or twenty people, every one of them an utter stranger! And there will be quite that number, I expect. Lady Blanche said they thought of asking a few others besides ourselves, and then there are to be visitors staying in the house as well."

"Two sets of visitors too, mamma," put in Laura. "I don't know when I ever heard of their having so much company at the Lodge."

"No indeed, nor do I," said Mrs. Arbuthnot, "they are usually so very quiet. They will have enough to do to entertain them all, I should think. You have heard me speak of the Honourable Mrs. Merton, perhaps, a great friend of Lady Blanche's; she is to be there for a few weeks with her two daughters, Edith and Fanny, though to be sure Fanny isn't much more than a child—somewhere about Cecilia's age, I dare say—so there won't be much trouble with her. But Edith expects a great deal of attention, I can assure you, and could make herself very disagreeable if she didn't get it, I should fancy, in spite of her sweet looks. She is considered a great beauty, you see, Miss Travers, and that does so spoil a girl's character.

. . . . Well, I don't want to say anything against Mrs. Merton, for I have always found her a very pleasant person, but I can't approve of the way she has brought up that girl to think herself better than everybody else."

"And I am sure she isn't," said Laura—"not in my opinion, at least. Of course if people can afford to dress as she does . . . . *I* should not be able to reconcile it to my conscience, that's all I know, if I had ever so much money."

"Nor I," said Frederica, the least good-natured of the two sisters, with a somewhat vixenish emphasis.

"I certainly never was able to see so very much in her myself," said Mrs. Arbuthnot, with a glance of maternal admiration at her daughters. "But she made a decided sensation in the neighbourhood when she was visiting at the Lodge last year, there can be no doubt of that." And the fond mother heaved a little sigh.

"I never could understand it," said Laura, and she too sighed slightly.

"You need not be surprised, my love ; men are never able to see through anything," rejoined Mrs. Arbuthnot consolingly. "Well, Miss Travers, as I was saying, it seems they expect to have quite a party staying at the Lodge. They are to have the Mertons, as I have told you, and then they have asked some friends of Lady Rosamond's, people who used to be her neighbours before she came here. I don't suppose you ever heard me mention them, Sir Arthur Ormond and his son— Philip Ormond, I think his name is."

Philip Ormond! This was the first time that Maud had heard that name spoken during all the weary months which had elapsed since she had left Hernebridge—the first time that she had had tidings of him in any way since the happy day that he had parted from her in front of the school- master's house with the hinted but well understood promise of seeking her father's sanction to his love. A tumult arose in her heart; her head grew dizzy and her eyes dim. Fortunately Mrs. Arbuthnot was too fond of hearing herself speak to notice the effect her words produced, and, without waiting for an answer, went on:

" Sir Arthur is not coming, I believe, for he has been rather out of sorts all winter, and does not like being put out of his way, but Philip Ormond has promised positively. A wonderfully fortunate young man that, to be sure! Only fancy, Miss Travers, the Ormonds have a magnificent family estate of their own, and lately they have come into another close by — the same indeed that would have been Lady Rosamond's if her husband had lived. So that they have two fortunes, in

fact, upon their hands, and they say Sir Arthur
has promised his son to put him in possession of
the new one whenever he marries."

A strange sense, as of compression, made itself
felt at Maud's chest as the last word struck upon
her ear. She had often told herself that Philip
Ormond would some day marry; and yet the idea,
now that she heard it suggested by another, was
as startling as though it had been altogether new
to her.

"What a catch he will be for some one, won't
he? with one splendid property actually waiting
for him to take pity on it, and another to look
forward to on his father's death, not to speak of
the title! It's only a wonder he has not married
long ago, especially as it seems his father is so
anxious about it. But that is the way with some
of these young men; the more you want them to
do anything the more they won't."

Maud breathed more freely. Perhaps he did
not intend to marry after all. Could it be that
the recollection of that last blissful parting was
still present with him as it was with her, steeling
his heart against all fascinations from without as
it would have steeled hers? She knew she had no
right to expect this, no right even to wish it; and
yet the thought that possibly it might be so made
her bosom glow with a momentary sense of plea-

sure. Only momentary, for immediately afterwards Mrs. Arbuthnot resumed :

"My opinion is—but of course you will understand this is quite between ourselves—that Lady Blanche wants to get him to fall in love with Edith Merton. Edith has always been a particular favourite of hers; she is a very haughty girl, you know, and I think Lady Blanche admires her manners. Well, there is no accounting for tastes. But I should not wonder a bit if we hear of a match being arranged ; she is a striking girl, there is no denying, and her fortune is very large. Is it not strange that the more money a man has himself, the more he looks for with his wife ? but it's the way of the world, I suppose."

Mrs. Arbuthnot sighed, and looked a little despondingly at Laura and Frederica, wishing perhaps that for their sakes the way of the world was less flagrantly unreasonable.

Meanwhile Maud sat mute, with swelling heart and reeling brain, as one who has just been warned of the near approach of a danger which nothing can be done to avert. She had never seen this Edith Merton who was the subject of conversation, and yet already she feared her as the mortal enemy of her peace.

"Well, all I know is that if I were a man, Edith Merton is one of the last girls *I* should ever think of falling in love with," said Frederica tartly, and Maud could almost have blessed her for the speech.

"I dare say, my dear, I dare say," answered Mrs. Arbuthnot sympathisingly, "but Mr. Philip Ormond may take a fancy to her for all that. You know how much the gentlemen admire her. However, we shall be able to judge when we see them together. Wednesday week is not very long to wait for."

Wednesday week came in due course, and with a beating heart Maud saw Mrs. Arbuthnot with Laura and Frederica set off for Ilscote in all the glory of blue tarlatane, pearl-grey moire-antique, and a private fly ordered from the hotel. She did not see them again that evening, having retired to her own room some time before their return, but on meeting them next morning at breakfast she found them inclined to be very eloquent on the subject of their experiences.

"Such a pleasant evening, Miss Travers!" began Mrs. Arbuthnot when the first salutations had been exchanged. "And I am sure you will be pleased to hear that nothing could have been better than the effect of the blue tarlatanes."

"I am very glad," said Maud nervously, for she was in a fever of anxiety as to what she might be about to hear of Philip Ormond. "I thought them very becoming dresses."

"And they light up so beautifully. I was quite pleased to see the girls looking so well, I was indeed. Though there were some very tasteful toilets last night, were there not, Laura?"

"It's easy to be tasteful, mamma, if people can think it right to spend a fortune on their dress," said Laura, tossing her head. "I wonder how much those lace flounces of Edith Merton's came to—they were real, I know."

"They were very beautiful," said Mrs. Arbuthnot meditatively. "And what a set of pearl ornaments, to be sure! Very becoming, I thought they were. Well, she is a handsome girl, that must be admitted."

"She knows how to make the most of herself certainly," said Frederica spitefully.

"Dress does a great deal of course, but I think she is what one would take for a good-looking girl anywhere," said Mrs. Arbuthnot, with a becoming assumption of candour. "Last night now—really I thought she was looking remarkably well, especially once or twice when she got animated. Did you notice her that time when she was sitting on the sofa and Mr. Ormond went up to ask her to sing?"

A sharp pricking pain quivered through Maud's

heart—the first distinct pang of jealousy she had ever known.

"How that girl does set her cap at him, to be sure!" said Frederica. "I should have thought she would have been above being a flirt."

"Come, come, my love, you must not be so censorious, really. She was very pleasant last night, I thought, and had more to say to you and Laura than usual; and Mrs. Merton I found particularly agreeable. Not but that were I in her place I should be sorry to see my daughter give such marked encouragement to any young man."

Maud was not addicted to forming harsh judgments, least of all on the strength of hearsay evidence, but she could not help passing a secret verdict of condemnation on Edith Merton.

"It is strange how young men can submit to be angled for in that manner," remarked Frederica, still unmollified, "but they like it, I suppose. Mr. Ormond seemed to do so yesterday evening, at all events."

"He is what you may call struck with her, certainly," assented Mrs. Arbuthnot. "I wonder whether it will come to anything."

"It won't be Miss Merton's fault if it does not," said Laura. "And really I think it will; he kept by her side almost all the evening. How pleased Lady Blanche will be!"

Alas! how each word seemed to sink into Maud's heart and settle itself there like a lump of lead! She had fancied that she had suffered so much in the past that she was fortified against the worst which the future could bring, but she found now that there was one kind of pain, as hard to bear as any, which she had not yet experienced—the pain of watching while the love which had been hers and which she had valued more than life was gradually transferred to another object. And yet she had often told herself that it must be so transferred one day, that her memory would not and ought not to stand as a perpetual barrier between Philip Ormond and a new love; ay, she had told herself, and even believed, that she would rejoice to hear that he had sought and found with another the happiness it had not been granted to her to share with him. Now she endeavoured to persuade herself that it was because Edith Merton was not worthy of him that she suffered so much from what she had heard; but it may be a question whether the most satisfactory proofs of Edith's worthiness would have brought her much consolation.

"How pleased Lady Blanche will be!" repeated Laura.

"I suppose she will," said Frederica; "though what pleasure people can find in match-making I am sure I can't understand."

"I think I know somebody who won't thank Lady Blanche," said Mrs. Arbuthnot. "That poor Captain Vivian!"

"What a goose he made of himself last night!" cried Laura. "So absurdly disconsolate, wasn't he? Though he may well think himself ill-used, for last year she seemed quite pleased with his attentions. People ought not to be so changeable."

"What can he expect if he chooses to attach himself to a girl who cares for nothing but rank and wealth?" asked Frederica indignantly.

"Well, as far as that goes, Captain Vivian is not to be despised," said Mrs. Arbuthnot. "He comes of a very good family, and will be well off, I believe, when his father dies. You know how he has been run after ever since he has been in garrison here. Miss Merton might do worse, I can assure her. And I don't think she dislikes him by any means, though she would prefer Mr. Ormond, no doubt."

Yes, yes, she would prefer Mr. Ormond, of course. How could any girl be loved by Philip Ormond and not give him unhesitating preference over any other admirer whomsoever, rich or poor, gentle or simple? So thought Maud, and her spirit sank within her, oppressed by a conviction that this irresistible Edith Merton, this fascinator of all men's hearts, was destined to win and to wear the love of which Maud Fleming had once been the proud and happy possessor.

"I am afraid Miss Travers must be quite tired out by hearing us talk so long about people she has never seen," said Mrs. Arbuthnot apologetically, noticing perhaps Maud's air of abstraction. "I forgot that we could not expect you to be much interested in Miss Merton's love affairs."

Mrs. Arbuthnot smiled pleasantly, and Maud, who could not have returned a spoken answer had her life depended on it, smiled too—faintly and artificially.

"But you are going to have an opportunity of watching their progress for yourself, and then perhaps you will take more interest in them. The Mertons have promised to come to a ball at our house this day fortnight, with Lady Blanche— Lady Rosamond never goes out to anything of that kind, you know. And I asked Mr. Ormond too—I could not do less—and as for Captain Vivian, I knew him a little already, having met him several times at parties since he was stationed here. So they are all coming, and you will see them of course, for I need not say how welcome you will always be to any little social entertainment that may be going on under my roof. I hope you like dancing, Miss Travers? I will take care you don't go without partners."

Stunned by the intelligence that Philip Ormond was once more to be brought so near her, Maud could find no voice to acknowledge Mrs. Arbuthnot's good-nature; but, fortunately for her, the omission was concealed by the timely interposition of Laura, who, pushing away her empty coffee-cup, exclaimed:

"I've done breakfast now, mamma. Shall I go and write out some of the invitations? We have no time to lose, with only a fortnight before us. And then there are our dresses to see after too, for we must have new ones of course. What colour are you in favour of, mamma? Blue becomes me best, I know, but that is not to be thought of after wearing it so much this winter. It must either be white or pale rose pink, and I think," &c. &c.

The important subject thus started soon absorbed the whole attention of both mother and daughters, and when shortly afterwards the party broke up from the breakfast table, Maud found an interval of liberty during which to familiarise herself as best she could with the idea of being under the same roof with Philip Ormond; and not only with Philip Ormond, but with the girl who, as it seemed, was to be her successor in Philip Ormond's love. Inexpressibly painful the idea was, and for the first time she could almost have found it in her heart to blame Nathaniel for not having foreseen the possible consequences of introducing her to a friend and neighbour of Lady Rosamond's. Not that she apprehended any danger of discovery; it would be easy for her to excuse herself from appearing at Mrs. Arbuthnot's ball, and so long as she avoided a face-to-face meeting with Philip her secret was safe. But the prospect of feeling herself so near him and yet so far—of knowing that in the same house with her, a few yards from where she would be miserably pondering on departed hours of bliss, he would be looking into another's eyes with that fond ardent gaze the very memory of which still thrilled through her! She had been very brave and patient hitherto, and she tried to be brave and patient still; but to find her wound thus violently torn open was a sore trial to her fortitude.

CHAPTER XV.

THE CONSERVATORY.

"MY dear Mrs. Arbuthnot, you must positively let me congratulate you on the perfection of your arrangements this evening. Such decorations, such lighting, such distinguished company! It is by far the most brilliant affair I have known in the neighbourhood this season," pronounced Miss Daukes, a middle-aged spinster of Grantwick, who, not being in the habit of giving balls herself, felt no scruple in making the admission.

"I think it is a success, certainly," simpered Mrs. Arbuthnot, and she glanced complacently, not to say triumphantly, at the scene before her.

A very gay glittering scene it was, and one which Mrs. Arbuthnot or any other hostess might be excused for contemplating with considerable gratification. By the aid of upholsterers and other functionaries receiving their inspiration from the taste of Laura and Frederica, the pretty dining and drawing-rooms at Fairlawn Cottage, ordinarily separated by folding doors, had been metamorphosed into a fairy bower resplendent with flowers and gauzy hangings, and sparkling with wax lights. The rooms were a little small, to be sure, for the number of guests now assembled in them; but they were amply redeemed from all charge of heaviness by the brightness of the chalked floors, by the fluttering festoons of muslin and artificial flowers that decorated the door-ways, and, above all, by the fresh green background furnished by the rare shrubs and exotics of the conservatory on which the folding windows of the drawing-room opened, and which had been tastefully lighted up for the occasion with Chinese lanterns hung among the verdure.

Then the company which animated that radiant scene was no less brilliant than the rooms themselves, and quite as imposingly got up. There were the Misses Arbuthnot, moving each in a haze of delicate rose-tinted drapery, and looking, it must be said, very well indeed. There was a very effective military group, consisting of Captain Vivian and three or four brother officers, and displaying the best-grown moustaches and shiniest boots of the company. There was Mr. Philip Ormond, who, if not remarkable for any speciality of attire, was universally known to be a baronet's son and the heir of two fortunes. There was

Lady Blanche Arden, magnificent in silk and diamonds and the consciousness of her noble birth. And yet none of these was the chief ornament of the ball-room or the admitted cynosure of all eyes.

"I don't think I ever saw Miss Merton look so well as she does to-night," remarked Laura Arbuthnot to a gallant young lieutenant who was her partner. "I have been admiring her all the evening."

"By Jove, so have I," was the answer, delivered through a pair of moustaches of extra thickness. "She's a fine girl and no mistake."

And then he fell to thinking, as perhaps Laura had intended, how pleasant it was to find a young lady so totally devoid of all trace of feminine envy as was Miss Arbuthnot in the presence of Edith Merton's charms.

She was indeed very beautiful, this Edith Merton, and looking so beautiful on this particular evening that other young ladies besides Laura were fain to make a virtue of necessity by acknowledging it. It was not only that a gracefully undulating figure was set off to more than ordinary advantage by the soft folds of the rich white lace robes in which it was enveloped, that the snowy whiteness of a perfectly modelled neck and pair of arms was heightened by the effect of the costly jewels which glittered on them, that greater elaboration than usual was displayed in the disposition of those thick silken masses of light auburn hair which formed the principal ornament of an exquisitely poised head, not only that exercise and excitement had enhanced the bloom of delicately rounded cheeks and ripe coral lips. There was this evening a peculiar character of softness and gentleness about her beauty which was not always there, and the charm of which could not but be felt even were it not understood. For Philip Ormond was by her side, and when she spoke or listened to him the clear blue eyes which were wont to look full and straight before them—surveying all objects from under "level-fronting eyelids" with a cold impartiality of gaze which on ordinary occasions formed the chief drawback on her beauty—were either cast modestly downwards or raised to his face with a subdued light shining in them which added infinitely to their power of attraction. Many ladies, and not a few gentlemen, thought Edith Merton a cold and haughty, almost repellent, beauty; but in truth no woman could be more graciously winning and fascinating than Edith Merton when she chose. And on the present occasion, in company with Philip Ormond, heir of Ormond Hall and Carleton Grange, Edith did choose.

And Philip was fascinated—not in love exactly, but fascinated, powerfully fascinated. He did not feel towards Edith as he had felt towards Maud. There was no involuntary vibration of his heartstrings at the sound of her voice, at the touch of her hand—no intoxication for him in the tenderest glances of her clear eyes. But he admired her beauty, he liked being in her company, he was gratified by the evident preference which this lovely much-made-of girl awarded him over a host of admirers and would-be suitors; and oftener and oftener he found himself considering whether the sacrifice of personal inclination demanded of him by his father when the old man urged him to take home a wife to the Grange would be indeed so great as he had anticipated—whether, such as it was, it would not be his duty to make it. Why should he not endeavour to blot the past from his memory— that past whose ineffable charm had, after all, been but the creation of his own imagination— and frankly accept the tangible blessing offered by the present in the person of a beautiful accomplished girl who apparently liked him and whom he greatly admired? as indeed who could fail to do? How many men had been disappointed in their first love and yet afterwards been happy husbands and fathers; and why should not he, Philip Ormond, be among the number? Certainly

Edith Merton, fair as she was, did not exactly answer to the type which in his early dreams he had made to himself of the woman he should marry; but then had not experience sufficiently proved to him that the standard which he had then set before his eyes was too high to be attained in the actual world? For a few short weeks he had indeed imagined otherwise; but when during his life had he been so miserably self-deceived? Was the ideal always to stand between him and the real? and what had Maud Fleming, the affianced wife of another—what had she ever been to him but an ideal? True, in marrying Edith he must bid farewell to dreams and memories which had constituted the poetry of his life; but then was not a great deal of enjoyment to be found in the prose passages of existence—so much that the majority of mankind are content to end their days without having tasted of anything else? What lot at once more honoured and more enviable than that of a country gentleman with large estates to improve, a numerous tenantry to care for, and a beautiful wife, who should always look well and dress well, to help him in the discharge of his social duties?— perhaps, too, a seat in Parliament some day, for somehow, when he contemplated himself in the possible character of Edith Merton's husband, he always looked forward to a stirring active life, making many and various demands on his time. Who would not catch eagerly at the prospect of such a destiny as this, and what right had he ungratefully to reject it when it actually seemed to offer itself to him?

"It is not difficult to see how things are going in a certain quarter, I think," whispered Mrs. Arbuthnot to her distinguished guest Lady Blanche Arden, while she nodded mysteriously towards the part of the room where Philip and Edith had taken up their places in a quadrille. "Miss Merton has made a decided conquest. I suspected as much a fortnight ago at your house, but this evening I am sure of it."

"Why, yes, I don't think there is much doubt of it," answered Lady Blanche, looking at the pair with evident gratification. "Well, all I can say is, Mr. Ormond's choice does credit to his taste, for Edith is a most superior girl, fitted to adorn any sphere which she may be called upon to fill."

"I am certain of it," said Mrs. Arbuthnot; "the fact that you, Lady Blanche, should have formed so high an opinion of her is quite a sufficient guarantee of her merits in my eyes. Then may I ask if they are engaged?"

"Not yet, I think—indeed I am almost sure I

should have heard if it was so. The truth is, Mr. Ormond has been rather more backward than I should have expected, but he has never been much of a lady's man. However, I don't think it can be long before he declares himself now— indeed I should not wonder much if he were to propose this evening," her ladyship added, with another look in the direction of her *protégés*. " I never saw him paying her so much attention."

And indeed the spell of Edith's fascinations had never been exercised on Philip so powerfully as on this evening. The admiration which he had from the first felt for the beautiful girl who smiled on him so winningly had been gradually growing stronger with every day spent in her society; and this evening the heightened attractiveness of her charms, the brightness of the surrounding scene, the inspiring tones of the music, the presence of other beauties not one of whom but was outshone by her, all contributed to create around him an enchanted enervating atmosphere through the slightly materialistic fumes of which the image of his ideal love waxed faint and ever fainter, and that of Edith loomed upon him as the destined, and after all sufficiently acceptable, companion of his life. Surely the moment of Edith's triumph was very near. Not only did Lady Blanche think so, but the Honourable Mrs. Merton, who sat watching

the progress of affairs with a keen maternal solicitude only equalled by her profound satisfaction;
and not only the Honourable Mrs. Merton, but the
young lady herself, who saw the impression she
had made and was well pleased with it.

And yet the beautiful Edith was all the time no
more in love with Philip Ormond than he was
in love with her. If she could, properly speaking, be said to be in love with anybody while she
was thus delighting her mother and Lady Blanche,
it was not with him to whom she inclined her ear
so graciously, but with a certain heavily-built
young man with a thick voice, luxuriant head
of hair, and shaggy moustache, who stood, in an
attitude which may or may not have been intended
to be Byronic, leaning against the wall and staring
half savagely, half ruefully, at her and the baronet's son. This was Captain Vivian of the
——th, who, the last time Miss Merton had
been in that part of the country, had monopo-
lised her good graces pretty much as Philip
Ormond was monopolising them now, and who,
if she had listened exclusively to the prompting of
her heart, might this evening have been occupying
Philip's place by her side. But the fascinating
Edith, sylph-like and almost ethereal as she looked
in her white gossamer robes, was not without a
share of sound practical common sense; and this

told her that as Lady Ormond of Ormond Hall and Carleton Grange she would occupy a much more desirable social position than as simple Mrs. Vivian of nowhere in particular. Not that, while she thus reserved the light of her smiles for Philip, her views were solely inspired by a vulgar or sordid ambition. It would have been unpardonable in her had it been so, seeing that her own fortune was amply sufficient to enable her to marry whom she would without danger of ever wanting for money or the social importance that money confers. But she had heard much of the obduracy of Philip Ormond's heart, and its resistance to all assaults hitherto made upon it; and she felt the same pleasure in setting herself to subdue it as does an enthusiastic member of the Alpine Club in setting himself to scale a summit hitherto held inaccessible. And then, as she had often told herself, Captain Vivian, though evidently so terribly cut up that she could sometimes have been almost sorry for him, had displayed such strange, not to say stupid, passivity under his disappointment! For a man with so splendidly developed a moustache and head of hair, the gallant captain was absurdly shy; and the appearance of a rival, instead of spurring him forward, as might have been expected in the case of an ordinary lover, had frightened him altogether into the background, where he remained in abject despondency, casting despairing glances at his partner of last season as though at a bright particular star which he had lost all hope of bringing down from its native heaven. What could the man expect, Edith asked herself, if this was the way he chose to take it? When people stand by and never lift up a little finger while other people carry off the prize they are sighing for, they do not deserve to be compassionated. So she continued to smile on Philip Ormond, and Captain Vivian continued to abide amid darkness and gnashing of teeth.

"How oppressively warm it is here!" said this belle of the ball to her partner Philip Ormond, as she paraded the rooms with him at the conclusion of a dance and gracefully unfurled an elegant down-tipped fan in the management of which were incidentally displayed to perfection the dainty curves of one of the whitest arms in the world. "Such small rooms are really not suited to dancing."

She glanced her eye a little contemptuously through the pretty suite the arrangement of which on that evening was the pride of poor Mrs. Arbuthnot's heart; but though it might perhaps have been better for the purposes of fascination if her expression had been a trifle less supercilious, a curl sat so naturally on that beautiful lip as not at all to disfigure it.

"May I get you an ice, Miss Merton?" asked Philip. "Or will you allow me to escort you to the refreshment-room? I think there seems to be a move in that direction at present."

"Thank you, I don't care about taking any-thing," said Edith, who knew that her immediate views were not such as a visit to the refreshment-room, made in company with a dozen other couples, would be likely to further. "A breath of fresh air is all I want, but it appears that that is a luxury not to be had this evening. These rooms must be very badly ventilated. The conservatory is pretty to look at, but I wish it were an open window instead."

"I wish for your sake it were. I am so sorry you do not feel comfortable."

"I wonder, by the by, if there is any open window there. That immense pile of shrubs completely shuts out one's view. I think I shall take the liberty of looking to see; some people are so afraid of draughts that I quite expect to find all apertures carefully fastened."

She glanced for an instant behind her. The room in which they were was almost deserted, such of the company as had not betaken themselves to the refreshment-room on the other side of the hall being clustered round the doorway dividing the two dancing-rooms, listening to a song which had just commenced in the apartment beyond. Then, withdrawing her neat little white-gloved hand from Philip's arm, she succeeded with some dexterity in so managing her flowing drapery as to convey it unharmed through a narrow alley formed, in utter disregard of the exigencies of feminine ball costume, by gigantic pots of flowering shrubs. This debouched into an open space behind, which was capable of containing some three or four persons with tolerable comfort, provided that they were careful not to put their elbows through the glass bow which separated them from the garden on one side, nor to stumble against the stand of piled-up shrubs and flowers which concealed them from the drawing-room on the other.

"I see, after all, they have not forgotten to make provision for a little fresh air," said Miss Merton, addressing Philip, who, as in duty bound, had followed her. "Here is a door looking on the garden which they have actually not neglected to leave open."

She went up and looked out; the night was very dark, and rain was falling in a thick steady drizzle.

"Dear me, I had no idea it was wet," she

added, and there was a slight tone of disappointment audible in her voice—perhaps she had expected to be invited to take a stroll in the garden.
" It is raining rather fast too ; I shall get quite
wet if I do not take care."

She closed the door as she spoke, with rather
inconsistent disregard of the effect on the tempe-
rature of the room behind, and then, looking round
somewhat languidly, remarked :

" I wonder Mrs. Arbuthnot did not think of
indulging us with a few chairs here. This is the
only habitable corner of the premises this evening."

For Philip to fly back to the room to fetch
a chair in obedience to the hint was the work of
an instant ; and Miss Merton was presently seated,
very comfortably and becomingly, under an arch-
ing canopy of ferns and foreign shrubs. Hardly
had she installed herself, however, when the first
notes of a set of quadrilles sounding from the adjoining room caused her to refer to an exquisite
little set of gold-mounted ivory tablets she carried
at her side.

" How very provoking ! There are the Lancers,
and I see I am engaged to that tiresome Major
Crump. So I must return to that torrid zone,
I suppose, and get through my duties as best I
can."

"I am very sorry," said Philip, and indeed so he was, for he was beginning to find the *tête-à-tête* with the charming Edith exceedingly agreeable.

"I wonder if it would be very wicked of me to be afflicted with a short memory for once, and let Major Crump go without his partner. He will find another, I dare say, for he is absurdly popular with the ladies, and if he does not I don't know that it will be any such terrible misfortune. What do you think, Mr. Ormond ? shall I be very reprehensible ? I am so much more comfortable here than I should be standing up with Major Crump."

There are few men so insensible as to be proof against flattery delicately administered by a pretty woman ; and there was more tenderness in Philip's voice than Edith remembered ever to have heard in it before as he assured her that she was not under the slightest moral obligation to sacrifice herself to Major Crump.

"No, no, Miss Merton, you must not think of going. Stay here—do pray stay here."

He made room for himself as he spoke on a low bench on which were arrayed a few vases filled with choice plants, and sat down almost at Edith's feet. And now indeed it seemed that the moment of her triumph had all but come ; for the memory of his lost love had melted into thin air, and he was conscious of nothing beyond the present, with its intoxicating appeals to his senses—the delicate perfume of voluptuous exotics, the sound of music mellowed by the intervening masses of foliage, the smiles of the fair enchantress whose eyes were beaming down upon him with a soft passion-inspiring radiance.

The darkest shadows are ever found in juxta-position to the brightest lights, and the minutes that flew by so pleasantly for the pair in the conservatory, and for the company from which they had separated themselves, counted as ages in a certain dimly-lighted room upstairs where a solitary watcher sat listening to the distant sounds of festivity that ascended from below. The room was the governess's bed-chamber, and the watcher was the governess herself, who, on the plea of a violent headache, the genuineness of which was sufficiently attested by her pale cheeks and languid eyes, had easily prevailed on Mrs. Arbuthnot to excuse her presence downstairs that evening. She had been recommended by that lady to lie down and sleep, but though she had once or twice thrown herself on her bed in the forlorn hope of finding a short oblivion from the pain which pressed like a load upon her heart, it was only to discover that com-

pliance with the last part of the prescription was
out of the question. How could she sleep, knowing that Philip Ormond was under the same roof
with herself, exposed to the spells of a beautiful
woman who was confessedly the admired of all
admirers, and who, as the Arbuthnots seemed to
think, was specially bent on attracting him?
Neither could she read, though several times she
had taken up a volume and desperately striven to
concentrate her attention on its pages. But her
throbbing brain refused to take in the sense of the
words on which her eyes rested, and persisted in
busying itself with thoughts of Philip Ormond and
of her who presumably aspired to be Philip
Ormond's wife. Perhaps now he might be leading
her out to dance, now whispering a compliment
into her ear between the figures of a quadrille, now
bending over her chair with that tender never-to-
be-forgotten expression in his eyes. Ah! if only
it were possible to slip on a garb of invisibility,
and see in very truth how he was occupied! The
worst reality could not be more tormenting than
these cruelly vivid pictures conjured up by a sick
imagination. But, do what she would, the pictures
haunted her still, making that evening which
passed so pleasantly for the company downstairs
a period of the most torturing unrest she had ever
known.

She was leaning back in her chair, wondering how she should get through what remained of the time during which Philip Ormond was to be in the house, when she heard footsteps ascending the stairs, and presently a knock sounded at her door. She rose to open it, and then, somewhat to her surprise, the resplendent figure of Laura Arbuthnot sailed into the room.

"I am so glad you are not in bed, Miss Travers," was the young lady's first exclamation. "Only see what that clumsy wretch, Mr. Potts, has done to my dress!"

She held up the garment in question very disconsolately as she spoke, and displayed a rent some three-quarters of a yard in length.

"Stupid awkward creature!" she commented, "he never looks where he puts his great rhinoceros feet, and then he thinks he has made it all right by saying he is very sorry. Would it be too much, Miss Travers, to ask you just to run it together? it won't take you more than two or three minutes, and I can't get at it myself without crushing the dress all to pieces."

Maud readily promised to do her best, and, having prepared a needle and thread, got down on her knees at Miss Arbuthnot's feet.

"It is so kind of you," said Laura. "Really I am quite ashamed of giving you so much trouble,

but the servants are busy laying the supper, and
Frederica is so selfish that I don't think she would
have given up the pleasure of waltzing with
Theodore Waddilove, not if I had been dying.
And then I knew that, not being very well, you
were not likely to be busy with anything of your
own. By the way, I hope your head is better,
Miss Travers?"

Maud murmured a few words in answer, but she
might have saved herself the trouble, for just
at that moment a martial strain was heard from
below, which caused Laura to tap the floor pettishly
with her foot, and exclaim impatiently :

"That delicious galop! I shall never be able
to forgive Mr. Potts if I can't get downstairs
in time to join it. And what will Lieutenant
Snappleton be thinking of me? he was so particular in making me promise him the galop. I
beg your pardon, Miss Travers, but I hope you
have not much to do now?"

"I am getting on as fast as I can, but I am
afraid I shall have to detain you another minute or
two; the rent was a very long one."

"That horrid Mr. Potts! Well, you will be as
quick as you can, Miss Travers, I am sure—I
don't want to disappoint Lieutenant Snappleton.
We are having such a charming evening, you can't
imagine. I have been dancing every time—four

quadrilles, three galops, two mazurkas, two waltzes, and one schottische, and I am engaged besides ever so many deep after supper. I never enjoyed myself so much in my life until that stupid man trampled on my dress."

It did not seem likely that Laura would spontaneously advert to anybody's pleasures or troubles except her own; and Maud, who was consumed with a feverish longing to hear some tidings, however scanty and indefinite, of Philip Ormond, ventured to falter out, while she bent her head over the luckless dress :

"I am glad you have been enjoying yourselves. Your friends from Ilscote Lodge are here, of course ?"

"Oh yes! of course. Oh! Miss Travers, I wish you could have been downstairs, if it had been only to see how extravagantly Edith Merton is dressed. Such lace and such jewels I never saw in my existence—I'm sure when one thinks of all the poor families that might be supported on them it is quite dreadful. But it isn't to be denied that the girl is looking uncommonly well this evening, and if what I hear is true she has made a conquest that it was worth her while to dress for."

Maud felt that a sudden rush of blood dyed her cheeks and brow crimson, and bent still lower over her task as she repeated inquiringly :

"If what you have heard is true, Miss Arbuthnot?"

"Yes. It was just before I came upstairs that Lieutenant Snappleton was telling me . . . . I hope you have nearly done now?"

"Very nearly," stammered Maud, her fingers so trembling with agitation that she could hardly hold the needle.

"I never was so surprised in my life as when I heard of it, but then he is such a wag, one is never sure whether to believe him or not. I had sent him to look for my fan—he is the politest of creatures, you must know—and when he came back he said he couldn't find it anywhere (and no wonder, for it was sticking all the time in my sash), but that if I heard of such articles as a lady and gentleman being missing he could put their owners in the way of recovering them, for he had just come across one of each sort in the conservatory. He is *so* funny, you know."

"A lady and gentleman!" gasped Maud.

"Yes, Mr. Ormond and Miss Merton—sitting alone in the conservatory—at least so he said. But perhaps it was only his fun, for just as I was going to question him about it, that clumsy man set his great anvil of a foot on my dress, and of course that put everything else for the time out of my head. You have done now, Miss Travers, I think?"

Maud had just enough strength left to murmur an affirmative, and Laura exclaimed:

"Oh! thank you—I am so very much obliged. Dear me, I hope stooping has not made your head worse; you are looking quite flushed—well, really I don't know how to thank you. You will excuse my hurrying away; I am so afraid of losing that darling galop."

And in another moment Maud was alone— alone to ponder on the doom conveyed in the words she had just heard. Philip Ormond and Edith Merton in the conservatory! Then surely the die was cast, and that love her faith in which, even since she had been banished from its light, had been the greatest treasure of her life, was lost to her for ever. She knew now what a hypocrite she had been to herself when she tried to think she would be happy in hearing that Philip Ormond had found a new love. She knew now that it was not only because the Arbuthnots had spoken disparagingly of Edith that her soul grew sick and faint within her as she pictured Philip at this unknown rival's feet. Not because she doubted Edith, but because she loved Philip, did she quail at the idea of having lost him.

And how she quailed at it! how intolerable a compression made itself felt at her heart as she thought of Philip and Edith in the conservatory, and the tender dialogue they might even now be holding there! If indeed it were true that they were there at all! For was it not possible that the report which caused her such infinite anguish might be nothing more than a silly jest, started by the gallant Lieutenant Snappleton to keep up his reputation for funniness? And if it were so, what a world of needless torture was she inflicting on herself! Oh! that she could but be sure, one way or the other—anything would be preferable to this heart-sickening suspense; and the sooner she knew the worst, the sooner she would grow accustomed to it, the sooner learn to purge her heart of all leaven of bitterness against the woman who was to be Philip Ormond's wife. But alas! how long might she not have to wait before her doubts could be resolved!

All at once, as though in obedience to a sudden impulse the wisdom of which she would not stay to consider, she sprang to her feet, threw a large shawl over her head and shoulders, and stole softly out of her room. A moment she listened on the dark landing; all was quiet save for the muffled strains of dance music sounding from below; and, gathering new courage from the stillness, she laid her hand on the banister and very cautiously began to descend.

The staircase was as deserted as she could wish, and uninterrupted she reached a landing at the bottom of the second flight, where a folding window opened on a balcony behind. With trembling hand she undid the fastening, and in a moment more she was in the open air, descending a flight of steps which led into the flower-garden surrounding the house. A soft fine rain was falling fast about her and upon her, but she was hardly conscious of it, and made her way rapidly through the darkness round to the other side of the house, only slackening her pace as she reached the front, and came in sight of the many-coloured lamps of the conservatory.

Her heart almost failed her now. It was as though the whole world depended on what should chance to be within that transparent bower of light and greenery. But after coming so far to learn the truth she would not turn back ignorant; and, with faltering steps, on she went over the sodden turf towards the light, attracted to it even as a moth by the illumination which is to mar the beauty of its life for ever. On she went until, protected from observation by a friendly creeper that was trailed inside, she came close up to the glass, and was able to look through it, at a place where the straggling branches left a gap. And then, after one convulsive throb, a strange aching

numbness crept over her heart, for in spite of
the rain-drops on the glass, in spite of the
dizziness that half blinded her, she saw enough
to know that what she had heard a while ago was
true.

Yes, it was true—true that Philip Ormond sat
with Edith Merton in the conservatory—true that
his heart was passing away from his old love
for ever; in spite of the rain-drops and the
dizziness, Maud saw enough to be sure of that.
There sat a radiant queen-like woman, with white
neck and arms issuing from fleecy clouds of lace
and blonde, and a profile fair and regular as a
statue's; and there, with upturned face gazing
into that of this peerless creature, sat the same
Philip Ormond who had tacitly plighted his faith
to Maud Fleming nearly a year before as he had
parted from her at the schoolmaster's door. The
same, and yet not the same, for the expression
was not quite that which on that day had stereo-
typed itself on Maud's heart. But, however the
expression of the present differed from that of
the past, it was one of unmistakable admiration,
and as she saw it the watcher felt that her doom
was sealed. Unable to stir, she stood riveted
to the spot with paralysed limbs and straining
eyes, gazing from her outer darkness at the
happiness that looked to be so near her, but

from which she was separated by what seemed a whole sea of calamity and shame. What had she done that her fate was so different from that of the well-born, well-dowered beauty on whose face those eyes were fixed which once had beamed upon her with a light dearer to her than life?

Suddenly she awakened from her torpor with an affrighted start, and shrank down terrified behind the thickest branches of the creeper. Edith had dropped her handkerchief, and, as Philip made a movement to recover it, those well-remembered eyes had for a second been turned full towards hers who gazed at him from amid the rain and the darkness; so that, as she hastily drew back, she could almost have believed that their glances had momentarily met. For an instant she cowered down in terror, and then, without daring to risk another look, sped away from the spot as fast as her trembling limbs could bear her—never stopping till she had locked herself in her chamber, thankful to find that she was not followed, and that she had not paid the penalty of her rashness by an exposure which would have undone everything that she had been labouring for during all those weary months. And then she threw herself on her bed and gave way to an agony of weeping.

CHAPTER XVI.

ASSURANCE DOUBLY SURE.

NEARLY a week had passed since the night of the ball—a week for Maud full of bitter recollection and yet more bitter anticipation, during which she wearily laboured to tutor herself into a spirit of something like resignation to the new trial which had overtaken her. She was sitting one morning in the school-room superintending Cecilia's lessons, when the door opened, and Mrs. Arbuthnot hastily entered.

"I am sorry to interrupt lessons, Miss Travers, but I must beg you to spare Cecilia from her studies for a few minutes. The Mertons have just called to say good-bye—they are to leave Ilscote to-morrow—and Mrs. Merton has very kindly brought her youngest daughter Fanny, so it would never do for Cecilia not to be there to entertain her. And you had better come too, Miss Travers; Lady Rosamond is with them, and has just been saying she would like to see you."

" It is very kind of her," stammered Maud, "but " . . . . She paused, hardly knowing how to excuse herself, and then added, in a voice which, do what she would, was tremulous with agitation : " Mr. Ormond is there too, I suppose ?"

" No, he isn't—Lady Rosamond has just been apologising for him. It seems he went home a day or two after the ball—got uneasy about his father's health, or something of that sort. But I can't help fancying he must have proposed to Edith first; she seems in such wonderfully good spirits. You had better come, Miss Travers; I should be sorry for Lady Rosamond to think I made any objection to your mixing with my friends."

" Oh yes ! do come, Miss Travers," cried Cecilia. " I should like you to see Fanny Merton. Laura says she is taller than me, but I say she isn't; it's only because she wears longer dresses. Do come."

Thus adjured, and relieved from the fear of being confronted with Philip Ormond, Maud made no further resistance. The society of Lady Rosamond always possessed a singular attraction for her, nor could she help feeling a vague desire to know how Edith Merton bore her triumph. With a beating heart, therefore, she followed Mrs. Arbuthnot into the drawing-room.

Lady Rosamond was not there when she

entered, having been conducted into the conservatory by one of the girls to see the progress of a rare plant contributed from the hot-house at Ilscote; so that Maud had full opportunity of taking note of the new acquaintances to whom Mrs. Arbuthnot, with rather more than her usual amount of patronising condescension, now introduced her.

"Here is Cecilia—only too glad to be allowed to come and see her young friend. And this is Miss Travers, the lady who teaches her, and whom I have succeeded for once in persuading to leave her post in the school-room. You see I make no stranger of you, Mrs. Merton, but our ways in this house are rather homely and old-fashioned, so you must not expect ceremony."

The Honourable Mrs. Merton, a stately-looking dowager, inclined her head a little stiffly towards the young person whom Mrs. Arbuthnot thus apologised for introducing to her; while, with more affability than was her wont, Edith bent hers also, and smiled a bright gracious smile. It was as though she were elate with some internal cause of gladness, and could not help letting some of her satisfaction overflow on those around her in the shape of smiles and extra courtesy and good-nature; much as great potentates feel constrained to let a share of their personal rejoicing descend on their subjects in the shape of largesse scattered among the populace. How that smile went to Maud's heart, reminding her as it did of the conservatory and the triumph presumably achieved there!

"Cecilia, my dear," went on Mrs. Arbuthnot, "had you not better ask Miss Fanny if she would like a walk round the garden? Young people always get on better by themselves," she explained, turning to Mrs. Merton; and indeed, from the sheepish manner in which the two girls sat eyeing each other from opposite corners of the room, it did not seem as if they were likely to get on very well in the oppressive presence of their elders. They both appeared much relieved by Mrs. Arbuthnot's proposal, and presently they might have been seen walking and talking together in the garden, with so confidential an air that it was evident the disparity in the length of their dresses did not operate injuriously on the friendly free-masonry apparently existing between all girls from the age of twelve to fifteen.

In the mean time Maud sat in an obscure corner of the room, watching the fair radiant face whose profile she remembered so well as seen between the pendent branches of the conservatory creeper with Philip Ormond's eyes fixed admiringly upon it. More hopeless than ever she felt when she looked on it now in the full light of day, without those eyes to distract her, and saw how exceeding fair it was—set off by an exquisite little spring bonnet of the latest Paris fashion, and wreathed with smiles which seemed to proceed from a very exuberance of satisfaction. She was indeed beautiful, this irresistible Edith, and apparently no less proud and happy than she was beautiful—proud and happy, as what woman could fail to be, Maud asked herself, conscious of being the object of Philip Ormond's love? And then a feeling of wild despairing anguish took possession of her, and it was with difficulty that she restrained herself from sobbing aloud in the bitterness of her heart.

But a few moments more, and the fierce impotent storm of bootless jealousy was lulled, as by a magic spell. She forgot Edith Merton and Edith Merton's triumph, and a sensation of peacefulness crept over her spirit as though she were suddenly made aware of the protecting presence of a guardian angel. For Lady Rosamond had re-entered the room, Lady Rosamond had gone up to her and pressed her hand, Lady Rosamond was sitting by her side looking into her face with kind mild eyes — eyes that exercised a strangely soothing influence on her heart even while they fluttered it. Perhaps the gentle lady, so accustomed to sorrow herself, divined that a load of care heavier than usual lay on Maud's mind that day; for, kind as she always was, she was kinder than ever now — asking after Miss Travers' health in a tone of earnest, almost tender, solicitude, and expressing regret at not seeing her oftener, in terms which showed that the earl's daughter kept no less strict note than the obscure governess of the length of the intervals which separated their rare meetings. But unfortunately for Maud, who would never have grown weary of the consolation which to her seemed naturally to reside in that sweet voice and those sympathising eyes, Laura Arbuthnot had placed herself on Lady Rosamond's other side, thus preventing her from bestowing so much attention on Maud as she was apparently disposed to do. And when Lady Rosamond looked away, Maud once more awoke to the presence of Edith Merton and to the drift of the conversation going on around her.

"And you actually return to London to-morrow?" said Mrs. Arbuthnot, addressing the Honourable Mrs. Merton. "I was in hopes you might be going to stay in the neighbourhood some time longer; the London season must be beginning to be on the wane by this time, so that I should have thought it was hardly worth while to return

to town.   But, to be sure, I suppose you are only
passing through London on your way to some
other part of the country ; I know what travellers
you are.   You will be starting again in a very few
days, no doubt ? ”

“ I hardly know,” said Mrs. Merton ; and Maud
noticed that she glanced in the direction of her
daughter.   “ Our arrangements for the next few
months are very uncertain.”

Was it imagination, or was Maud right in thinking that there was an expression as of slightly
embarrassed self-consciousness on Edith’s face as
this was said, accompanied by a decided heighten-
ing of the tints of her cheek?   Mistaken or
not, the fancy was a fresh suggestion of her
rival’s triumph, and as such cost Maud a new
pang.

“ We had arranged a tour in Switzerland this
summer,” continued Mrs. Merton, still looking at
her daughter, “but I think I may say certainly
that that is given up now.   We shall none of us
be able to leave the country for the next few
months, at all events.”

There could be no doubt this time about the
blush that rose to Edith’s cheeks, and Maud
turned sick at heart as she looked.

“ You were thinking of Switzerland ! ” exclaimed
Mrs. Arbuthnot regretfully.   “ Oh dear! I am

quite sorry to hear you have given it up, for if you had been going it is just possible we might have had the pleasure of meeting you, and that would have been so nice. I have almost decided to take the girls abroad for three or four weeks this summer — there is nothing like a little foreign travel for young people — and of course we should pay a flying visit to Switzerland before coming home. I have never been there myself, but I know I shall so delight in those charming mountains. Indeed I think I might say that our going was positively fixed, only that I can't quite make up my mind how to manage with Cecilia. She is so anxious to accompany us, poor child, and she is just at the age to be interested by the journey, you know; but, as I tell her, it would seem so very rude and unkind to leave Miss Travers in the house by herself, that really " . . . .

She looked at the governess as though expecting to be helped out with the sentence, and Maud felt herself compelled to take the hint.

" You are very good, but there is not the slightest occasion to think of me, I assure you. I shall not mind being left alone at all."

" So you are always kind enough to say, I know, my dear Miss Travers, but really I feel quite a delicacy about taking you at your word. However, we shall see about it. If we go at all it won't be

for another week or two, so we have plenty of time
to make up our minds."

The truth was, Mrs. Arbuthnot's mind was
pretty well made up already, so much so that
Cecilia's outfit for the journey was at that moment
in course of preparation ; but being a kind-hearted
little woman, and withal very fond of obtaining
full credit for her good impulses, she missed no
opportunity of expatiating on her reluctance to
leave Miss Travers alone, especially as she was thus
always certain to elicit assurances which helped to
set her conscience at ease on the subject. After
all, as the worthy lady herself did not fail to
remember, it was very kind of her to have a conscience at all in the matter. It was certainly no
fault of hers that Cecilia's present instructress did
not happen to have friends to go home to for the
holidays ; nor was it her fault either that no provision existed enabling governesses to travel gratis,
in which case Miss Travers' company on the
journey would have been very acceptable.

The conversation lasted only a short time longer
—mostly dealing with such topics as the hardships
imposed on female travellers by Custom-house
regulations, and the immense economy of laying
in a good stock of Brussels lace or French silk on
what the ladies rather vaguely spoke of as " the
spot ; " and in a few minutes, the two young people

having been duly recalled from the garden, the visitors rose to take leave. Once more Maud had the pain of enduring Edith's radiant yet unsympathetic smile; once more she had the pleasure of feeling the warm pressure of Lady Rosamond's hand; and then the excitement both of pain and pleasure died away, and she was at liberty to bestow attention on the remarks which Mrs. Arbuthnot freely passed on her visitors as soon as the retreating sound of their carriage wheels became audible.

"What a magnificent shawl that is of Mrs. Merton's, to be sure! fifty pounds at the very least, I am confident. Well, it has been a pleasant call on the whole. That dear Lady Rosamond, she is always so nice. What did you think of Edith Merton this morning?"

"I thought she was looking particularly well pleased with herself," answered Laura. "Oh! mamma, did you notice what Mrs. Merton said about the change in their arrangements? She must be engaged, I should think, shouldn't you?"

"To that Philip Ormond, of course?" said Frederica.

"Oh! of course, if she is engaged at all," rejoined Laura. "I wonder whether she really is or not?"

"Nobody thinks of asking me," said Cecilia,

tossing her head with an air of pique. "And yet I'm the only person in the room who can tell you what you want to hear."

"You, Cissy! what do you know about it?" asked Laura in surprise.

"Everything," said Cecilia, and nodded mysteriously.

"Oh! I see — you and Fanny have not been talking so long together for nothing. Tell us all about it then, Cissy dear," coaxed Laura ; "what has Fanny been saying?"

"Ah! but that's a secret," said Cecilia, pursing up her lips tightly. "She made me promise first not to tell."

"You tiresome child! she never meant you not to tell your own sister."

"Yes, she did though—it was a very great secret indeed. And don't call me a child, please, or you shall never get it out of me."

"Come, don't be cross, Cissy, there's a dear. Tell me what Fanny said, I really want to know."

"We will never tell it again to anybody," added Frederica persuasively.

Mrs. Arbuthnot said nothing ; it would have been contrary to her notions of propriety to take an active part in encouraging her daughter to a breach of confidence.

" I must not tell you what she said," persisted Cecilia, shaking her head in intense enjoyment of her secret. " But you may guess if you like, and I'll let you know if you guess right."

"She said that Miss Merton was going to be married," promptly hazarded Laura, quite satisfied with the arrangement.

" That's it," said Cecilia, nodding vehemently in the affirmative. Apparently she felt now quite relieved from all obligation of secresy, for she instantly went on to volunteer fresh information.

"They're thinking of a Honiton lace dress for the bride, and white tarlatane with blue trimmings and forget-me-not head-dresses for the bridesmaids. Fanny is to be one of course, but it isn't quite fixed yet how many more there are to be, for they haven't known long that there was going to be a wedding at all—it was only settled on the night of our party."

If there had been any doubt before, there was none now. Maud thought of the conservatory, and shivered.

" Our party ! so it was made up at our party ! " said Laura. She paused an instant, and looked very pensive, perhaps thinking a little bitterly of the eligible matches that might have been, but were not, made up at the recent entertainment;

then added with renewed vivacity: "The gentleman is Mr. Ormond, of course?"

"Oh! we may be sure of that," said Cecilia, "but there was no time to talk about everything. I wish Lady Rosamond and Mrs. Merton had not been in such a hurry—I should have heard ever so much more."

Cecilia's tidings were very terrible for Maud. Why, it might have been hard to say, for after all were they not a wholly superfluous confirmation of an hypothesis already sufficiently demonstrated by what she herself had witnessed in the conservatory? But then it sometimes happens that when a man is being tried for his life, the pronouncing of the capital sentence affects him more than even the verdict by which that sentence has been determined.

So it was with Maud now, after learning as an indubitable fact that Edith Merton had been wooed and won on the night of Mrs. Arbuthnot's ball. She did her best through the remainder of that dreary day to bear up bravely and continue to show a cheerful front in the presence of the Arbuthnots; but this new blow, coming after what she had already suffered, was almost too much for her strength, and, in the absence of anything that could serve as a diversion to her thoughts, might perhaps have broken it down altogether. Fortunately, however, such a diversion was even then preparing for her. The next morning's post brought her a letter addressed in a graceful flowing hand that was not Nathaniel's, and when she opened it, lost in wonderment as to who could be her correspondent, she found the following :—

Ilscote Lodge. Ilscote.
Wednesday Evening.

My dear Miss Travers,

From a few words I heard this morning while I was with you, I understand that should Mrs. Arbuthnot decide on going abroad this summer you are likely to be left with a few weeks of leisure, of which you have as yet made no disposition. Ever since then I have been thinking how much pleasure it would give me if I could prevail upon you to spend them here, and I write these lines to beg that you will, if possible, so far oblige me. Please to give my best regards to Mrs. Arbuthnot, and tell her that I am sure she will think this arrangement a good one, since, from what I heard her say to-day, I know how much she would have regretted the necessity of leaving you alone.

I do hope, my dear Miss Travers, that you will be able to give me the pleasure I am asking for. A little change cannot fail to do you good, and I was sorry to see this morning that you were looking paler than usual. My sister desires to be kindly remembered to you, and, in the hope of seeing you with us as soon as you are able to leave Grant-wick, believe me to be,

Your very sincere friend,

Rosamond Carleton.

Under ordinary circumstances, Mrs. Arbuthnot might perhaps not have been too well pleased at the signal honour thus conferred upon her governess. But Lady Rosamond's note relieved her from a dilemma which really had been rather embarrassing to her conscience; and then the discreetly worded message which it contained was so polite that she could almost persuade herself that the invitation had been given rather to facilitate the domestic arrangements of the Arbuthnot family than to gratify any feelings of personal consideration for Miss Travers.

"Very kind and polite of Lady Rosamond, upon my word," she said, handing back the note to Maud, who had lost no time in taking her opinion upon it. "You must not forget, if you please, to tell her how very much obliged I feel, and how delighted I am to think that you will be so comfortably provided for during my absence. You will go of course?"

"I—I think so," said Maud, hesitatingly. And indeed why should she not—with Philip Ormond busy at Hernebridge preparing a home for his betrothed bride, Edith Merton in London selecting her trousseau, and the safe retreat of Fairlawn Cottage ready to fall back upon in the improbable event of a new influx of company at the Lodge?

"Oh yes! of course you will," rejoined Mrs. Arbuthnot decisively.

And thus it was settled that the invitation should be accepted—Maud well satisfied to find that no other choice was left her, and looking forward to the time she was to spend in the companionship of that gentle mourning lady at Ilscote almost as a fever patient longs for the cool refreshing touch of a tender nurse's hand on his brow, almost as a sick child longs to rest its weary head on the bosom of its mother.

CHAPTER XVII.

THE BANK PARLOUR.

THE summer sun was shining in its full after-noon glory on the green fields and waving woods round Linchester, making it seem an absolute waste of life to remain cooped up in narrow streets and dingy counting-houses; but Mr. Fleming sat contentedly in his dull back parlour at the bank, working his way through long columns of figures with as untiring a patience as though the whole universe of nature contained no place or occupation more attractive. A gloomy room at all times and seasons was this same back parlour at the bank, but perhaps never so gloomy as on a bright summer day like this, with the obscured sunshine beating reproachfully against the dusty panes, and suggesting how wide was the contrast between the world without and the world within. A gloomy room—meagrely furnished with a thread-bare carpet, a collection of straight-backed horse-hair chairs, and one or two tables and tall office desks groaning under piles of papers and ponderous ledgers; a gloomy room —destitute of all ornament or decoration, unless the heavy spectral-looking drapery garnishing the single narrow window, or the disused inkstand and superfluous paper-weights arrayed on the high mantel-piece, could be reckoned as coming under that designation. A gloomy room—almost prison-like in the aspect imparted to it by the compli-cated bolts of the huge iron safe occupying one of its dark corners, and by the solid grating protect-ing the window on the outside; more prison-like than ever when the sun shone as it did to-day, projecting the shadows of the bars without in thick dark stripes on the dirty-yellow walls and wainscotings.

But, gloomy or not, the place seemed to suit Mr. Fleming, and he sat doggedly at his desk, turning his back on the sun-light and the blue sky, and keeping his eyes fixed on the columns before him as though greedy of work. Thus he had sat and toiled since the morning, with the exception of a few minutes devoted to a hurried meal, and thus he intended to sit and toil far into the night. They were busy just now at the bank with the making up of the half-yearly balances, and, the head clerk being absent on sick leave, Mr. Fleming found himself with an amount of work on his hands by which most men would have been overwhelmed. But nothing in the shape of work overwhelmed Mr. Fleming, and, so far from complaining, he almost revelled in the quantity of labour before him, gathering increased energy and spirit from what would have been a martyrdom to others. Not that his mind was so abnormally constituted that he could find a greater absolute pleasure in work than men in general; not that the processes of addition and subtraction were more intrinsically fascinating to him than to the average of mankind. But his home was cheerless and desolate, and his leisure was haunted by memories which he had to thrust from him perforce lest they should turn his brain; and therefore it was that he was never so well contented as when sitting thus in the bank parlour with an untold quantity of labour both of his own and other people's to get through.

It was growing late in the afternoon when one of the two noiselessly opening and shutting doors which, with their covering of moth-eaten green baize, slightly relieved the monotony of the dirty-yellow walls, and respectively communicated with the public room in front and with a small ante-chamber leading to the private part of the house, was, after a premonitory tap, thrown open. Mr. Fleming looked up with a more benign air than was usual with him, expecting that Bob, who had all that day been doing wonders of work at his post behind the bank-counter, had come to consult him on some matter concerning his department. The intruder, however, was not Bob, but a short pursy-looking man with stubbly black hair and a face inclined to be red, imposingly dressed in a long-tailed coat with brass buttons and scarlet collar — Grimble, for more than twenty years porter of the establishment. On sight of this personage all appearance of interest faded from Mr. Fleming's face, and he bent down once more over his books, demanding absently as he went on with his calculations:

"Well, Grimble, what is it now?"

"Gentleman to see you, sir," said Grimble, who piqued himself on being a man of few words.

"What gentleman?" asked Mr. Fleming, without waiting to look at the card which Grimble laid on the table as he spoke. "A customer, I suppose?"

"A new one then; I never seed him afore. That's his card, sir."

Mr. Fleming glanced at the card, and a cloud black as night gathered on his brow. It bore the name, "Mr. Francis Godfrey."

"Not in, sir?" demanded the observant Grimble.

"No, no, there is no need to tell him that," said

Mr. Fleming, regaining his self-possession with an effort. " It is a great inconvenience of course, but I must make time. Show him in."

Grimble departed, and for a moment Mr. Fleming leaned back in his chair as though overcome with sudden exhaustion. He recovered himself, however, almost instantaneously, and was sitting erect and composed as usual when Grimble returned ushering in the visitor.

The past few months had not changed Francis Godfrey for the better—Mr. Fleming's keen scrutiny told him that at once. There had always been more or less of a truculent swagger about the man, at least according to Mr. Fleming's experience of him, and this had never been so conspicuous as now when he entered the bank parlour. Formerly, indeed, there had been blended with it a kind of polish and softness of manner which, if too evidently constrained and artificial, was so far satisfactory that it showed a certain desire of conciliating the opinion of others, a certain instinctive caution which to some extent must operate as a check on the force of evil passions. But now it appeared that either the will or the power to dissimulate had been impaired, if not destroyed altogether. There was a reckless dare-devil air about his face and bearing that had not been there before—an air that spoke at once of defiance and menace. Apparently he had even lost respect for the world and its opinion to the extent of not caring whether he passed for a gentleman in gentlemen's society. There was no negligence in his attire; on the contrary, it was perhaps more jaunty than ever; but there was an unmistakable sporting cut about it which a few months before he would have had the good taste to avoid. Evidently he had not been mixing lately with his social equals, and both his manners and appearance, no less than the slightly inflamed features of his still handsome face, bore witness to a loss of refinement.

A stiff inclination of the head was the only greeting which Mr. Fleming bestowed on his unwelcome visitor, who, seemingly quite unabashed by the frigidity of the salutation, made his way towards a chair by the table and seated himself.

"Well, Fleming, here I am again, as they say in the pantomime. Still in the land of the living, you see."

"I see," said Mr. Fleming drily, and he looked at the new-comer as though he would have been well pleased to have had the fact otherwise.

"So this is the hive where all the honey is made, is it?" said Francis, looking about him while he lazily tapped the tip of his brightly varnished boot with a dandified little bamboo cane surmounted by a fox's head in ivory. "Rather a musty fusty kind of place, it must be confessed, but all the better adapted for the purposes of honey-making, no doubt. A curious coincidence, by the way, that honey should rhyme with money."

"Mr. Godfrey, I am busy," said Mr. Fleming sternly, touching up some of the figures before him with his pen. "Perhaps you will be kind enough to state the object of your visit at once."

"That you may be the sooner relieved of my company, I suppose?"

"Precisely; that I may be the sooner relieved of your company."

The quiet contempt of Mr. Fleming's manner seemed to be felt and resented by the young man, for he ceased his bantering tone, and, coming to the point sooner than perhaps he had intended, answered sullenly:

"Well then, the object of my visit, as you are in such a hurry to know it, is to tell you that I am in the hands of the Philistines—that is, of a damned infernal fellow of a Jew who holds my acceptances—and that you have got to help me out of them. An immediate supply of the needful, to keep me on the right side of the post—that's what I want, and that's what I must have."

"You mistake; I am not in your debt at present. The last half-yearly remittance was paid to you on the first of this month; I have your receipt to prove it."

Francis contracted his brows savagely—it was plainer than ever that his powers of self-control had not improved of late—and his fingers visibly tightened round the bamboo.

"You needn't try to come over me with your cursed coolness. You'll find me another sort of customer than I was last year when I let you walk over the course so neatly, I promise. I'm in a mess, I tell you, and if you think I shall be content to go to the wall while I've got a rich banker's hand to look over, you don't know what it is to do with a desperate man, that's all. I don't intend to rot in a jail, or out of one either."

He paused, but apparently Mr. Fleming wished to gain time for consideration before committing himself one way or another, for he stooped over the page of figures before him as though to conceal the angry glow that rose to his face, and merely answered, in a tone of constrained calmness:

" Indeed!"

" Yes indeed, and I'll tell you what, if you don't answer me with something better than your confounded sneering 'indeeds,' I'll let you find out pretty soon that you've staked your money on the wrong horse. My affairs are supremely uninteresting to you, I have no doubt, but it is quite as much

worth your while to bestow a little serious attention on them as on any of the business you have
got yonder. You have not forgotten that I hold
the trump card, I suppose, and by George if you
insult me with any more of your damned supercilious airs I'll play it, I will. I wonder in what
light your worthy partner would view my little
story, or the ingenuous youth in the next room,
who I presume is one of your clerks, or the fellow
outside with the brass buttons. It would rather
astonish them—eh ?"

Perhaps the mental wear and tear of the past
few months had somewhat broken down the proud
spirit which had once asserted itself successfully
against Francis Godfrey's overweening arrogance.
Perhaps Francis Godfrey himself, brutal and des-
perado-like as he looked, appeared a more formidable antagonist than he had done then. Or
perhaps the threat of public exposure sounded
more terribly in Mr. Fleming's ears here—in the
place of business where with years of toil he had
sought and achieved the universal respect of
Linchester and its neighbourhood, almost within
hearing of those among whom his daily lot was
cast—than it had done in the dining-room at the
Grange. However this may have been, certain it
is that the defiance which rose to his lips was not
uttered. He cast an anxious look towards the

door that separated him from the large room in front, perhaps at that moment full of customers to each and all of whom the name of Gilbert Fleming was as a very synonym of respectability, and then, after a few moments' reflection, forced himself to say, in a voice hoarse with suppressed passion:

"You have brought some account or memorandum of what you owe, I suppose. Let me see it."

The young man tossed a paper across the table.

"Here it is—in old Isaacson's own handwriting, if that is any additional satisfaction. I thought I should get you to interest yourself in my business at last."

Mr. Fleming returned no answer, keeping his eyes fixed for the next two or three minutes on the document handed to him. At last he turned his pale face towards his visitor, and said sternly:

"So! the man has, or says he has, claims on you for twelve hundred pounds—six times the amount of your income squandered in less than a year. And you look to me to bear you unharmed through the consequences of your recklessness?"

"Certainly I do. Who else have I got to look to?"

"And suppose I refuse?"

"Oh! I am not afraid of your refusing. I should have to go to a debtor's prison probably, and you . . . . Well, really, I don't know what precise statutory penalty you have incurred; but you wouldn't be able to hold your ground here at all events, with a romantic little story like that attached to your name."

Mr. Fleming winced, and visibly hesitated.

"And if I make up my mind to give the money," he said at length, "of what use will it be? If I could be sure that this application would be the last—that you would change your mode of life . . . . But I know you too well."

He shook his head; still it was plain that he was yielding, and Francis hastened to follow up the effect of his menaces by a little seasonable persuasion.

"Come, come, you must not give a fellow over because he makes a false start or two to begin with. Where would you have been, I should like to know, if you had found nobody willing to give you a second chance? And suppose I have been running a trifle wild, it's only natural I should need a little relaxation after working as I did to get my picture ready for the Exhibition. You read what the critics said of me, no doubt—a gratifying reception, wasn't it? And you ought to see the piece I have got on the easel now."

Mr. Fleming leaned back in his chair, pondering deeply. Business had been unusually prosperous of late, so that the payment demanded of him, however inconvenient, was not altogether beyond his power to make. And if he did not make it—if he obeyed the impulse which urged him at any risk to resent and resist the insolent intimidation of that man—was not the prospect utter ruin and annihilation? Then who could say but that Francis Godfrey might possibly be capable of profiting by experience, might be brought by motives of self-interest to keep his dissipation within bounds, might set himself seriously to cultivate the abilities which he undoubtedly possessed? Surely the experiment was worth trying when the alternative was so desperate.

"For this time, then, I will help you," he said aloud, after a few moments spent in deliberation. "But remember this is your last chance, so be careful that you make a good use of it."

He looked up as he spoke at the flushed triumphant face before him. Alas! it was not the face of one likely to profit by a last chance, likely to be turned from evil by the striking of the eleventh hour. Mr. Fleming felt as he looked that he was hoping against hope, that he might as well seek to fill up a bottomless abyss with his hard-earned gold as spend it in making a respectable character of Francis Godfrey. The man was born to sink, let who would strive to hold him up—to sink till he reached the very depths of social and moral infamy. And this was the man with whose fate Gilbert Fleming's was inextricably entangled !

"Well, since I have promised that the thing is to be done, I will lose no time about it," he went on after a pause. "I will go up to London to-morrow and make terms with this man Isaacson —he is open to negotiation, of course."

The young man's countenance fell.

"I must have the money in my own hands," he said moodily. "I'm quite as competent to strike a bargain with old Isaacson as you are, and if there should be a trifling margin over, I've plenty of uses to turn it to. It's twelve hundred pounds I want, and not your good offices with Isaacson, damme."

"And I cannot afford to pay twelve hundred pounds when I can reduce them to eight or six by negotiation," said Mr. Fleming coldly. "I have promised to pay this debt for you, but I must do it in my own way."

"Then you may as well save yourself the expense of doing it at all," Francis answered fiercely. "By Jove, I'm not going to stand being treated like a baby, and you needn't expect it. Give me the money at once, and let me go."

Mr. Fleming cast a quick scrutinising look at his visitor, and then glanced downwards at the memorandum before him. Might it be possible that the document was not in the money-lender's hand-writing, after all? The theory would account for the young man's violent objection to Mr. Fleming's plan of undertaking a journey to London, while it was only too consistent with what appeared of his character. Again the shrewd man of business looked into his companion's face, and the look confirmed him in his distrust. In any case it would be madness to confide a large sum to a man with a face like that; for even were the memorandum genuine, where was the security that the money would not be squandered on objects other than its proper destination?

"I have yielded so far," said Mr. Fleming quietly, "and I cannot afford to yield further. You have my promise that I will go to London to-morrow to settle this business, and that must satisfy you."

"But by Heaven it will not satisfy me," exclaimed the other passionately, striking the table violently with his clenched fist. "You have promised me the money—it is mine—and I will have it—will have it, do you hear me?"

A tap at that moment sounded at one of the doors, and Mr. Fleming became deadly pale.

"If you are not quite a madman, you will hold your peace now," he whispered in hoarse accents;

and then, in a voice struggling to regain its natural tone, he cried :

"Come in."

The door opened, and Grimble appeared.

"Sir Gregory Winklethwaite wants to see you, sir."

"I am busy just now," said Mr. Fleming with a nervous glance at his companion. "Ask him to step upstairs. Mr. Walford will be kind enough to attend to him."

"Mr. Walford is gone for the day, sir, just this minute left—with his compliments, and to say that he would have been too late for dinner if he had waited to see you."

Mr. Fleming was not surprised; he knew that under no pressure of work could his partner be induced to trifle with his digestion by lengthening his hours of business.

"Ask Sir Gregory to wait a few minutes. I will see him as soon as possible."

"I shall not detain you more than two seconds —two seconds at the very most," said a cracked falsetto sounding from behind the portly form of Grimble. "Allow me, if you please."

The last words were addressed to Grimble, and at the same moment, to the great disturbance of that functionary's dignity, there pushed past him into the room a thin wiry little man, with sparse iron-grey hair, sallow complexion, and a peculiar restlessness in the management of his legs and arms, indicating either that those members were hung upon springs or that their owner was endowed with more than usual nervousness of temperament. This was Sir Gregory Winkle-thwaite, long known at Walford and Co's. as one of their best customers, and Mr. Fleming had no help for it but to resign himself to the intrusion as well as he could. He looked uneasily in the direction of his other visitor. To his relief it appeared that the young man, with all his violence of temper, understood that the best policy for the present was one of self-control, for he had taken up a newspaper, and pretended to be absorbed in its perusal.

Sir Gregory fussed up to Mr. Fleming with his usual elasticity of tread, though a less energetic man might well have been tired by the weight of a large tin case which he carried under his arm, and which with some difficulty he deposited on the table in company with a smaller case—likewise of metal, and furnished with a padlock almost as big as itself—which he took from his pocket.

"I know how valuable your time is, but you will spare me half-a-minute, I am sure," said Sir Gregory. He jerked his head with a friendly nod in the direction of Mr. Fleming, and, before the banker had sufficiently recovered himself to answer, rattled on :

"There are a few little articles here which I want to have taken care of for the next month or two while Lady Winklethwaite and I are on the Continent.   You will oblige me, eh ?"

"Certainly," said Mr. Fleming, constraining himself to speak. "You can leave the things here in all confidence ; I will see that they are put in secure keeping."

"You are very kind," said Sir Gregory. But still he showed no intention of going away, and, clearing his throat nervously, continued :

"It wouldn't be giving you too much trouble to ask you to lock them up now, would it ? There is nothing so satisfactory as one's own eyes in such matters, you know, and I think I should feel happier in my mind if I could tell Lady Winklethwaite I had seen the things put by myself."

"Very well," said Mr. Fleming, making an effort to swallow down his impatience, while he took a curiously shaped key from his waistcoat pocket and proceeded to open the prison-like apparatus in the dark corner.

"I am very sorry to hinder you," apologised Sir Gregory, "but taking into consideration what there is at stake . . . . Why, in this biggest

box, now, all Winklethwaite Park is contained, as
one may say."

" All Winklethwaite Park ! " said Mr. Fleming,
elevating his eyebrows.

"The title deeds, I mean," explained Sir
Gregory, patting the box caressingly. " And in this
little one, though it isn't much to look at . . . .
You have seen Lady Winklethwaite's diamonds, of
course ? "

Mr. Fleming confessed that he had not had that
privilege.

" Haven't you really ? well, you do surprise me.
They are pretty well known in the county too, I
flatter myself. Thank you, thank you, I am very
much obliged," added the baronet, as he saw his
treasures deposited in a space cleared among the
books and papers in the safe. " You have made
me feel so comfortable in my mind, you have no
idea."

" I am very glad to have been able to serve
you," said Mr. Fleming, bowing.

" You are very good, I'm sure. But I said
I would not keep you beyond five minutes, and
I won't; I know how busy you are. Good day,
good day—I feel quite grateful really, and so will
Lady Winklethwaite."

The little man bustled out of the room, hardly
waiting for his adieux to be acknowledged, and

Mr. Fleming was again alone with his abhorred visitor. He paused a moment to lock the safe, and then turned round to confront him. The young man put down his newspaper, and returned Mr. Fleming's look with a glance more defiant and threatening than ever.

"Well, what have you to say to me now?" he asked sulkily. "You'll hardly pretend you can't afford to pay me the money, I suppose, with a key in your pocket which gives you access to half the ready cash in Linchester, to say nothing of Lady What's her name's diamonds. I wonder, by the way, if they really are such fine ones."

A strange look of doubt and distrust, almost of fear, crossed Mr. Fleming's face as these words were spoken, and with a slight, apparently mechanical, movement of his hand he pushed a small packet of notes which was lying beside him so that it disappeared under a mass of loose papers.

"It is nothing to you what amounts pass through my hands in the way of business," he said calmly. "What I have promised I will perform —that is, I will go to London to-morrow and settle with your creditor; but more, I repeat, I cannot afford to do. And now let me advise you to go quietly back to London. If you delay much longer you will have to wait for a train till two o'clock in the morning, and we have absolutely nothing more to say to each other just now. I will see you to-morrow afternoon in London, when I have arranged matters with this man Isaacson. Good day."

"But it shall not be good day," exclaimed the other furiously, starting to his feet and approaching with an expression of menace in his face which made Mr. Fleming instinctively look round for a weapon of self-defence. "Damnation! do you think that when I know where the money is to be got" . . . . . .

He paused suddenly, recalled to himself by a sound of footsteps outside, and, rounding off the unfinished sentence with a long low whistle as unconcerned as he could make it, sauntered off to a chair some way from Mr. Fleming's, where he had just had time to sit down when Bob entered the room, having first announced himself by a modest tap.

"Please, sir, I want to ask you about the account of Mr." . . . . . .

He became suddenly aware of the presence of a stranger, and discreetly stopped himself—getting very red in the face, however, under his sense of the awkwardness of the situation. A year at Walford and Co's., though it had sharpened Bob's wits and considerably brightened up his personal appearance, had by no means rubbed off his native shyness, and an incident like this put him terribly out of countenance. But the question he had to ask was one for which it was necessary to get an answer; so, while wishing himself anywhere rather than where he was, he still stood his ground, eyeing his employer with a piteous look of entreaty.

Mr. Fleming saw how the case lay, and glanced anxiously towards his visitor.

"Will you be kind enough to step into the next room for two or three minutes, Mr. Godfrey? I will be with you as soon as possible."

A dark dissatisfied look rose to the young man's face, but he made no objection, and left the room in moody silence.

"Well, Mr. Bates, and what did you want to know?" asked Mr. Fleming, turning encouragingly towards Bob.

"The state of Mr. Hobb's account, if you please, sir," faltered Bob, finding his voice with difficulty. "I am so very sorry for disturbing you, sir."

"It is no fault of yours," answered Mr. Fleming. He turned over the leaves of a ledger before him, and then, singling out a particular entry, laid his finger on it, and said:

"Here is what you wish to know. You had better copy the figures."

Bob proceeded to make a note of the amount, while Mr. Fleming inquired :

" Well, how are you getting on yonder? I am afraid you have a pretty long day's work before you still."

He always spoke kindly to this young clerk—more kindly than to any other member of the establishment. As Mr. Naggles, Bob's absent colleague, often remarked with a touch of bitterness in his voice, it was plain that Mr. Bates was a favourite.

" There's a good bit to do, thank you, sir," said Bob, blushing as he always did when thus noticed by either of his employers. " It will last me till twelve or thereabouts, I dare say."

" Never mind," said Mr. Fleming, good-naturedly, " even then you will get away an hour or two before I shall. And the extra work will be all over by next week, you know."

" I don't mind it, sir, thank you. I like having plenty to do."

" That is fortunate, for you will have more than ever on your hands to-morrow. I am going from home for the day."

" Indeed, sir ! " Such a thing as his patron allowing himself a holiday had hardly entered into Bob's experience, and the intelligence surprised him not a little.

"Yes, on business"—a shadow crossed Mr. Fleming's face as he thought of what the business was—"so we must both do what we can this evening towards reducing the work for to-morrow. Have you got the figures down right?"

"Yes, thank you, sir." Bob prepared to leave the room, but Mr. Fleming detained him; any pretext was welcome which delayed the renewal of the sinister conversation so seasonably interrupted.

"By the by, Mr. Bates, in case I forget to mention it, you may as well tell Grimble there will be no need for him to sit up. I know he does not like to be put out of his regular way, so he can go to bed at eleven as usual, and when I am ready to leave I will call him down to lock the door after me."

"I'll be sure to tell him, sir," said Bob.

"Thank you. Well, I see you are in a hurry to get back to your work, so I won't keep you longer. I am sorry you should have so much of it just now, but it can't be helped for the present, and when Mr. Naggles comes back to his desk I will speak to Mr. Walford about giving you a holiday for a few days. You have worked well for it."

"You are very kind to say so, sir. I shall never be able to thank you enough, I know."

Bob made a clumsy salute and withdrew, penetrated with gratitude, and revelling in the prospect of a short holiday to be spent in the bosom of his family. A minute or two longer Mr. Fleming remained seated, nerving himself for an interview which, as he felt, might only too probably terminate in an open quarrel and the consequent disclosure of the secret he had striven so hard to keep. Then at last, summoning up all his resolution, he rose and laid his hand on the door of the room where he had bid Francis Godfrey wait for him. It had been left unlatched, and flew open at his touch. But, to his surprise, when he entered the room no Francis Godfrey was there.

He stood for a moment on the threshold, hardly believing his eyes, then crossed the room to a door on the other side, leading into the narrow hall used by Mr. Walford and himself as a private entrance, half expecting that Francis, tired of being left so long in that dark little ante-chamber, might be sauntering to and fro in the not much less lugubrious passage. Still no Francis was there, but only Mrs. Grimble, who—just emerged from the lower regions with a couple of dirty-faced children following reluctantly at her heels—was going upstairs according to her wont to put the two young Grimbles to bed. Naturally enough she could return no answer to the question as to when the gentleman had gone away, not having indeed known that any gentleman had been there; and, wondering more than ever, the banker went to the front door and opened it, looking up and down the street for some moments in the expectation of finding his persecutor loitering outside. But except Grimble, who was pacing to and fro in front of the bank with his hands clasped majestically behind his back, nobody was near whom Mr. Fleming knew.

"So the gentleman, my—my friend, is gone?" he asked, accosting this dignitary.

"Gone, sir—is he?" said Grimble, condescending to halt for a few moments.

"That's just what I want to know from you," said Mr. Fleming impatiently. "I can't find him in the house at all events."

"If he isn't in the house he must be out of it, sir," said Grimble axiomatically.

"You did not see him leave then?"

"I didn't just happen to see him, sir. My eyes can't be everywhere, and the boys to-day is more owdacious than ever. But of course he must have come out when I wasn't looking."

"Of course," said Mr. Fleming, and shutting the door he drew a long breath of relief. So the young man's desperate words had been mere rodomontade after all, and he had gone back on his way to London, content with the promise of assistance which he had extorted. The banker returned to his room, and settled himself down to his work with indomitable energy and an aspect almost of serenity. He had once more escaped—for the present.

CHAPTER XVIII.

AFTER MIDNIGHT.

LONG after the ponderous iron shutters at Walford's had been closed, long after Mr. and Mrs. Grimble had retired to seek repose in their distant attic, long after all sounds of traffic were hushed in the street without, Mr. Fleming was still in the bank parlour, toiling at his appointed task. Opposite to him sat Bob, who had been allowed to bring his accounts thither for the sake of greater facility of reference to the books that his patron was using. Together they sat and worked till long past midnight; for Bob had either under-rated the amount of the business before him or had over-rated his powers of getting through it, and twelve o'clock came and passed without finding him near the termination of his labours. Indeed, even when, more than an hour later, Mr. Fleming put away his books and announced himself ready to go, Bob found that it would still be a considerable time before he should be able to follow.

"I must finish to-night, sir, whatever I do. I should never be able to get through my work to-morrow if I didn't, to say nothing of not liking to go to bed with all these arrears behind me."

"In that case finish by all means," said Mr. Fleming, smiling. "I am glad to see you so zealous, though I am sorry too you should be kept up so late."

"I don't care a bit, thank you, sir," said Bob stoutly. "It's a great deal pleasanter to have too much to do than too little, at all events."

"Well said, Mr. Bates, you are made of the right metal for business. You will be a prosperous man yet, I don't doubt."

Bob blushed up to the roots of his hair, and Mr. Fleming continued, laying a key on the table:

"You will need this to lock up the books. It is lucky I have remembered to leave it with you; it would have been terribly awkward for you all to-morrow morning to find I had carried it off. See, Mr. Bates, it is the key of the safe. I never trusted it with a clerk before, but I am sure you will take as much care of it as I should myself."

Bob eyed the key as reverentially as if it had been the Great Seal of England which had been confided to his charge.

"I think I shall, sir," he said earnestly.   "It won't be for want of trying, anyhow."

"I am certain of that," said Mr. Fleming. "There is nothing to detain me longer, I suppose? No chance of your feeling nervous, I hope, sitting up so late by yourself?"

"I never feel nervous, thank you, sir.   And as for sitting up late to work, I rather like it; everything is so nice and quiet."

Mr. Fleming reached down his hat, and prepared to leave.

"I need not say anything more to you about taking care of the key, I am sure.   And don't forget to call down Grimble to lock up after you; you will have hard work to waken him, I dare say; I know from experience he is a heavy sleeper."

"I shall be very particular.   I should never be happy again thinking I had done anything to make you repent your trust, sir."

Mr. Fleming smiled.   Mr. Naggles was not wrong in believing that he regarded the junior clerk with peculiar favour.

"That's right, Bob.   Well, I will say goodnight now."

He was not often so unbusiness-like as to call the young man by his Christian name, but he had heard Maud use it in speaking of him, and it sounded pleasantly in his ears.

"Good-night, sir," said Bob gratefully.

Mr. Fleming nodded good-humouredly, and in another moment the iron-plated door opening on the street had closed heavily behind him, and Bob was alone, listening to his patron's retreating footsteps as they resounded on the deserted pavement. For more than a minute he could distinguish them, so absolutely hushed and still lay the sleeping town in the silence of the calm summer night. At last they died away in the distance, and Bob, having taken one or two turns through the room to stretch his limbs, consulted a cheap silver watch to which he had lately treated himself, and returned to his desk to work with renewed ardour.

Nice and quiet! Yes, Bob working at Walford's at that hour of the night might well say it was nice and quiet. According to his watch it was now a few minutes past one—that is, during summer, as nearly as possible the middle of the night for all practical purposes in a country town of the status of Linchester, where, in the absence of theatres and music-halls, the last stragglers are generally cleared from the streets by eleven, and the first signs of life in the shape of a stray market-cart or two are sure to make their appearance with the first rays of daylight. Thus everything was at its very quietest, and when Mr. Fleming's footsteps had at last become inaudible in the distance, no sound was heard to break the stillness save the ticking of Bob's watch and the scratching of his pen over the paper. If Bob had been a philosopher engaged in the elucidation of the abstrusest of problems, he could not have desired more absolute tranquillity. For a nervous person, indeed, the silence would have been a little too profound to be pleasant, but then Bob had said that he was never nervous.

Yet had not Bob, in so saying, somewhat over-rated his own fortitude? Certain it is that he had not been writing many minutes when a very slight sound mingling with the watch-ticking and pen-scratching made him look up from his work with a decided start. A very slight sound it was—so slight that it would not have been audible at all but for the death-like quiet of the hour—a slight cracking sound coming from overhead as though a plank creaked in the room above. Once, twice, thrice it was repeated, and for a minute or two Bob forgot his figures to gaze up at the ceiling and listen. But again all was silent, and, conscious that the sound was one which, had Mr. Fleming still been in the room with him, he might have heard fifty times and never noticed, he smiled at himself and resumed the thread of his calculations.

During a few minutes he went on steadily, and

then again he looked up and listened. For once more a sound had struck his ear other than the watch-ticking and pen-scratching—a slight cracking sound such as he had heard before, only this time it seemed to come rather from the staircase than from the room above. Perhaps it was that he was unnerved by his long day's work; perhaps that he was not accustomed to sit up alone far into the middle of the night, and did not know what a trick beams and rafters have of playing practical jokes at the expense of a solitary watcher. But however that may have been, it is not to be denied that, though not lacking physical courage, Bob grew seriously uncomfortable; more uncomfortable still when, after a few moments' interval, he heard the sound again, and again, and yet again—always, as it seemed to him, coming from the direction of the staircase, and each time from a point nearer the bottom.

If Bob was not naturally nervous, he had sadly tampered with his mental constitution during his boyhood by an unlimited consumption of ghost stories and other tales of the horrible; and scores of such came to his recollection now, crowding upon him with a vividness that made him wonder at his own powers of memory. He despised himself for his weakness; but despising himself did no good, did not chase from his brain any of the tall white-robed figures which swarmed there—walking about with clanking chains fastened to their feet, or ghastly wounds gaping in their throats, or poniards plunged to the hilt in their bosoms, or with some equally unpleasant personal peculiarity—did not stop his heart from beating with quicker pulsation than its wont.

Crack, crack—still the sound continued, very softly and gently, hardly louder indeed than that made by Bob's watch, always creeping, as it seemed to his excited ears, nearer and nearer, until at last he could almost fancy he heard it stealing across the floor of the little ante-room behind him. Then it was that, indignant at his own folly, he made a grand effort, and, turning his head valiantly round, called out in a moderately firm voice:

" Who's there ?"

But no low sepulchral groan, no rattling of chains, such as he had almost expected to hear, answered him. All was perfectly still, and, listening amid a silence which would have made audible the dropping of a pin, Bob could hear no sound save the ticking of his watch and the beating of his heart. Through the comparative darkness made in the room by the shade of the lamp, he strained his eyes towards the door communicating with the adjoining chamber; but the green baize panels continued immoveable, and no spectral figure holding its hand on its heart appeared on the threshold. He began to recover himself on this, and, heartily ashamed of his recent sensations, turned round to his work again, muttering something about rats. And then he set himself to whistle " The Ratcatcher's Daughter" as loudly as he could, beating on the floor with his feet; and he heard no more of the cracking which had so annoyed him.

He soon found, however, that " The Ratcatcher's Daughter" was not favourable to concentration of thought, and in three or four minutes more gradually relapsed into silence; and again nothing was audible save the ticking of his watch and the scratching of his pen.

Nothing ?—was that so ? Was there not something more—a faint irregular sound as of suppressed breathing ? It almost seemed to Bob that there was.

His heart gave a strange throb, and then seemed to cease from beating altogether, while with straining ear he listened, unable for very horror to turn his head. Perhaps after all it was only his own breathing that he heard; but, strive as he would to throw it off, a belief had somehow taken possession of him that he was not alone.

With a quick convulsive movement he sprang to his feet and looked round. Not alone—no,

merciful Heaven! he was not alone. A man stood
behind his chair, holding with both hands a gun,
the butt end of which seemed ready to-descend
on his head.

Instinctively Bob stretched forth his fingers
towards the key which had been entrusted to
his keeping, and which had been lying at his
elbow while he worked. It was all he was able
to do, for the next moment the uplifted hands
came down, and Bob knew no more.

END OF VOL. II.

LONDON: PRINTED BY WILLIAM CLOWES AND SONS, STAMFORD STREET
AND CHARING CROSS.